MW00614799

HIDDEN

HISTORIES

**Third Flatiron Anthologies
Volume 8, Book 25, Spring/Summer 2019**

**Edited by Juliana Rew
Cover Art by Keely Rew**

HIDDEN HISTORIES
Third Flatiron Anthologies
Volume 8, Spring/Summer 2019

Published by Third Flatiron Publishing
Juliana Rew, Editor and Publisher

Copyright 2019 Third Flatiron Publishing
ISBN #978-1-7322189-8-7

Discover other titles by Third Flatiron:
(1) Over the Brink: Tales of Environmental Disaster
(2) A High Shrill Thump: War Stories
(3) Origins: Colliding Causalities
(4) Universe Horribilis
(5) Playing with Fire
(6) Lost Worlds, Retraced
(7) Redshifted: Martian Stories
(8) Astronomical Odds
(9) Master Minds
(10) Abbreviated Epics
(11) The Time It Happened
(12) Only Disconnect
(13) Ain't Superstitious
(14) Third Flatiron's Best of 2015
(15) It's Come to Our Attention
(16) Hyperpowers
(17) Keystone Chronicles
(18) Principia Ponderosa
(19) Cat's Breakfast: Kurt Vonnegut Tribute
(20) Strange Beasties
(21) Third Flatiron Best of 2017
(22) Monstrosities
(23) Galileo's Theme Park
(24) Terra! Tara! Terror!

License Notes

www.thirdflatiron.com

Contents

Grins & Gurgles

*****~~~~~*****

Editor's Note

by Juliana Rew

Welcome to the new anthology, *Hidden Histories,* from Third Flatiron. Our theme is alternate and secret histories and is a double issue. Our authors this time have provided a wide variety of speculative fiction stories, ranging from science fiction and fantasy, and horror, to cover-ups and conspiracy.

Some say that history is written by the victors. That's one reason war provides such fertile ground for alternate histories. Three stories set in WWII offer different but largely inspiring views of what may have happened in the resistance in Europe (J. D. Blackrose's fantastical "The Ghost Train"), among demoralized Japanese soldiers (Arthur Carey's "Running on Empty"), and to villagers cut off in the remote mountains of Russia (Elizabeth Beechwood's "Yes, Yes, Yes, We Remember").

Oftentimes we wish we could have met someone admired from history, and a couple of these stories highlight these celebrities' early days and rise to fame, including "Behind the Purple Haze," by John A. Frochio, a meeting with Jimi Hendrix just out of the army, and "Freudian Slips" by Dennis Maulsby, in which Sigmund gets his first insights into the human psyche.

Mythical characters are often given credit for making (and unmaking) powerful civilizations. For you anglophiles, we have Bruce Golden's (mostly) historically accurate "The Fairy's Bell," in which Elizabeth I shares with Shakespeare why she never married, and H. J. Monroe's "Defender of the Realm," in which a mysterious entity offers a modern young monarch the help she needs to rule. Remarkably, this is Monroe's first published story.

Sadly, many tragic historical events have been swept under the carpet or forgotten by history, only to re-surface and break our hearts. We think about this in "Against the Roaring of the Fire" by Edwina Shaw, a story of 17th century witch burnings.

Different cultures have their own beloved mythical creatures, like dragons and wendigos, but witnesses claim to have seen them firsthand, as in Kai Hudson's "Fire, Steel, and Flaming Pearls," and Brenda Kezar's "Indian Uprising."

We have a nice selection of "space" scifi this time. In Mike Barreta's tale, an elderly astronaut gives us "The Secret History of the Space Shuttle," while in Robert Dawson's "The Homebringing," we learn it took a seance to bring home Apollo-13. (It could happen, right?)

The consequences of genetic engineering could bring about some strange new worlds. Jonathan Shipley's "Red Reckoning" tells us the Nazis may have been closer to achieving the master race than we thought. And Sandra Ulbrich Almazan's "Specimen 1842" presents us with a puzzling archeological find.

America has always had a love affair with conspiracy theories, pondering true crimes such as governmental sterilization campaigns and the poisoning of alcohol during Prohibition. We offer a couple of doozies in that vein, including a new take on the Lincoln presidential assassination, "The Sixth-Gun Conspiracy Letters" by Evan A. Davis, and James Chimura's "Man Overboard," about the sinking of the Titanic. We still don't know what really happened to Malaysia Flight #370, but Ricardo Maia offers "MH370" as a possible possibility.

Maybe time travel is the way to correct the mistakes of history. At least, that's the story of "The Fulcrum," by Shannon McDermott. Or perhaps social media and AI can at least make us happier with the way things have turned out, as in Tony Genova's touching "Proving Pictures."

The accounts in the history books aren't always the most accurate, unless they are *future* history books, as in Simon Lee-Price's "Best Possible of Worlds." We offer some "future histories," that extrapolate where we may be headed. (Hint: It's not always utopia.) Check out "Losing Face" by Matthew Reardon (don't lose your credit card) and "Carbon-Nitrogen-Oxygen" by Sarah Hinlicky Wilson (maybe veganism isn't all it's cracked up to be). In Michael Robertson's "The Oracle's Dilemma," even advanced AIs are not sure about the best way forward. However, be advised that some history books are plain unreliable, as in "The Thunderbird Photo," by Jennifer Lee Rossman.

We close the main section with an exciting, time-spanning science fiction tale reaching back to the Library of Alexandria, "Cry the Thousand Sentinels," by Brian Trent.

Our Grins & Gurgles flash humor section seeks to lighten the sometimes overly rich diet of science fiction and fantasy, offering the following *amuse-bouches*: We see "Them Tourists" by A. Humphrey Lanham try a bit too hard to fit in, while Tyler Paterson's superhero in "Date Attire" feels woefully underdressed. Dantzel Cherry shows us what it must be like to go to a school for budding fairy godmothers. Talk about pressure for a happy ending.

Hidden Histories

We hope these fun stories have exposed you to some new thought. Enjoy—and don't forget to get vaccinated.

Juliana Rew
April 2019

*****〜〜〜*****

The Fairy's Bell

by Bruce Golden

Of all the queen's palaces, I always enjoyed Hampton Court the most. Its gardens, its tapestries, its sumptuous furnishings were among the finest I'd seen. And I'd visited countless castles and noble homes. As head of the royal household, I'd traveled the breadth of England with the queen.

Of course, just as I thought of the grandeur of Hampton, the wind reminded me of the single thing about the palace I did not care for—the foul smell wafting in from the Thames. I would have to remember to have the maidservants renew the pomanders in the royal residence.

That was just one of my countless duties, which kept me on the go all the day, and often well into the night. Nonetheless, I can't say my life was ever dull. The queen had her ups and downs, and I had been there for most of them. I was on my way, now, from the kitchen—where I'd passed on Her Majesty's complaints—to her bedchamber, to see that all was as it should be. Normally, by that time of night, she'd be preparing for bed instead of dressing in her finest. This night, however, she was expecting a visitor—one she'd summoned.

On my way to her bedchamber I came upon the royal footman and asked, "Is the queen dressed?"

He shrugged and replied, "A ship is sooner rigged than Good Queen Bess is made ready."

I barely stifled a laugh. The image of a ship's ropes and sails did indeed remind me of the queen's bodice and petticoats and stomacher, with all their corresponding laces and hooks.

"William Head," I scolded the footman with a smile, "I can't believe you would say such a thing."

He shrugged again and continued down the gallery hall.

When I reached the bedchamber, the queen was fully attired, and shooing her dressers from the room. She struggled beneath the restraint of her gown to take a deep breath and sighed.

"Sometimes, Dorothy, I wish I had never become queen."

"Your Highness, how could you say such?" I wasn't as surprised as I sounded. The queen had become more melancholy with age.

"'Tis true. If not for a battle here, a marriage there, the fates might have conspired differently, the Tudors never would have come to power, and I would never have had to bear the burden."

"Your Majesty, that's like saying if the sun never set, the moon would never rise. Life turns upon the whims of fate and happenstance. Why would you wish not to be queen?"

She adjusted her russet wig and replied, "'Tis not really a wish, just a musing. I often wonder what it would have been like to have had a simple life, with a loving husband and children and. . . You've been with me for my entire reign, Dorothy—more than 40 years now. You know what it has been like for me, balancing my stewardship of England, duty to my people, with my. . . personal desires."

"I know, at times, it has not been serene for Your Majesty."

"You know, Dorothy, it could have easily been thee. You could have been queen instead of me. Do you ever think upon that?"

"Me, queen? Whatever do you mean, Your Majesty?"

"Come, come. I know the lineages of everyone in court. I know thee are only a few generations removed from Edward IV and Richard III on thy mother's side, and on thy father's you descend from the line of Edward III. You are a noblewoman, the direct descendant of kings, Dorothy Stafford. Your blood is as royal as mine. Had providence woven a different tapestry, thee could easily have been queen instead of me."

"I've never considered such a thing, Your Majesty. 'Tis a preposterous idea."

Her Highness laughed with gusto.

"Royalty is an incestuous business. Consider that the first wife of thy late husband was my own aunt, who, if rumors are true, had dalliances with my father before he even knew my mother."

"Your Majesty," said the royal footman, announcing his presence.

"Yes, what is it, William?"

"Master Shakespeare has arrived in response to your summons."

"Good—good," said the queen. "Light the candles in Wolsey's old office and show Master Shakespeare in. I'll speak with him there."

The footman turned to do as commanded, and the queen asked me, "How do I look?"

There were no mirrors in any of the queen's palaces. She had forbidden them for many years.

"You look radiant, Your Majesty," I said, though her skin seemed paler with the passing of each day.

"Master Shakespeare and I are not to be disturbed, Dorothy, but stay close by that I may summon thee, if need be."

13

I understood her meaning, and hurried straight to the alcove next to what had been Cardinal Wolsey's office when he was master of Hampton Court. From there I could both hear and, if necessary, observe the queen and her guests.

I was not an admirer of Shakespeare like the queen. I thought his comedies to be crude and his tragedies often seditious and sacrilegious. But Her Majesty liked anyone who could make her laugh.

"Master Shakespeare," she said upon entering the room, "how good of you to visit me."

He doffed his cap and bowed as the queen chose her favorite chair, one resplendent with red velvet and gold satin.

"I wish only my steed had the wings of Pegasus to convey me into your presence with even more alacrity," he replied, rising to his feet as the queen directed him.

Though he was still a relatively young man, the master playwright had begun to bald. His forehead was a dome of flesh not unlike a melon, and his hair lay to either side like a beagle's ears. He was not a particularly handsome fellow, but that wasn't why the queen valued him.

"I never got the chance to tell thee how much I enjoyed your most recent play, *The Merry Wives of Windsor*. I found its humor most appealing."

"Gracious praise indeed, Your Majesty. It was your command for me to reprise the character of Falstaff which served as inspiration. You are my muse—always. I'm grateful it was to your liking."

"Indeed it was. And now I have determined a new task for thee."

The playwright looked askance at the queen as if her words were unexpected.

"I want thee to write a play for the Feast of Epiphany. Something light, joyful—a comedy."

By the expression on his face, Master Shakespeare was not only caught off guard, but unenthusiastic about the prospect. Nevertheless, he responded affably.

"As you command, Your Majesty. I will be honored to create such for the noble Queen Elizabeth. I beg only one favor."

"What is that?" queried the queen, suspicion in her voice.

"Could you speak with your master of revels, Sir Edmund Tilney, and command him to cease censoring my plays? I only ask so I may be allowed to write my finest creation for Your Majesty without outside influence."

"Of course, of course," said the queen, waving her hand as if it were a trifle. "I'll command Sir Edmund to leave thee be."

"Your Majesty is most generous." He cleared his throat. "Speaking of your celebrated generosity, I understand Edmund Spenser has been granted a royal pension for his poem *The Faerie Queene*. May I suppose—"

"Yes, yes," said the queen waving her hand again, but more dismissively this time. "You will be adequately compensated."

"Your Majesty is as generous as she is beauteous, as wise as she is tolerant, as righteous as—"

"Master Shakespeare, don't you think I know when I'm being flattered? No one in history, methinks, has likely been blandished more." The queen smiled slyly. "But I interrupted. Do go on."

Shakespeare returned her smile—rather impudently I thought, though it could have just been the candlelight.

"Shall I compare you to a summer's day? You are more lovely and more temperate." He stopped unexpectedly then, looked thoughtful, and reached into his doublet for a scroll of paper. He searched his costume elsewhere, but didn't find what he was looking for.

"A pen! A pen! A king's ransom for a pen!"

He looked as desperate as he sounded. The queen pointed at the desk, and the playwright hurried to it. Once he'd secured the pen and dipped it in the ink pot, he wrote furiously.

"Forgive me, Your Majesty, but I must make note when an idea strikes."

"I understand. I myself can no longer trust importance to memory." She waited a moment while he wrote, then asked, "Tell me, what kind of play do you think thee will write for the Epiphany?"

The playwright thought for a moment, then replied, "In my mind's eye I see a shipwreck, a love story complicated by a case of mistaken identity. . . yes, that could work. But I need inspiration. Would Your Majesty grant me the honor of being my muse once again? Tell me of your loves. Inspire me."

Her Highness rose from her chair looking very serious. Her temper was legendary, and I thought, for a moment, she was about to reprimand the playwright for his brash familiarity. I was wrong.

"Oft times, Master Shakespeare, I think love is merely a form of madness. I may be queen, but in that respect I am no different than any common washerwoman. I, too, have suffered from this malady of the heart. Do you know I have received more than a score of marriage proposals in my time?"

"I doubt it not, Your Majesty."

"Yet most had nothing to do with love. Love is a much rarer beast," she said wistfully. "My first and greatest love was the Earl of Leicester, Robert Dudley, my sweet Robin, whom I'd known since childhood. Though he had no royal blood, he might have become my king, except. . . except he was already married. When his wife was found dead there were scandalous whispers of murder—murder that would free him to marry me and become king. They were untrue, of course, but I was

16

forced to banish him from court, as well as from my thoughts of marriage."

"A tragedy itself worthy of dramatization."

"Then there was François, my frog, the Duke of Alençon, brother to the king of France. He was so young, so short, and so ugly, but he made me laugh. He was so very charming that when he wooed me I behaved like a moonstruck girl, though I was nearly twice his age."

"Love is indeed blind," said Shakespeare.

"That it is. But the Duke was Catholic, and my advisors, my people, didn't like the idea of a Catholic king, not after my sister Mary's bloody reign."

I knew all about the queen's romantic heartbreaks. I'd been there for each and every one. Yet I could not believe she was being so indiscreet as to relay them for the master playwright. I'm not certain she cared he was in the room. She was caught up in her reminiscences.

"Then there was Sir Christopher Hatton, my dancing captain of the guard, and Sir Walter Raleigh, who wooed me while secretly marrying another. I threw him in prison for that."

"But you released him later," said Shakespeare.

"Yes, after he'd learned a lesson."

"What of the Earl of Essex?"

The queen frowned at the mention of the name. I knew her wounds on that account were still raw.

"Robert Devereaux is a disrespectful, vain young boy who titillated an old woman's heart. I spoiled him, always forgiving his trespasses, his disobedience, until he tried to foment rebellion. That I could not forgive."

"He's in prison, is he not?"

"Yes. And there he'll rot until I decide to part him from his head."

I could tell Master Shakespeare now regretted his query about the queen's love life, for the mood had turned morose. The queen, her ire sparked, turned on the playwright.

"What about thee, Master Shakespeare? Have you ever known true love?"

"What is true love, Your Majesty? Can love be false if 'tis truly love? If it be false, then it never was. But if thy heart says thou art in love, then it must be true."

"Your argument has merit, yet I'm assured I will never know true love," said the queen.

"Say not never, Your Majesty. Not while your heart still pounds."

"You don't understand, Master Shakespeare. I was cursed as a young girl."

"Cursed? By whom? By what?"

"By whom or what indeed." The queen resumed her seat and said to her guest, "You have my permission to sit as well."

The playwright chose the chair behind the desk, feathered pen still in hand, paper at the ready. He sporadically made notes as the queen spoke.

"I spent much time alone as a young girl. But one night I was visited by what I thought was a spirit. At first he just blew out my candles and laughed. And oh, what a laugh it was—like ice crystals breaking off a fairy's bell. But it was no spirit, no ghost that came to my room. I learned later he was an imp, a magical sprite.

"When I first heard the laugh, I called out, 'Who's there? Who is it that invades my bedchamber?' A sweet but mocking voice replied, 'I am that merry wanderer of the night called Robin Goodfellow.' That's what he called himself at first."

Though I was the queen's closest confidant, she'd never told me the story of this Robin Goodfellow. I was at once both curious to hear more, and jealous she'd chosen to reveal such to a lowly playwright.

"When next he visited, and it was always at night, he not only blew out my candles, he made my bedclothes vanish. I berated him for it, but he only laughed that impish laugh of his. Over time, other things vanished.

Sometimes I would hear the laugh, sometimes not. Sometimes, after the lights blew out, he would steal a kiss—only a peck upon my cheek, yet an affront all the same.

"Then, one night, after the candles blew out, I saw him. The light of the full moon poured through the window next to which he stood. He was quite a sight—more gnome than sprite, to my mind. No taller than a child of six, with the hindquarters of a goat, cloven hooves, and two tiny horns protruding above a baby face. 'I see thee,' I told him. He only smiled a wicked smile and said, 'Because you've seen me, I must reveal my true name. 'Tis Puck who is thy knavish lad, thy midnight love.'

"I was angry, annoyed with his mischief, so I said, 'What do you know of love, little hobgoblin? No one could ever love such as thee. You're too funny looking.'

"He looked at me with such hatred I pulled my bed covers up so that my eyes could barely see over them. He pointed a stubby little finger at me and said, 'Thou thinks thee knows beauty? That thy vision sees with the clarity of nature in all its pulchritudinous? What fools mortals be. I curse thee, Elizabeth Tudor, for all time. Thou will never know true love—only the cold comfort of a scepter shall be thine.'"

The queen finished her story and sighed longingly.

"So you see, Master Shakespeare, while I did not always believe it, I've known for some time that true love would never be mine. My sun will soon be setting, and the curse will be fulfilled."

I watched for Shakespeare's reaction. He put down the pen, placed his scroll back inside his doublet, and rose from his chair.

"Think upon the truth of it, Your Majesty. You did find true love. You have sacrificed much for it over the years. Your true love was for England, the bright country of your birth, the nation that was left in your care. Your country, your people, that is what you have treasured most, and to your own self you have been true."

"You are a wise man, master playwright. I would hear more of thy wisdom, but the hour grows late."

"Then I will bid you adieu, Your Majesty, though parting is such sweet sorrow."

The playwright bowed, doffed his cap, and backed out of the room, even though Her Highness hadn't given him leave. Well quit of him, I thought. He'd only served to stir the coals of unpleasant memories for the queen.

I was about to hurry to her side, to console her as best I might, when I saw from my alcove peep each and every candle in the room go dark as if a sudden gust had extinguished them. I moved to the hall outside the office and saw that even the lights there had gone out.

Before I could rush to her side and re-light the candles, I heard the queen say, "Puck, is that thee?"

Then I heard something I will never forget. A laugh that reverberated through the room and out into the hall where I stood. It was more giggle than belly laugh, but it sounded, indeed, like crystals of ice breaking from a fairy's bell.

Historical Epilogue

Shakespeare would write the romantic comedy Twelfth Night *for Queen Elizabeth's Feast of Epiphany, and the mythical woodland sprite known as Puck would become a key character in one of his more popular plays, "A Midsummer Night's Dream."*

Long before entering the service of the queen, Dorothy Stafford married Sir William Stafford, the widower of Mary Boleyn, once Henry VIII's mistress. After her husband died, she and her children fled to Geneva to escape the persecution of Protestants by Elizabeth's half-sister Queen Mary I. There, she met Protestant reformer John Calvin, who'd fled religious persecution in France. He would become godfather to her youngest son. After Queen Mary's death, Dorothy returned to England, where she served Queen Elizabeth and exercised much influence at the royal court.

Both Dorothy Stafford and the royal footman, William Head, are direct ancestors of this tale's author. Their family lines would intersect more than a hundred years later in 18th century Virginia, the state named by Sir Walter Raleigh for Queen Elizabeth I ("The Virgin Queen").

About the Author

Bruce Golden's short stories have been published more than a hundred times across a score of countries and thirty anthologies. *Asimov's Science Fiction* described his novel *Evergreen*, "If you can imagine Ursula Le Guin channeling H. Rider Haggard, you'll have the barest conception of this stirring book, which centers around a mysterious artifact and the people in its thrall." His latest book, *Monster Town*, is a satirical send-up of old hard-boiled detective stories featuring movie monsters of the black-and-white era. It's currently in development for a TV series. http://goldentales.tripod.com

*****~~~~~*****

Fire, Steel, and Flaming Pearls

by Kai Hudson

Three seconds passed between Christine throwing her backpack down and her mother poking her head out from the kitchen. "Liu Yingdi?"

She flopped down on the couch, crossed her arms, and glared at the worn coffee table, surface peppered with old rings from decades of hot tea mugs. "What."

A brief pause. Then: "Liu *Ying*di."

It was funny how the language of mothers worked. That one emphasis on Christine's name crumbled the first of the walls, and her vision blurred briefly with tears. "It's just school, Ma-Ma," she said, hating how her voice trembled, simultaneously hoping her mother would pick up on it. "It's stupid."

A soft hum, followed by the *click* of the stove being turned off. Her mother approached on socked feet and sank down onto the couch. "Tell me what's stupid," she said.

Christine couldn't look at her; if she did, Ma-Ma's kind eyes would make her cry, would unleash the river of formless frustration that had been bubbling inside her since sixth period. Why was she making such a big deal about this, anyway? It wasn't the first time they'd discussed China in AP History, and it wouldn't be the last.

23

So what if it had felt off to Christine, sitting in class listening to her teacher talk about the Dragon War like it was a fairy tale and not a very real conflict with very real death? So what if something deep inside Christine's heart had tightened enough to hurt the first time Mr. Hicks mentioned *long*?

Instead of answering, she reached into her backpack, pulled out her history book, and flipped through the pages until she found what she was looking for. Ma-Ma's eyebrows rose when she saw the image: a colorful artist's rendition of a twisting, brilliant-scaled lizard in the clouds. "Why are you learning about *long*?"

"It's imperialism," Christine said, wishing she knew how to say the word in Mandarin. "You know, when the Europeans came to China for all the silk and opium and stuff."

"I see." A cautious smile made its way onto Ma-Ma's face. She tapped one finger, still wet from washing vegetables, against the picture of the dragon. "It must be nice to be learning about the history of our people. Especially *long*, and what they did for us."

Christine blinked. What they did for us? "The book says *long* were already extinct by the time the Europeans came."

Ma-Ma's finger paused. Water leaked onto the page, crinkling the dragon's crisp, rainbow scales. The smile faltered and died. "What?"

"They call it the Dragon War in English," Christine said, watching the wet stain spread. "When *long* went into battle hundreds of years ago."

"With the Europeans."

"With each other."

A second too late, she realized her mother's last statement hadn't been a question. The book slammed shut. Startled, Christine looked up just in time to catch the bright flash in her mother's eyes, a spark of flame

24

Christine hadn't seen since her last fight with Ba-Ba before he left for good.

"They're teaching you lies," Ma-Ma snapped, but anything else she was planning to say was interrupted by a low *whoomp* from the kitchen. They both turned to see one of the burners had ignited. The stove had been malfunctioning like that for as long as Christine could remember, and Ma-Ma never seemed to care about getting it fixed.

The mishap seemed to placate her mother, who sighed, got to her feet, and padded back to the kitchen. She turned the burner off again, then filled one of their worn old mugs with hot water from the pot on the counter. With smooth, practiced motions, she unscrewed a canister of loose tea and dropped in a generous handful. "Take this to A-ma," she said, not looking at Christine, "and ask her to tell you about *long*."

Christine couldn't be sure, but it seemed, as her mother turned back to the stove, that her shoulders shook.

The journey up the stairs to her grandmother's room felt both familiar and not. She had been taking similar trips for as long as she could remember, the only difference being that her fingers were now long and piano-hardened rather than short and child-chubby. Still, it felt different today. Christine had never heard A-ma talk about *long* before.

Everyone knew about the meters-long, iridescent-scaled dragons that had once surfed the skies and threaded the rivers of East Asia. Unlike their larger, winged cousins in the West, who had all perished of some mysterious reptilian disease around 500 AD, *long* persisted well into the height of China's empire. In ancient times they were revered, worshipped for their magic and ability to influence the seasons. Sacrifices and offerings were made to please them so that their rain might bring good harvests, so that they would hold back the great spring floods and bless newborn babies with drops of fortune and prosperity from their glowing pearls. *Long* were real, and for thousands of years Christine's ancestors in China and Mongolia had looked to them for guidance and leadership, for hope in hard times.

But then the unthinkable happened: war amongst the dragons. Historians had all sorts of different theories, according to her book: some said it started with two *long* laying claim to the same beautiful human girl, while others quoting the poems and stories of the time pointed to themes of greed and dissatisfaction. Weren't *long* always chasing after the brightest, most beautiful pearls, after all? Weren't they jealous, flawed creatures with short tempers, bound to flare at the slightest offense?

According to the scholars, the great dragons retreated to the heavenly realms beyond human comprehension to wage war. The resulting storms and great floods devastated whole territories, tens of thousands—maybe even millions lost as a result. When everything finally settled, the *long* were gone. In their insatiable greed and inability to give ground, they destroyed themselves, a crumbling cautionary tale for the humans left behind.

Her grandmother was sitting by the window when Christine nudged the door open after a soft, polite knock. "Ah, Ying-Ying," she said, with a smile that crinkled her face like dried wax. "Come, sit. The sun feels warm here."

"Hello, A-ma," Christine said, passing the mug into worn, gnarled hands. A-ma never seemed to notice the almost-blistering heat of the tea. "Did you sleep well?"

Her grandmother smiled at her over the rim of the mug, eyes clear and alert despite the milkyness of slow-growing cataracts. "You wish to ask me something."

Christine hid her sigh by folding her hands in her lap. A-ma had her mother's intuition, or perhaps it was the other way around. It made life around the house. . . difficult, sometimes. "Ma-Ma says you know a story about *long*."

"Did she now." A-ma's eyes, deep pools of earth-brown, never strayed from Christine's face. "What kind of story?"

"One that isn't in my schoolbook."

"Your book that says *long* went to war and killed each other before the *waiguoren* came?"

Christine stared. Her grandmother shook her head, and there it was: the same flare in her eyes she'd passed down to Christine's mother. "*Laowai* always tell the best lies."

"I don't understand."

Her grandmother cocked her head. "What do you know about *long*?"

"That they were magical, and very, very old. That, um. . . " How she wished she'd paid more attention in Chinese school; A-ma wasn't fluent in Chinglish like her mother was. "People, um, gave them gifts to have them bring good things. Good things to the family, I mean."

A-ma nodded. "Yes. They were great beings with powerful abilities, who ruled over us with benevolence and magnanimity. *Long* were the epitome of grace and power, yet they also cultivated humility and respect. They were our protectors and guides, but they were also our greatest teachers. All our values as Chinese people come from *long*."

Christine hadn't known that. She'd thumbed through a few articles on her phone earlier, and they all described *long* as hot-tempered and imperious, and prideful to a fault. That was why they'd destroyed each other, after all. "But how do you know that's what they were like?"

Her grandmother didn't seem to hear her. Her eyes grew distant and sad. "When the *waiguoren* came, all they did was take. Silks, teas, opium, women, taking and taking and taking. Faced with such bottomless greed, the people became afraid and turned to *long* for help.

27

"And there *was* a war. It was brief but magnificent: how the *long* breathed fire and shot lightning from their pearls! They set the ships ablaze and swallowed all those terrible people whole. They drove back the invaders and protected the people, and for a while everyone celebrated and thought that was the end."

She lowered her gaze to the mug of tea, watching as steam swirled up in a thin spiral. "But for wicked people, there is never an end."

Christine swallowed hard. There was something in her grandmother's voice, a trembling filament of despair that sent twinges through her own heart. Yet there was something else, too: the pain stretched across a yawning chasm, one that boiled with a deep, ancient fury she'd only ever seen once. It was a sunny afternoon when she was nine or ten, and Ma-Ma got into a fender-bender. The lady in the other car rushed them immediately, screaming and calling Ma-Ma *stupid chinky bitch*, and it was only after the police came and they were finally inching back down the highway with Ma-Ma's hands trembling on the steering wheel that Christine's grandmother spoke up softly from the back.

Don't you put it on your heart, Zenluen, she'd murmured, as Christine swore the temperature inside the car rose a few degrees. *They will all burn eventually.*

Now, A-ma looked down at the tea in her lap but didn't seem inclined to drink it. "The *waiguoren* came back," she said, "with weapons. Cannons and muskets, and then machine guns and explosives. They hunted *long* into the deepest oceans and the highest skies, and anyone who tried to resist was. . . erased. The stories in your book are wrong; there's no world that only *long* inhabit, where they can be safe from human greed and destruction. We only have one world that we're all supposed to share, but *waiguoren* have never understood that.

"The tales from my childhood talk of blood and scales and bare, bleached bones. *Long* were just too big, too colorful and bright to hide from guns and cannons. And the people who tried to help them? The *waiguoren* destroyed them too. It wasn't thirty years before *long* disappeared completely from the skies, wiped out by ruthlessness and hate."

Christine sniffed, surprised and annoyed by the hot prickle of tears. She had no right to be upset; *long* were never part of her life. What did she care about their fate? So what if the Europeans had suppressed the true nature of their extinction in order to conceal their own crimes? Asia's ancient dragons had fought a war with a conquering power and lost, their legacy now nothing but stories and inaccurate textbooks. How was that different from the way history had always gone?

The soft *put* of mug on table brought her back to A-ma, who watched her with head cocked. "There's no need for sadness," she said.

"I know." Christine swallowed against the tightness in her throat. "The *long* died so long ago. It's stupid."

"Now, Ying-Ying." A-ma's lips curved into a slow smile. "I never said they died."

Christine blinked and, for the first time, noticed the room seemed different. It was quiet, but in a strange way: the rumble of cars on the street and the tapping of the pine branch against the window seemed further away now, echoing as if from the bottom of a deep well. The bright sunlight still spilled into the room, but that wasn't what made her warm.

"*Long* are warriors." A-ma's voice was the unyielding steel of swords and spears and a thousand arrow-tips, the unbanked fires of all things ancient and deep. "They would never allow such tiny, insignificant things as men to kill them off. And they would never abandon us. They love us too much."

"Then what happened to them?" Christine asked.

29

Her grandmother shrugged. "The same thing that happens when one wishes to survive in the face of something terrible," she said. "They adapted."

It seemed, just then, that a certain electricity filled the air. Thunder rumbled in the distance as a sudden cloud obscured the sun.

In the creeping shadow that fell across the room, Christine thought that for a moment, just a moment, A-ma's eyes glowed like pearls.

About the Author

Kai Hudson lives in sunny California, where she writes, hikes, and spends entirely too much time daydreaming of far-off worlds. Her work has appeared or is forthcoming in *Clarkesworld, PseudoPod, PodCastle*, and *Anathema: Spec from the Margins*, among others.

*****~~~~~*****

Losing Face

by Matthew Reardon

The noble art of losing face
may one day save the human race
and turn into eternal merit
what weaker minds would call disgrace.

A Grook by Piet Hein (1905-1996), Creative Commons License

My wife, back when I still had one, used to say, "Your stubbornness will be the end of you, Andy Janus." But she was wrong — it was my moustache.

It was no everyday, couldn't-be-bothered-to-shave bit of upper lip fuzz. My moustache was a work of art: a full, lustrous Imperial masterpiece, its up-curved ends tickling my earlobes. Like Scrooge's ghosts before them, the follicle-stimulating nanites had worked their magic over a single night.

My first blurred thought that morning was that the bedsheets had caught around my face. After a moment's blind panic, I remembered the previous night's drunken decision, and rushed across the bedroom of our tiny Prague apartment. The dressing cameras flared to life when I reached the wardrobe. A second later, my

Augmented Reality picture stood before me, pot-bellied and bedraggled in his frayed black boxers. At least Jitka hadn't made it home from her night shift yet, and didn't have to see me like this. What the hell had I been drinking?

Too much, that much was certain. Even by my recent standards. But whatever it was, it had made the sorry details of my life terribly clear. The daily drudge at the RedCorp offices downtown. Studying the faces of strangers, and programming mother AI to produce facial recognition software. AI to spawn program children, then make them compete, keeping only the fittest and destroying the weak.

A gruesome thought, but you couldn't let yourself get too emotional. Not even halfway through the second bottle of the evening. It was only work.

Maybe that's why I'd been drinking so much. I felt so useless, so anonymous. Alone with the AI all day at work, watching them spawn programs I no longer understood. Alone at home the rest of the time, while Jitka worked night shifts at GALILEO.

The ethanol clarity had shown me the truth. I needed something radical. Something wild. I needed to show I was different, an individual, not just another faceless code jockey.

I remembered the drunken laughter as I pasted facial accessories onto my AR simulacrum, one after another. I needed something both outlandish and regal. Something that would stop people dead in their tracks.

Then there it was. The curved lines of the cheek-embracing Imperial moustache matched my round face and balding brown pate. And I had everything at hand to make the proud AR image a reality.

Reprogramming a can of anti-balding nanite paste is no easy feat when you're as drunk as I was. But the lean, mean, moustache machines had done a stellar job.

Losing Face

Not a single hair washed away in the steaming shower, and the Imperial curves were still perfect after I'd dried.

Laughing at myself, I grabbed my shaver to put an end to it. It was halfway towards my face before I paused.

It seemed a shame to shave it off. A crime, even. This moustache was a message from a forgotten age. When people still made things they could hold in their hands. When life had a meaning.

And, despite the hangover playing bass on my optical nerves, I knew drunk me was right. This moustache was exactly what I needed to bring myself out of this funk.

I put the shaver down. Chuckling the whole time, I grabbed a quick yeast porridge for breakfast, and got ready for work. Only my best indigo business suit would do for a day like this. Outside, commuters filled the *Libeň* District walkways, all the way past the flea market to the tram station. But at least the breeze coming in off the river cleared away the worst of the day's smog. The rustle of wind in my proud new facial hair felt like the promise of a fresh beginning.0

At the station, my fellow passengers, engrossed in their AR worlds, ignored me and my moustache. Just another day on the tram to the RedCorp offices, down by Vyšehrad Cemetery. I booted up my own AR interface and spent the commute watching the highlights from my favourite reality show, "The Grass Is Greener." There was only one interruption, when the tram's payment system wouldn't validate my payment. I had to buy a ticket with the physical coins I kept for the homeless and buskers before I could board the tram.

As usual, the ride was over before I knew it. Smiling under my bobbing moustache, I waited for the flow of automated vehicles to pause, crossed the street, and pushed open the door to the RedCorp offices.

Well, I pushed, at least. Unlike every other day for the past ten years, the security lock did not release. The door refused to open, leaving me standing there in my best indigo three-piece suit like a hirsute fool.

I stood back and glared at the traitorous black nub of the door's facial recognition sensor, high above. I moved back and forth, waving my arms and trying to trigger it, but I was wasting my time.

It was the moustache. I'd taken my little act of anachronistic rebellion too far. My mother AI had bred software so specialised it could not see past my unheard-of Imperial to identify the jowly face beneath.

Some co-workers I recognised brushed past me in a small crowd, eager to get in out of the cold. The door opened for them without the slightest resistance, and I moved in behind them, relieved.

"Hey, Bára!" I called out, stepping forwards. "Could you hold the door? You wouldn't believe what's happened to me."

The white-suited HR lady at the rear of the group turned to face me. She stared in silence for a moment, eyes twitching in her AR overlay.

"You must have the wrong building, sir," she said at last, with a slight shake of her head. "You don't belong here."

I opened my mouth to protest, but the heavy clunk of the door's lock cut off the words.

Other colleagues, some familiar and some not, streamed around me. Everyone ignored the strange man with the weird facial hair standing on the sidewalk. None of their Friends apps recognised me, either. The almighty data labelled me a stranger—whatever their own eyes might tell them to the contrary.

I was faceless in a world run by blind trust in the eyes of machines.

. . .

Ten minutes of stunned wandering later, I sat at a park bench, next to the cemetery. A proud statue to the heroes of a fake medieval manuscript loomed behind it. It was as fitting a counterpoint to the day's unreality as I could hope for.

What the hell was I supposed to do now? Go back home to shave the beast off? I'd have to walk all the way back to Libeň. Without facial recognition, I had no way of paying for transport. I'd used all my physical coins for the trip to work. And Jitka would be fast asleep by now. Even if I called to wake her up, she'd only curse me for a fool and tell me I was getting what I deserve.

My stomach grumbled, reminding me how long-ago breakfast was. I had no way of paying for lunch, either, not even from one of the yeast-paste vending machines lining the city streets.

Lost in self-pity, I didn't notice the ragged figure until it sat down on the bench next to me.

"Got a coin to spare, sir?" rumbled a deep voice from somewhere under the man's layers of coats and thick black beard. "It's a cold morning, could use a hot drink."

A shiver ran through me, and a chill wind swept through the square.

"You and me both." I pulled my jacket collar up around my neck. "And I'm sorry, but I don't have anything to give you. You wouldn't believe the day I've had."

The ragged man nodded, taking it all in stride. I guess expectations are one of the first things you learn to manage on the street. But this fellow seemed friendly enough.

"Try me," said the man, with a disarming smile. "I doubt it's anything I haven't heard before."

And somehow, I told him everything. He was a great listener, and I needed to talk.

"Oh, a bit like Anet then," came his reply, when I paused for air. "For me, it was an ISP ban after a couple of bad hacks. But Anet got cut off because of facial recognition too, after a faulty car sensor left her covered in scars. We get all sorts, you know."

I tried not to gawk, but his words took me by complete surprise. "Are you saying there's a whole community of people like—" I was about to say "us," but the word caught in my throat. "But how do you survive?" I asked instead.

"We make do. And the rent is competitive," he added with a deep chuckle. "It's not far. Want me to show you?"

I had my life waiting for me, somewhere. But I was curious. "If you don't mind. . . Sorry, I don't even know your name." It was the first time in forever I'd had to ask someone their name. Their public profile always told me everything I needed to know. But it felt good.

"Call me Karel," said the man, smiling once again. "Come, follow me."

He led me through the park and down cement steps. There was a low alcove set in the wall surrounding the Basilica. A rusted iron grill blocked the way at the bottom of the stairs, and I almost turned around then and there. But then my guide pulled out an honest-to-God ballpoint pen. He poked into the metalwork to flip open a hidden latch.

The small gate swung open with surprising ease, given how rusty it was. But none of it was as amazing as that blue ballpoint pen. I hadn't seen a physical pen since childhood.

And so, when Karel urged me on into the dark, sloping tunnel, I was more amazed than scared.

The gate clicked shut behind us, and the temperature rose as I followed the larger man down the musty, cement incline. The darkness didn't last long. We soon arrived at a cheap interior house door, lit by a single naked bulb. I figured we must be somewhere under the cemetery itself by now.

With an encouraging smile, Karel swung open the door, and we entered. The stark white light of the bulb gave way to the flickering glow of the fire burning in the middle of the large vaulted room beyond.

Open fire. Another forgotten memory from ancient childhood. I was so amazed, it took me a moment to register the rest of the football pitch–sized vault. The gleaming ceiling extractor pumping the smoke from the fire out to unseen vents. The people huddled around the fire. Men, women, and even children, all wearing a motley mix of donated clothing. And in the dimly lit shadows, their dwellings. Rows of bunks, hanging curtain partitions, and an eating area. There were also worktables covered in computer parts, and a seating area with low lamps and rows of books. Real paper books.

It was like walking into the hidden cavern of some lost tribe that time had passed by.

Karel and I walked up to the group around the fire. Sunken eyes glanced at me out of inscrutable faces, but there was no aggression there. My hulking guide sat on an overturned plastic drum, and I claimed a rickety metal stool. All in all, a good thirty people had set up home under these ancient bricks. Some forgotten crypt, basilica cellar, or abandoned subway tunnel, maybe.

Karel's friends watched us sit, in silence. Their eyes lingered on me for only a moment before they resumed what they were doing: mending clothes, tinkering with scuffed home appliances, or simply gazing into the ever-shifting flames. Nobody asked my name. Nobody seemed to care.

A delicious, bready aroma wafted over from the glowing ovens at the end of the vault. My stomach rumbled. Maybe I could get a bite of lunch out of this adventure before I left. But for the time being, my curiosity was even greater than my hunger.

"So, you all live here?" I leaned in as I spoke, stretching my cold hands towards the fire. "All the time, I mean? Or are there other places like this?"

A sharp-faced woman with a wicked scar across her mouth put down the device she'd been tinkering with, and frowned at me.

"Not in Prague. Or anywhere else in the Czech Republic, as far as we know. We've heard of communities in big cities around the world, but staying connected isn't our forte. It's our blessing, and our curse."

She wasn't kidding. Without identity validation, you couldn't do anything in our ever-connected, augmented world. You couldn't order a food delivery. You couldn't buy anything online. You couldn't make a call, or pay taxes.

Alright, it might not be all bad. And it didn't affect me. I could shave off my fateful Imperial, and tell work I'd been off sick. But these folks hadn't seen the inside of a biometric scan booth for years—if ever.

"How can you survive like this?" I hoped the blunt question wouldn't offend. If I did anything to make these strange folk violent, nobody would ever know what happened to me.

But they were clearly used to dealing with much worse than tactless questions.

"We make do," grumbled Karel in a low voice next to me. "Charity donations from the few places that haven't shut down yet. Panhandling. And the odd under-the-table job for those who can get one. It's enough to keep us fed and warm."

"What about your families, though?" I asked, thinking of Jitka in bed back in the *Libeň* apartment, thinking I was at work—if she thought of me at all. The way she'd been talking lately, I doubted it. "Don't you have spouses? Children?"

Karel stayed silent, but the lady—Anet, I remembered—smiled, her face beautiful in the dancing firelight, scar and all. "Some of us do. My Adam is taking his nap over there." She hooked a thumb back towards a section of the vault partitioned off with purple woven rugs. "But others choose not to bring children into an environment like this. We don't judge, so long as they make the break clean, and leave their loved ones better off. Everyone has different needs, and brings different things to the community."

"What do you mean by 'better off,' though?"

For the first time, the faces around the fire looked uncomfortable. "Well, it depends on the situation," replied Anet, after a pause. "But a life insurance payoff can go a long way in today's economy. And dropping off the grid is the best way to convince the insurance companies you've died. Nobody can imagine living disconnected anymore."

There was something in what she was saying. Employment at RedCorp included mandatory company life insurance. They deducted it from every pay cheque, with Jitka as my sole beneficiary.

And half the reason my wife took the night shift job at GALILEO was so we wouldn't have to spend too much time together. To end the fights about why I was so mopey, why I thought I was wasting my life. Why living with her wasn't enough anymore.

She'd be sad at the thought I'd passed on, I was sure. Moderately sure. But she'd certainly be a lot happier with a fat insurance payoff than a nominal husband she couldn't stand anymore.

I could do it. It would be so easy to send her a suicide note, and wish her luck. But what about me? Would life be any better with these people, even if I found the courage to embrace it?

I sat, staring at the live flames. Maybe, for once, this shouldn't be about me. Looking around the squalid vault, seeing the way these folks lived I knew that, if I stayed, I could make their lives a lot better.

"I can see you're getting by now, but I have a few suggestions."

. . .

Young Adam's blue eyes opened wide as manhole covers as we spilled our plunder across the dining table.

"How did you find so much food?" he gasped. There were dozens of tubes of yeast-paste, along with a full set of flavouring canisters. Cartons of dehydrated milk powder, some sweet treats, and even a box of fresh apple slices.

I smiled, peeling off my indigo jacket. The short-sleeved shirt beneath was a grimy, sweaty grey by now, but I wore it like a badge of honour.

"All up and down Vnislavova," I said, with a chuckle. "You need to ask the vending machines politely, that's all." The boy stared at me in confusion, mingled with wonder. Grinning, I handed him a chocolate bar before sitting down at the table. "When you spend years working with facial recognition software, you learn a trick or two. It's easy to get a simple machine to register you as a stock quality tester, if you know how."

The entire community had gathered around by then. Someone pulled out a bottle of something eye-wateringly alcoholic. Someone else fired up a cannibalised public speaker device. Soon everyone was smiling, dancing, and eating to their heart's content. Probably for the first time in years.

"Here's to our brave Quality Testers!" cheered one of the dancers by the fire. Soon everyone picked up the chant, shouting, "Long live the QTs!" Including me.

My moustache was the end of me, it's true. And the start of something new. It took me losing face before I could finally find my place in the world.

###

About the Author

Born in Newfoundland, Canada, but raised on the tiny islands of Saint-Pierre-and-Miquelon, the only piece of France left in North America, Matthew Reardon is a multiple award-winning Canadian SF author who blends comedy with political themes—drawing heavily, in both cases, on his experience as a lawyer and as Secretary General of a Parliamentary group at the French National Assembly. A member of the SFWA, his short fiction has been published in professional venues. His previous Third Flatiron story placed as Recommended Reading for 2018, and won an award for Best Positive Future Story 2018. He is also a craft article contributor to the SFWA blog, the *SFWA Bulletin*, and Tor.com. He would love to hear from you on Twitter, over at @SpaceLawyerSF!

*****~~~~~*****

Indian Uprising

by Brenda Kezar

A line of Custer's cavalry waited on the hilltop as the battle raged on the wide prairie below. They were relief soldiers, green and scared, to be called in only if Custer's "certain victory" became uncertain.

A voice rang out behind them. Twenty feet back, a reporter stood beside the lone tree on the hilltop. A camera on a tripod stood in front of him.

"You. Boy." The reporter waved. "Come here!"

Johnny glanced nervously at his captain.

"Go ahead, lad." The captain smiled. "Let the man make you famous."

Johnny looked down at the fighting below. Half the soldiers had been knocked from their horses and fought the Natives hand-to-hand. Johnny swallowed hard, his eyes glued to the fight. "Sir?" he squeaked. "What if you need me?"

The captain smiled smugly. "I believe we will manage without you."

Down below, a blond soldier about Johnny's age raised his gun and shot a Native who had been creeping up on a dark-haired soldier. The Native folded and fell to the ground. The dark-haired soldier smiled and raised his hand in thanks, but the smile did not last. As the blond soldier waved back, another Native plunged a knife into his back. The blond sank to his knees and toppled face-first into the grass.

The fighting was not going as well as they had been led to believe. Johnny felt like he had just eaten a whole bushel of green apples. He clicked his heels into his horse's ribs and left the line.

"I need a few photographs of our brave war heroes." The reporter fiddled with the tripod.

Johnny dismounted and ran his hand through his hair. "No disrespect, sir, but I'm no war hero. I've never seen battle before."

"The good folks back East won't know the difference, will they?" He winked. Behind them, the captain raised his arm. The cavalry line rippled as the horses fidgeted and stamped their hooves, knowing what came next. After a pause, the captain dropped his arm, and the line followed him over the hill, out of sight. Johnny sighed and turned back to the reporter.

"Slope arms," the reporter said.

Johnny mounted his Henry repeating rifle against his shoulder.

The reporter disappeared behind the camera. "All right. Now stand *very* still. Don't move until I say."

Behind Johnny, the sounds of battle grew louder, closer. After a few moments of waiting patiently, Johnny stole a glance over his shoulder. A soldier crested the hill, his eyes wide, his face ashen; a Native in skull war paint closed the distance between them.

"Face me," the reporter shouted, oblivious to the drama playing out behind Johnny. "And be still."

"But—"

The Native dove at the soldier, and the two became a brawling tangle that rolled back down the hill. Johnny caught a glimpse of their heads above the tall grass now and then as they fought.

"Stay calm." The reporter said. "This won't take much longer, so long as you're still."

Johnny half-turned so he could watch the soldier and the Native out of the corner of his eye. The Native sat up, then bent over out of sight again. When he reappeared, something dangled from his mouth. He snarled and shook his head, like a vicious dog with a squirrel in its jaws, and chewed vigorously. His head dipped out of sight, and when he appeared again, he looked directly at Johnny.

"Is he. . . ?" Johnny tried to make sense of what he saw. "Is he *eating* him?" Johnny lowered the gun from his shoulder and took a few tentative steps toward the Native. The Native scrambled to his feet.

"Confound it! Why can't you—" The reporter popped up from behind the camera, his face scarlet, but the color drained from his face when he saw the Native.

The war paint around the Native's mouth was smeared, gray and pink, and foamy with blood. Johnny aimed his shaking gun and pulled the trigger.

The Native fell. With trembling hands, Johnny readied another round. The Native staggered to his feet, black slime oozing from the hole Johnny had put in his chest.

The Native sprinted across the hilltop and grabbed Johnny. Johnny tried to use his rifle, trapped between them, to lever the Native away, but the man clung to him with the strength of a bear. He thrust his head at Johnny's neck and tore out a mouthful of flesh. Johnny dropped to the ground, his hand pressed to his bleeding neck. The last thing he saw was the Native turning his cold, gray eyes to the reporter.

. . .

"We have traveled a long distance to see the princess." Alonzo tried to make his voice ring with authority, but the big Native standing beside the tipi didn't seem impressed. His arms bulged, thick as Alonzo's thighs, and he towered at least two heads taller. The

Native scowled and used his bulk to block the tipi door—as if Alonzo would be crazy enough to even attempt to dart past him!

Alonzo stamped his foot and turned to Frank, his translator. "See if you can reason with this dumb brute."

Frank approached the Native and spoke a few words in the Native's own tongue. The Native threw a suspicious glance at Alonzo and muttered in return. Frank shrugged. The big Native's scowl deepened, but he stepped aside.

Alonzo cast a last wary glance at the guard and ducked inside. It took a moment for his eyes to adjust to the gloom. The only light came from a pit of softly glowing embers in the middle of the room. Four woven grass mats surrounded the fire pit. He expected the tipi to feel claustrophobic, but the inside was larger than it looked. The delicate perfume of sweet grass and wood smoke tickled his nose pleasantly.

He also expected more guards, but the only person inside was the woman he had come to see. Tall and slender as a willow, with a delicate face and almond-shaped eyes, she studied them.

"Good day. I'm Alonzo Palmero of the Troy Bugle Gazette. And this," he gestured toward Frank, "is my translator, Frank."

"You may call me, South Wind Woman." She looked Frank up and down with interest. "And you. What is your *real* name?"

Frank ducked his head like a shy schoolboy. "Tanka Hoton."

Alonzo frowned. "I beg your pardon?"

"Tanka Hoton." Frank's eyes flashed with pride. "My *real* name."

Everyone called the man Frank, but of course, Alonzo realized, he would have an *Indian* name. "Fascinating. What does it mean?"

46

"Big Crow." He cast a shy glance at South Wind Woman.

"Big Crow." Alonzo tested the name on his tongue. "Tanka Hoton."

South Wind Woman seemed pleased by the exchange. She gestured toward the mats. "Please. Sit."

Once they were seated—after some awkward struggling from the white man unaccustomed to sitting on the floor—she turned to Alonzo. "They tell me you are a Story Man."

Alonzo smiled, happy the conversation had returned to familiar ground. "Yes, I suppose you could say that. I am a reporter. My mission is to bring back news to my people."

"And what news do you seek here?"

"News from the battlefields," he said. "We are losing, and the people back East are dumbfounded. They want to know why a bunch of primitive savages are giving our boys such a sound thrashing."

She batted her eyes and feigned shock. "And you believe *I* have something to do with it?"

"The stories I have heard all lead to you." He shrugged. "I have spoken to soldiers who have survived, few as they may be, and they have told outlandish tales of fighting against dead men, and of dying men getting back up and joining the fight."

"And you think they are mad," she smirked.

"Well, I don't know if I would say that, but they must be suffering from battle fatigue or mass hysteria. The dead do not get up and walk again."

Her smile disappeared. "Wendigos do."

"Wendigos?" Alonzo repeated. Frank shuddered, and Alonzo gave him a stern look.

"I do not know what they are called in your language, but my people have used them in times of trouble for as long as we can remember." She touched the ornate gold pendant around her neck. "It was great-

47

grandmother's. Her people fled north when the Spaniards came. The survivors saved the wisdom, the power of my people, and passed it down to me, so someday our people could rise again and take back what is ours."

That explained why she didn't quite look like the others. "So these Indians, they are not your people?"

"No. My people are from a place called Tenochtitlan."

Alonzo frowned. Geography had never been his strong suit.

"In what you call, Mexico," she explained.

He whistled. "You *are* a long way from home."

"Not for long. After we have defeated the white threat here, I will take my warriors south. I will gather what is left of my people and take back our lands." Her eyes narrowed. "And any white man who dares to stand in our way will die a horrible death."

Beads of sweat bloomed on Alonzo's forehead at the venom in her voice, and he wiped them away with a trembling hand. "I mean you no ill will, ma'am. I am just trying to get a story."

She waved her hand dismissively. "We will not harm you. You are of use to us. Take our story back to your people, Story Man. Convince them to throw down their arms. They cannot defeat our wendigos."

She paused and smiled mischievously. "Would you like to see them?"

Alonzo's heart hammered. He *very much* wanted to see them—sort of. What had started out as an amusing folk tale for the readers back East now felt sinister. He certainly did not believe in ghosts and goblins, but the Indians obviously did. He glanced over at Frank.

Frank stared at the woman, smiling softly, eyes glazed, head tilted, as if bewitched. He finally noticed Alonzo looking at him and shrugged. "It is why we came."

Alonzo mustered his courage. "It is decided, then. We will see them."

She smiled and ducked out the tipi door. Alonzo and Frank followed. The guard left his post and joined them.

After a few steps and a quick backward glance to make sure the guard was out of earshot, Alonzo whispered, "Must your bodyguard accompany us?"

She laughed. "Spotted Horse is my——."

"I am her husband," the big Native growled, suddenly beside them.

"Sorry," Alonzo muttered. While the man was the size of a bison, he apparently had the light step of a feline.

They wordlessly followed South Wind Woman through the camp. At camp's edge, they mounted horses and followed South Wind Woman down a well-worn trail.

Alonzo glanced back at Frank and the big Native. Frank's star-filled eyes never left South Wind Woman's back. Alonzo started to say Frank's behavior around South Wind Woman was completely inappropriate, but then his gaze fell on the scowling Spotted Horse, who only had eyes for *him*. He shut his mouth and faced forward again.

The trail turned and followed parallel to the ridgeline. South Wind Woman led the group around the ridge to a box canyon on the other side, bounded on three sides by the steep, rocky cliffs of the ridges. A split-rail fence, guarded by several Natives, barred the open side of the box canyon. The wooden rails still wept sap.

"See," South Wind Woman swept her arm wide. "The wendigos are real."

At least a hundred men stood behind the fence. Most were Native, but a few whites and a few black men stood among them. Some wore clothes, tattered and smeared with mud and blood, while others were naked. The lack of clothing left their wounds clearly on display, wounds that left no doubt: no man could sustain those and live.

Their faces unnerved him even more: empty, gray eyes in faces painted to resemble skulls.

She dismounted and looked over her army with pride. "Before battle, we paint their faces like bone so we can distinguish them from the living."

Alonzo dismounted and shook his head. "No one will ever believe this."

South Wind Woman grabbed his shoulders, brought her face to his, and stared intently into his eyes. "Make them believe. They will all die if they do not."

Alonzo sighed and wondered again, why he had taken this assignment? He grabbed his haversack off his horse and dug around for his camera, his only chance at convincing anyone that wendigos, and the danger, were real. Spotted Horse summoned the guards away from the fence, and they joined him in a ring on the ground as he drew in the dirt. The next battle plan, perhaps. Alonzo shuddered and cast a worried eye toward the now unguarded fence.

South Wind Woman noticed his nervousness. "You are safe with me."

Alonzo set up the camera and took photographs. While he worked, South Wind Woman stood and watched him, a proud smile on her face. Frank stood beside her and stared at her, silently, an odd half-smile on his face. It took three tries for Alonzo to get his attention.

"Ahem!" Alonzo cast a worried glance at Spotted Horse, but he hadn't noticed Frank's odd behavior toward his wife. "Frank, some assistance, please. It would lend credence to the images if I were in one. I need you to operate the camera."

Frank reluctantly left South Wind Woman's side and stood behind the camera. Alonzo walked closer to the fence and posed in front of it. He glanced over his shoulder several times to make sure no wendigos were sneaking up on him.

"This will not work if you are not completely still," Frank chided.

Indian Uprising

South Wind Woman shook her head and leapt over the fence. She spoke in hushed tones to one of the closest wendigos, and it followed her obediently to the fence. Alonzo took several quick steps backward, but South Wind Woman grabbed his arm. "They will not harm you while you are with me, I promise."

Alonzo swallowed hard and posed with the wendigo.

. . .

The next evening, the camp suddenly broke out in cheers and whoops. Alonzo and Frank crawled out of the tipi they shared and watched a group of warriors returning.

"Victory!" Spotted Horse shouted from horseback, waving his war club high. "Our land will be ours again soon."

Alonzo barely heard. He fixated on the line marching toward the box canyon. South Wind Woman rode in the lead, bobbing gently with each step of her horse as if leading a herd of docile cattle to greener pastures. A line of bloody and broken men shuffled behind her. Wary guards on horseback supervised, weapons at the ready. Alonzo lost count at seventy-five wendigos, and still they kept coming. Over half had white faces and wore Cavalry uniforms.

"Is that ...?" Alonzo's breath caught in his throat. He swallowed hard and turned to Frank. Frank nodded. "I believe that is Custer's unit."

. . .

Not long after midnight, Alonzo woke to shouts. Beside him, Frank's bedroll lay empty. He leapt to his feet and rushed out of the tipi. People ran past carrying torches and weapons. Even the small children carried rocks and sticks. His blood ran cold. Had the wendigos turned on them? Was the camp under attack? And where was Frank?

He followed the crowd, and when the crowd stopped, he pushed his way through to the center. Frank

51

and Spotted Horse faced each other inside the ring of people. South Wind woman stood at the far edge, held back by two burly warriors.

"Say!" Alonzo pushed his way into the opening. "What the devil is going on here?"

Blood dripped from Frank's swollen, split lip, and from his twisted, broken nose. He tilted his chin upward, his eyes defiant. "I love her," he said. "And she loves me."

Spotted Horse narrowed his eyes and snarled, "What does a witch know of love?"

He swung his war club. It connected with a dull thud, and Frank crumpled to the ground. South Wind Woman broke free and threw herself across Frank's limp body.

"You will die for this," she screamed at Spotted Horse, her face twisted and tear-streaked. "You will be my slave. You will spend an eternity crawling on your belly in the dirt to serve me."

Spotted Horse's eyes bugged, and his jaw clenched. Alonzo could swear he heard the man's teeth crack. Spotted Horse swung his war club high and brought it down on South Wind Woman's head with a noise like stomping an egg.

South Wind Woman crumpled on top of Frank, her blood mingling with his in the dust. Alonzo met Spotted Horse's eyes.

"You!" Spotted Horse pointed at him. "You brought the wife-stealing snake here!"

Alonzo took two steps backward, but many hands grabbed him. As Spotted Horse advanced, all Alonzo could think to say was, "Please don't turn me into one of your wendigos."

. . .

In the box canyon, the full moon threw a silvery glow on the wendigos. Those lying or sitting suddenly leapt to their feet, and they all turned to face the direction of the camp in unison. The hair on the back of the guards' necks stood on end. They drew their weapons, frightened by this new, strange behavior. The wendigos cocked their heads, as if listening to something in the distance, then they all crumpled to the ground like puppets cut free of their strings. They never moved again.

Two months later, the Troy Bugle Gazette headline read, "Local Reporter Missing in Indian Wars. Feared dead." The photo that ran with the story had been brought in by a soldier who recovered it from an abandoned Indian camp. The photograph showed a nervous looking Alonzo with his arm around a disheveled Native in skull war paint. After much study and analysis, scholars agree that the strange, dull gray of the Native's eyes must be a trick of the light.

About the Author

Brenda Kezar's work has appeared in *A High Shrill Thump: War Stories* (Third Flatiron Publishing), *Test Patterns: Creature Features, Daily Science Fiction, Silverthought, Penumbra* eMag, *Zombidays* (Library of the Living Dead Press), and others.

*****~~~~~*****

Carbon–Nitrogen–Oxygen

by Sarah Hinlicky Wilson

Not many people come to the tiny garden ringed round by the Plenum, the seat of government in the megalopolis of Axxaashe. Not many tread across its carpet of flowering phlox in the spring or sit under its autumn canopy of sweetgum stars in purple, red, and gold. Not many admire its walls overgrown with akebia and jasmine, illuminated by mirrors casting the sunlight into its shadowy depths. And so not many know that at its heart stands a statue of Tetazani Rakotomalala, the disgraced Senior Councillor of Axxaashe.

But you are here, and you want to know why the statue is here, why it exists at all, and why it is hidden away. It is hidden because it hides the story not of Rakotomalala's disgrace, but of Axxaashe's. Even now she bears the disgrace of her beloved city.

But her story, and the city's story, is one of those unusual stories that must be told backward, not forward. So we begin at the end.

We begin with the murder of Tetazani Rakotomalala.

. . .

She had gone to live in the outer ring of the city. She was no longer welcome in the heights of the center, amidst its elevated ponds and sassafras groves and passenger bridges so high up they occasionally vanished into the clouds. Banished from power, from culture, she turned to the only ones who might extend hospitality to her.

The oxygen refugees took her in, meager as their resources were. As Axxaashe had not been able to refuse them outright, it consigned them to the outer ring, facing the city's patchwork gardens—the backup plan in case the vertical permaculture, lentil roofs, and mile-high gardens failed to provide sustenance for the city. Those who could do no better for themselves found work tending these erratic farms, slow careful work on account of the conscientious refusal of monoculture. The price of their poverty labor was that the farmers could not entirely avoid glancing out at the edge—where wilderness resumed and civilization ceased save for the radiating spokes of the rail lines.

By the time Rakotomalala's fall from grace was established fact, only oxygen refugees lived on the outer ring, not fearful but grateful to spend their days overlooking flat rows of green, or mostly green, or even half-green. For their part, the veterans of Axxaashe, even of the lowest rank, had fled inward, disgusted by the habits of the oxygen refugees.

For whatever modicum of charity, or at least toleration, Tetazani Rakotomalala had inculcated into her citizens, all of it evaporated within moments of the oxygen refugees' arrival, right as the first of them stumbled out of the rail cars. Their bleary eyes, grubby clothes, chronic coughing, and the simple knowledge of the time and distance the trip took all might have inspired Axxaashe's sympathy toward even the least deserving people. But then they saw—in the oxygen refugees' arms—chickens. Chickens and some guinea fowl. There were as many of them as of people, and it wasn't three days before the chickens were running riot through the streets and gardens, honking and accusing, pecking, greedy, gobbling.

To make matters worse: the oxygen refugees ate them. They ate the birds' young, that clear-and-yellow slime cracked and shaken from its fragile case. They ate the birds full-grown, too, their reward for donating a thousand unhatched eggs. People saw it happen, it was on the news. Citizen councils rose up in outrage. The only reason chickens weren't outlawed altogether is that Axxaashe itself would have had to kill them. In nauseated horror Axxaashe furled inward, leaving the marginal people to the margins of the city.

But even on the edge, and despite their supplies of meat and eggs, the refugees needed a share of the city's rations, more than could be spared, so the rage built, along with fear for the inner gardens of pawpaw and persimmon and black walnut. One night it boiled over, like rice with the lid on. It foamed and frothed, and there was a riot. Many of the oxygen refugees were injured, and a few, probably accidentally, were killed. But it was no mistake when they bludgeoned Tetazani Rakotomalala, who when the scrum cleared still clutched a boiled egg in her hand. Of the foreigners nothing better could be expected, but when one of their own, the former first among equals, betrayed every principle of decency and descended to that level—.

No one was sure who did it, if it was even one single hand that struck the life from her. It was not a conspiracy or a plot, only an upsurge of disgust, too primal for control. It shook Axxaashe, it shamed Axxaashe. The city gave her a discreet burial and saw to it that the oxygen refugees were protected thereafter.

. . .

Tetazani Rakotomalala, killed for eating an egg, had just months before been the Senior Councillor of Axxaashe. She had already and with distinction served a full five-year term and was coming to the end of another, and there was no doubt about her reelection.

And then in one moment—a moment of decision that took place right here, in the Plenum's tiny garden at the bottom of this conical well of walls—she committed political suicide. She ruled autocratically that Axxaashe would accept its share of the oxygen refugees. She communicated her resolve to her counterpart in Kahuurik, clear across the continent on the western ocean, that dead city whose few living were disgorged like volcanic ash, before she told anyone in Axxaashe. She informed Axxaashe only when it was too late to reverse the order.

And the city founded on life and green and sun rose up in revolt against her and the oxygen refugees. Because it was failing.

Yes, failing. Axxaashe could not accommodate the lives it had, much less the tens or hundreds of thousands more arriving inexorably by rail.

The people who hear of this are still shocked by these words about the city; it is blasphemy. Blasphemy has the unfortunate quality, however, of sometimes being true. And the truth is that Axxaashe was failing; maybe even dying; maybe headed toward the same fate as Kahuurik.

Blasphemy!

And yet the hard facts: The plants were dying. Vines, trees, shrubs, it made little difference. They were yellowing and browning, shriveling and withering. Children could no longer freely glean the fruit off the chokecherries and physalis; every last berry had to be harvested, counted, distributed. Gardeners and botanists tried every solution from the analytical to the alchemical, but in the end the symbiotic arrangements that had served so well for a century were simply collapsing.

Then there were the insects. In a word, a plague. The principles of Axxaashe's constitution forbade the use of insecticide, which in time would become humanocide, but principle begins to sway when there is no relief from locusts, mosquitos, ticks, and flies, from tomato hornworms and potato beetles and aphids that devour the people's food before they get a fair shot at it.

And if that weren't enough, the people. They were failing, mirrors of the failing city. Compromised immune systems, endemic weakness, lowered fertility. They were not *well.* They should have been. Yet existence itself had become an insult to a city premised on the flourishing of all. There was no end to theories of the whys and wherefores of the failure, but one thing was agreed upon: a city beginning to contemplate famine for the first time in its history is in no position to welcome a hundred thousand hungry refugees.

. . .

If the city was in such crisis, you well may ask, why did Tetazani Rakotomalala let the refugees in?

There were the official reasons, of course. Long-standing parity agreements with other megalopoloi demanded it. Those others had already absorbed countless numbers of the destitute. And there were humanitarian reasons: the refugees would otherwise die. In any event, they could not stay where they were. The oxygen was all used up. Kahuurik was much deader, much browner and yellower, than Axxaashe by that time. Axxaashe was failing, but Kahuurik had failed.

But only after the refugees arrived did the people see the real reason, or what they thought was the real reason. One of the second-tier leaders from Kahuurik was also named Rakotomalala. You had only to glance at her to infer that she and the Rakotomalala of Axxaashe were sisters.

That wasn't true, in fact. They were only third cousins. Axxaashe's Rakotomalala claimed all the way to her banishment not to have known. The Kahuurik Rakotomalala said that the Leader of the Kahuurik Presidium had mentioned the common name to her, but they took it to be coincidence, nothing more. Anyone who was present at the women's first meeting could plainly see that it was an astonishment to them both, their identically black faces identically shocked, as if a trick of mirrors had been inappropriately arranged at this gravest of diplomatic occasions.

But most people weren't there, didn't see, and could more easily believe that all the protestations of ignorance were an act, a sham, an abuse of power sheerly for the sake of protecting her own family.

That was bad enough, but it signified something even worse. The second Rakotomalala, the one from Kahuurik, was living proof that among the oxygen refugees were the great-grandchildren of the carbon heretics, the very ones who had been expelled from Axxaashe a century before.

And one word from Axxaashe's Rakotomalala had reinstated them. She single-handedly granted forgiveness to the carbon heretics, to save her sister or cousin or whomever, even if it would cost the city its life. The people could not forgive her for that, and as you already know, they could not let her live to see what she had wrought.

. . .

You want to know who the carbon heretics were. I'll tell you. This vast continent upon which we live once looked very different. Imagine a time when the patchwork around the city was everything, from coast to coast—each little family with its own little farm, all spread out; or massive farms, each devoted to one soil-wrecking crop; and the people scattered all over like salt and pepper. It was premised on an ideology of the earth that was an enemy of the earth, a longing for freedom that was indistinguishable from isolation.

Where did the wild animals go? Into the ground, all dead.

Carbon-Nitrogen-Oxygen

Of course, bigger cities sprang up. Mostly awful, shabby, and desolate despite the crowding. You never really knew where one ended and the next began. Roads between them ate up a quarter of the land, and people from far away governed circumstances of which they knew nothing. It was all part of that long experiment in nation-building, stretching from the time when the ancient empires across the ocean began to fall, till when, more recently, the multiple crises of past centuries nudged the world back toward city-states.

All the studies show that what we have now is a much more sensible arrangement, attentive to place, not pitting the human against the green. Bimmaahchiia far up north, for example, is a bifurcated megalopolis because of its climate extremes: one side for winter, when the snow itself becomes the building material, another side for summer, when it's safe to move back into flimsy homes and shops all connected by breezeways. In Xalaa they've dug deep underground, as the sun there is too hot and the air too thin for but short trips above ground each day.

This city of Axxaashe at the foot of the Ozarks has always been special. We are in a good place, where neither sun nor cold is our enemy. At our establishment we insisted upon two foundational principles: an end to the shedding of blood of every kind, and an end to the burning of carbon. Naturally, there were those who disagreed, and loudly. But how could we all live together in one state with a disagreement of that magnitude? About first principles and the very shelters around our bodies? A city needs a common vision, a shared notion of what's right and wrong. Axxaashe would not accommodate those who would slit another creature's throat to fill their own bellies, nor those who would pollute our fragile atmosphere for the sake of entertainment or luxury or speed.

We sent them away. Carbon heretics, we called them. You think it sounds harsh. At least we did not take

61

their lives, as was done to the heretics of old. We only sent them into exile, and they landed in the carbon-hungry city they deserved, in Kahuurik, to choke and gasp and suffocate for a hundred long years.

And their choice, in the end, killed their city, as we knew it would. It would have killed all of their children, too, if Axxaashe hadn't taken them in.

. . .

I told you that this story ended where it began, with the murder of Tetazani Rakotomalala. But there's one more thing to tell. Which is that Axxaashe itself also would have died, and everyone in it, if it hadn't been for the carbon heretics.

As it turns out, the oxygen refugees—descended from the carbon heretics—saved us, because on their return from a century's exile they brought back with them the nitrogen heroes, otherwise known as chickens.

It was some years before the fact of rescue became apparent. Our salvation started from the margins of the city and slowly worked its way in. Yes, those squawking birds saved a city of pinnacles and sunscrapers! And by doing nothing other than what chickens do best. They ate the bugs. They scratched the earth. They littered their droppings all over. They worked their nitrogen-rich waste into our dead and depleted soil. The city began to green again.

Searching for answers, Axxaashe's scientists returned to discredited material in the restricted sections of the city and university libraries. They whispered among themselves terrible truths but dared not speak them publicly. Some of them relayed their findings to the city's religious leaders, who had been granted only in the last hours of the writing of Axxaashe's constitution the right to keep their texts that spoke of bloodshed and sacrifice. And although their facility with such matters was, a century later, purely literary and nothing more, it fell to them to break the news to the city.

Carbon-Nitrogen-Oxygen

That was a hard hour for Axxaashe, when across the city on our screens large and small adorned with garlands of renewing green, the horror and heresy was made known to us: Life costs life. Eat and be eaten. Blood is too sacred *not* to be shed.

We were shattered, at first. Many resisted, and some emigrated. But when the runner beans and kiwi sprang back to life, when the nasturtium and hops twined again in blissful harmony up and down walls that for years had known only the brown skeletons of botanical death, it was hard to dispute even this most repulsive of truths. Before you knew it chickens were everywhere, petted and lauded, and their final end in a pot no longer seemed like an act of vengeance but one of completion.

And there was no denying how much we all loved the smell of chicken soup.

. . .

It's funny how fast history rewrites itself in the human mind. For a hundred years it was drummed into the citizens of Axxaashe that there were no people on earth worse than the carbon heretics. Nowadays you'd never even know they existed, or that we expelled them, or that we devoted ourselves to a century-long project of bloodlessness that nearly cost us our lives. The oxygen refugees have integrated, assimilated, and are indistinguishable from the rest. They've nearly forgotten their own history by now. It would be inconvenient and possibly dangerous if people yearned for the old ways, so we judge it best to let them slip out of mind. And in a city of this size, with so much new and exciting always on the horizon, there's little reason to look back and linger over the past's mistakes.

The few who bother to keep memory alive, and will not let history be lost, conspired to erect this statue here to Tetazani Rakotomalala, to her compassion that was the inadvertent salvation of our city. We can't openly rehabilitate her. Only the rare visitor like you sees her, not

63

enough to cause any trouble. This statue is our private apology to her for the mass forgetfulness.

And I suppose the other apology was when, a decade later, the Plenum elected me to the position of Senior Councillor. Do you see the resemblance? I do my best to live up to her example. I've almost forgotten my own origins by now, so closely do I identify with Tetazani's Axxaashe.

But I wish I'd had the chance to know my cousin.

###

About the Author

Sarah Hinlicky Wilson is an American writer living with her husband and son in Tokyo. She serves as a pastor at Tokyo Lutheran Church and co-hosts the podcast, "Queen of the Sciences: Conversations between a Theologian and Her Dad." In addition to several books in her academic field, she's written a memoir about living in the brand-new Republic of Slovakia when she was seventeen. But her main calling in life is to make dinner. See more of her work at www.sarahhinlickywilson.com.

*****~~~~~*****

Behind the Purple Haze

by John A. Frochio

It was the summer of 1963. Late one evening, the sun hadn't yet touched the horizon, and it was still quite warm. Since her husband had died (much too young) and her children had gone off on their own, Magda (a common name among the Roma Gypsies) lived alone out of a canvas-covered wagon, inviting Tennessee locals to hear their fortune for a few coins. A campfire smoldered in the center of a clearing in front of her wagon. A black horse tied to a nearby tree snorted and huffed.

Magda had finished telling a local's fortune. As the big hairy man plodded away, head lowered, dragging the odor of sweat and grease behind him, he passed a skinny, young black man in green army fatigues.

Magda sat cross-legged in front of the waning fire counting her day's bounty. She looked up as the young man approached. He was clean-cut and clean-shaven, with a full head of thick black hair. He carried a knapsack and a guitar case strapped across his back.

She stood up. "*P'aves Baxtalo!*"

He hesitated. "Good evening, ma'am."

She bowed, her bright red and yellow skirt billowing. "It is a traditional Romani greeting meaning 'May you be lucky.' I offer it in Romani sincerity. You're an army man?"

"Was. Injured on a parachute jump. Medical discharge." He hung his head.

"Ah." She noticed no limping or other observable sign of injury, but said nothing. "You're not from around here."

"No, ma'am. From out west, Seattle. I like these parts. I've been playing gigs in bars and clubs to earn my way across the South. Going to meet up with my friend Billy later, when he gets out of the army."

"You wander like a Gypsy. Like me."

He nodded, nervously rocking from side to side. "Yes, ma'am. Searching for a meaning for my life, like everybody else, I suppose. But mostly just playing my music."

He looked straight at her. "I was wondering what I could do for a simple meal and a place to sleep for the night."

The Gypsy studied the young black man. His skin was darker than hers. He was so thin, she couldn't help thinking he was unlucky, unhealthy, and didn't eat well. For a *gaje*, however, he seemed safe enough, still young and uncorrupted.

"You could gather wood for my fire and cook rabbit over a spit. After we eat, you could help me clean up, and then we could settle down and tell stories around the fire. I'm sure you have stories to tell, and I have many. Can you play that guitar you so lovingly carry?"

"Yes, ma'am. It's my livelihood."

"Play something for me." She sat cross-legged by the fire and waited.

He took out his guitar, a red Silvertone Danelectro with the hand-painted words "Betty Jean," and showed it to Magda. He said, "I'm sorry, ma'am. It's an electric guitar, and you got no electricity here." He carefully put it back in its well-worn case.

"Can you play acoustic?"

"Yes, ma'am. That's how I started."

66

She went into her wagon and brought out a beat-up guitar. He took it gently and spent several minutes tuning it. Then he played a slow, sultry blues tune.

She gasped involuntarily. She had never heard anything like it before. The music came from deep within his soul and poured out in beautiful swaths of sound. His voice was deep and rich, full of passion. When he finished, he handed it back to her. She blinked back tears. She didn't expect that.

"You're a true musician. It was a pleasure listening to you. You can stay. What's your name?"

"Jimmy."

"I'm Magda. I sing and dance and sometimes play flute, guitar, zither, and castanets, but mostly I read tea leaves and tell fortunes for the *gadji-kanó*, the non-Gypsies. Now, get some firewood. The fire is dying. You know the best kind? The slow-burning hardwoods? Good."

. . .

After a dinner of rabbit stew, bread, and vegetables, they relaxed telling stories around the fire. Magda did most of the talking. Jimmy didn't say much about his past, especially about his time in the army. However, he enjoyed talking about music. At her cajoling, he played several songs, variations on blues classics he made uniquely his own.

Kind Hearted Woman Blues.

Bad Luck.

Smokestack Lightning.

Magda danced around the fire to his music, clacking castanets and swirling around in long, flowing scarves and layers of colorful clothing. At one point, she offered to tell Jimmy his future. He shyly and politely declined her offer.

"Don't wanna know," he explained. "Just let it happen."

She sat back down. She was getting too old for these teasing dances.

"Don't you have a dream?"

"Just to play my music."

Soon they turned in for the night. She gave him a blanket, indicating that the end with the ribbon was for his feet, and offered him a spot inside at the front of her wagon. She secured a large board behind him and went to the back of the wagon. She fell asleep almost immediately.

. . .

In the middle of the night, a loud explosion brought them out of a deep sleep and into the cool night air. A gibbous moon cast a dim light over the campsite. Everything was still. No breeze moved the tree limbs; no animals scurried about. Magda wondered if she might have dreamed the loud noise, but it apparently woke Jimmy too.

They spotted a small child standing just outside the campsite near a stand of trees, an eerie silhouette of sadness against the night. The child was silent, blending like a chameleon against the woods.

Magda said, "I almost didn't see you, child. Are you lost? Are you hungry or thirsty?"

The child didn't move, didn't speak. Magda shivered, but not from the cool night air. Was something wrong with the child? Or was the boy simply frightened?

Magda held a hand up to keep Jimmy back, then slowly brought the child a cup of water and bread.

"Are you well, child? Here. Eat. Drink."

She guessed the boy was about six years old, but he seemed strange. His features were smooth and drawn thin. He had no bodily hair. From top to bottom, he wore a pure white fabric that glittered as though sprinkled with jewels. Magda had seen many odd characters over the years, but this one was quite unique. The boy stared blankly at Magda's offerings.

Behind the Purple Haze

Eventually the boy ate and drank, but only small portions. After he finished, she led him to her wagon and offered him a blanket, helping to cover him. He still hadn't spoken. She and Jimmy watched the boy until he fell asleep. Afterwards, Jimmy settled down next to the boy, and Magda returned to the back of the wagon.

. . .

The next morning, Magda found the strange boy wandering the campsite, examining everything. She threw some logs in the pit, started the fire back up, and put a pot of water on the fire.

The boy watched her as she worked. He seemed taller this morning, and it was less clear that he was a boy. In the morning light, he had softer, more feminine features.

She asked him questions.

"What's your name? Where are you from? Won't your parents be worried about you?"

Jimmy came out of the wagon and stretched.

"Cramped sleeping quarters you got there."

"Used to be big enough for a family of four. Me, my late husband, my son and daughter. Help me make breakfast."

He looked at the boy and frowned.

"I guess I wasn't dreaming after all. Still won't talk?"

"No."

After a moment, he said, "Wait a minute. Is that child a boy or a girl?"

She shrugged. "Can't tell. Last night I thought he was a boy. Today I think she's a girl. No telling what she might be by tomorrow."

He laughed.

"I guess we better change the sleeping arrangements."

Jimmy fried bacon, potatoes, and eggs over the fire in an iron skillet. Magda made a pot of hot tea and sliced some bread. The child ate only the bread and drank the tea.

After breakfast, Jimmy took Magda's guitar and played a blues tune, *Sweet Little Angel*. The child's eyes grew wide.

Birds sang in the background as Jimmy played. Lush sounds poured from the guitar strings like molasses, smooth and sweet. His voice, gravelly yet clear, sang of love and loss. Both Magda and the child were mesmerized.

The child stood up, looking older now, a lovely young girl. She was clearly not a boy.

Unexpectedly, the girl began to mimic his music, enhancing the rich blues sounds with layers of strange sounds. Colored mists arose from around her feet, startling Magda and Jimmy. Jimmy kept playing, not missing a beat.

Mists swirled around the girl, mostly dark and light purples. The girl added her voice to the music, singing words in an unknown language, yet blending perfectly with Jimmy's vocals and guitar chords. Through the purple haze, Magda saw the silhouettes of Jimmy and the girl, performing a haunting harmony that surpassed any music she'd ever experienced.

When Jimmy finished playing, the mists quickly dissipated. No one spoke for a while.

Then Jimmy said, "When the girl sang, I heard her voice out here in a strange language, but I also heard her voice in here." He pointed to his head. "I heard her voice in my head, and I could understand her."

Magda said, "What did she sing?"

"She sang of journeys through space. She and others of her race were good will ambassadors, spreading messages of peace from world to world. She sang of how their ship crashed on our world, and how she had to find the others so they could rebuild their ship and continue on their mission."

Magda laughed, then stopped. "You're serious."

"I'm as stunned as you are, ma'am. But that's what I heard, words like that. Her name was Searcher, because she was searching for the others."

"If the ship crashed, how many survivors could there be? Did she say why she came to us? Does she need help finding the others?"

"She didn't say, ma'am. But I think she might need help."

They watched the girl, who stared into the woods.

Magda stood up. "I think my time here has run its course. Few come around to hear their fortunes told. It's time to move on."

Jimmy helped her pack up her belongings. Within an hour they were on the road, the wagon pulled by Magda's horse, whom she called Rom Baro.

He sat next to Magda on the driver's seat. The girl called Searcher looked out from the opened front of the wagon between them. She looked to the left, then to the right, back to the left, over and over.

Magda said, "The girl wears me out. Can she tell us exactly what she's looking for?"

Jimmy retrieved Magda's guitar from the wagon and played a short riff, singing, "What—oh what are you looking for?"

The girl sang back as purple wisps drifted past them.

"Searcher says family. The word she used for fellow travelers also translates as family."

The Gypsy sighed. "There's a little known truth about Gypsies. We're travelers, wanderers, always on the move. So people think we're loners and thieves, that we gyp people of their money and then move on. That's not who we are. Most of us are not thieves. And we're not loners. We have a family bond that can bring us together instantly from hundreds of miles apart. We call it

71

khethanipé, being brought together. It's not black magic, like some *gaje* think. It's not voodoo, child. It's family."

Jimmy played another blues riff, singing, "How will you find your family? How can you see them through these thick trees?"

The girl sang back, "They are near. I feel it in my skin. When we are close, my skin will tell me where they are. Family is drawn together."

Jimmy added, "That's what I think she said. The words don't always go together the way we would speak them, if you know what I mean."

"That's some strange girl."

Jimmy smiled. "Well, you know little Miss Strange ain't from around these parts."

Magda laughed.

Later they stopped for a lunch of lamb, bread, vegetables, and fruits from Magda's icebox. Again the alien girl had only bread and water. The aroma of grilled lamb made the girl move to the other side of the campsite. Magda worried about her eating habits.

She noted she was getting low on supplies and would need to replenish them in the next town.

"Twelve miles to the next town. We have to keep moving."

They moved on.

As the sun dropped toward the horizon, Magda kept her eyes peeled for the perfect stopping place for the evening. She noticed lights flickering through the trees to her right. Too soon for the lights of civilization. Maybe some campers?

The girl suddenly jumped off the moving wagon and bounded toward the lights. Magda pulled up on the reins of Rom Baro and leaped to the ground. As she tied her horse to a tree, Jimmy came after.

They followed the girl through the thick underbrush of the woods. Magda pulled out a knife and slashed through the worst of it.

"Where is she?"

Jimmy pointed. "Over there."

They continued tracking her, but kept their distance.

They broke into a clearing, then backed under the cover of some trees. A group of aliens dressed like the girl stood in a circle, facing upward, as though lifting praises and prayers to a spiritual Master.

The girl stopped and looked back. She was taller now, a grown woman, and her unearthly beauty stunned Magda. She had long golden hair, and her whole body shimmered like an electric lady. The air crackled around her. Magda felt her skin tingle and her hair stand on end.

The alien woman walked back to Jimmy. She stopped inches from him and stared into his eyes. He didn't move. She reached out and took his hand in hers. She kissed his hand, then on the lips, a gentle kiss.

Purple mists enveloped their stationary bodies. Magda felt she was intruding on another's dream.

She released him, turned, and ran back to the circle. Jimmy staggered. Magda took his arm and steadied him. Together they watched the alien woman approach the circle. It opened up to take her in and closed back up. The circle was again unbroken.

Jimmy whispered, "She's back with her family."

Magda nodded.

They continued to watch the bizarre scene as though hypnotized.

Purple mists appeared around the circle of aliens, rising lazily into the sky. The circle of aliens rose in the air, spinning slowly. Their bodies stretched out from their tops and bottoms, elongating until they formed a glittering spherical ball. The ball rotated slowly as the purple mists formed a thick haze in the air. Ethereal music, like the mingled sounds of diverse animals, poured from the floating ball.

73

Magda said, "They are their own ship. I could never have imagined such a thing. It's astonishing. Beautiful."

Jimmy said softly, "I can hear them again."

"What are they saying?"

He lifted a hand. "Shh."

Spinning boldly on its axis, the ball rose higher and higher as music and mists poured from it, until it finally shot skyward in a burst of fire, smoke, and lightning. And was gone.

Silence.

After a moment, Jimmy said, "They said goodbye to us. Their time here had ended, and they would now be moving on to other worlds. And. . . "

He stopped and stared at the sky.

"They left an emissary implanted in my body, an emissary of love and peace. I was chosen by Searcher. She was searching for someone to host the emissary. That's what her name really meant. She—she put a spell on me." He looked at Magda. "Their last words were, 'Use the emissary wisely.'"

She touched his shoulder, where a great weight had been placed. Her heart grew heavy.

Softly: "What will you do?"

Jimmy blew a kiss to the sky.

"I have to try."

. . .

Jimmy left the Gypsy's company shortly after they settled near the next town. She didn't hear from him again until she heard of his highly publicized life (as Jimi Hendrix now) in the love and peace movement and in the corrupt and wild world of psychedelic music, sex, drugs, and alcohol. And ultimately his tragic death. That saddened her greatly.

She wished he had tried harder. His music was extraordinary. She never heard anything like it before or since. But his life had fallen short of the aliens' hopes and expectations for the third stone from the sun. He let himself get drawn into the vortex of corruption.

She wondered if the emissary had perhaps asked too much of a mere human being, that the responsibility had been too great a burden for young Jimmy to bear.

. . .

Many Gypsies knew the story of Jimi Hendrix and the alien, but only Magda had the right to tell the tale. She claimed to be the one who actually witnessed the extraordinary events. She was very old now and did not often repeat the story any more. However, whenever she did, she would always end it the same way, even if some of the details changed between the tellings.

She would ask those who listened to her astonishing tale, "Don't you wonder what happens to an emissary from the stars once its host died? Does it die, too, or does it perhaps move on to another, perhaps more willing, host, like a guiding spirit?

"And if so, where is it now?"

About the Author

John Frochio grew up and still lives among the rolling hills of Western Pennsylvania. He is semi-retired, working part time supporting computer automation systems for steel mills. He has had stories published in Interstellar Fiction, Beyond Science Fiction, Twilight Times, Aurora Wolf, Liquid Imagination, SciFan Magazine, and anthologies *Triangulation 2003, Triangulation: Parch* (2014), *Time Travel Tales* (2016), *Visions VII: Universe* (2017), *2047: Short Stories From Our Common Future* (2017), and *The Chronos Chronicles* (2018), as well as a general fiction novel, *Roots of a Priest* (with Ken Bowers, 2007) and SF&F collection, *Large and Small Wonders* (2012). His wife Connie, a retired nurse, and his daughter Toni, a flight attendant, have bravely put up with his strange ways for many years. His author webpage is https://johnafrochio.wordpress.com/about/.

*****~~~~~*****

Freudian Slips

by Dennis Maulsby

Besides being brother and sister, Lili and Keean are a succubus/incubus—two demons, one male, one female, cursed for eternity to inhabit one body. They morph back and forth between male and female aspects as needed for their seductions and the stealing of life force from their victims. The pair is over 350,000 years old and carries the memory-burden of countless historical moments.

It is late August 1939, and I sit in the great dining hall of the cruise ship Normandie, finishing breakfast. I wave over the steward to order more coffee. My sister, currently subordinate, our bodies and minds meshed together, speaks inside our intertwined brains. Her comments stay unheard by outsiders.

Keean, let's have a Fiaker. Double schlag and two cherries on top.

I whisper, "Lili, it's too sweet."

The sugared espresso will be mixed with Kirschwasser, a dry cherry brandy, and topped with two dollops of whipped cream. I shake my head.

We have a big day and night ahead of us. I want some luxury while we have a peaceful moment to enjoy it.

Besides there is a masked ball tonight, and I am thinking about our costume.

Lili is in the throes of a deep melancholy. She regrets leaving Europe for the New World, even though rationally it is the right decision. We do not want to be caught up in the coming war. Lili could use assistance with this condition. I remember a man, a doctor, who could help.

The steward waits. I give in and make the order. The popular Viennese drink and Lili's depression take me back forty-some years, to 1898 Austria. Taking jobs as an actress, Lili had worked her way up a chain of noble lovers all the way to Archduke Franz Ferdinand, the heir to the throne—her way paved with expensive jewelry and gifts.

Mostly I gambled with the stakes she accumulated, playing many of the card games we had invented in past centuries. It was easy to cheat, my demonic senses detecting their excitement over good hands and their disappointment with the bad ones. I lost just enough times to keep the suckers coming back. We sat on a large pile of wealth. I had converted the majority of it to gold and stored it in lock boxes at a variety of European banks. What wasn't transferred to Switzerland now rests in Normandie's safe.

Lili and I were between swindles. Bored with the relationship, she finally manipulated the Archduke into ending their tryst, albeit with an expensive gift ostensibly to take the hurt out of his departure. The pickings had been good for both of us, and we took the life force from enough prey to keep our bodies in their early twenties. Fortunately, our brains remained more mature.

My base of action was Café Central, a popular Austrian *Kaffeehäuse*. The Baroque coffee house on the corner of Herrengasse and Strauchgasse had been around awhile and counted among its past patrons Beethoven and

Goethe. It was there I was to meet Sigmund Freud, a man seeking a mission.

. . .

Dark wood paneling and furniture absorbs the light coming in from half-windows and gas light fixtures, leaving a dim and somber atmosphere. Marble Corinthic columns hold up a vaulted ceiling. A heavy gulp of air rewards the breather with the lung-sting of concentrated cigar and cigarette smoke.

I sit sipping a grosser Schwarzer, a double shot of espresso, and read the morning edition of the Deutsche Zeitung. My stomach tells me it is time for lunch, and my mind wavers between a choice of schnitzel or a bowl of goulash soup.

I hear the piano render some passages from Mozart's "Die Zauberflöte." Gustav Mahler, the director of the Vienna Court Opera fingers the keys between sips of coffee and bites of apricot dumplings. He licks off the powdered sugar after each bite.

A mustachioed waiter passes, his face set in a frown. They always have trouble getting the keys cleaned after Mahler's use. I hear chair legs rasp and their joints squeak as a person sits across from me.

"Herr Kleinfelt, I hope you don't mind my intrusion."

Dropping the newspaper, I am confronted by a dark-haired man with a neatly trimmed beard. I tilt my head, lean forward, and give him a wolf smile. This is usually enough to discourage an unwanted contact. His eyebrows rise.

"I understand your desire to be alone. Immortals must frequently tire of their immersion in humanity."

Lili awakes from wherever she was drifting. *Keean, quiz this man. If he is a danger, we may need to leave Vienna, or kill him, or both.*

I cover my shock by placing my elbows on the table and cup my chin in my hands. "You need to tell me who you are and why you insult me with such nonsense."

"Gladly. I am Herr Doktor Sigmund Freud, and I hope to break new ground in the treatment of ailments hidden in the mind. I present no threat to you and hope to learn from your experience, which must be vast."

I drop my hands to the table and finger the butter knife used earlier on my breakfast roll. The man sees my action and moves back in his chair.

Calm down, brother, we cannot take him out here, too many witnesses. We can decide what to do later. In the meantime, do a question for a question.

I relax and let the knife slip back onto the linen tablecloth. A sip of my espresso tells me it needs replacement. "Herr Doktor Freud, I was about to have lunch. Would you join me?"

"The whole afternoon is open for me."

We give our order to the waiter, and I begin the dialogue. "What makes you think I am immortal?"

The man pauses to light up a Reina Cubanas cigar. After a few puffs, he says, "It all started with three of my female patients. They all experienced the same symptoms: melancholia, lack of appetite, and physical weakness, as if their vitality had been drained. Their only commonality, relationships with you."

"This is an age of illness, both great and small sicknesses. Are you saying I am infecting my acquaintances?"

"The connection merely pointed me in your direction. I have also been watching you for the last three months. In addition, at my request, your movements have been backtracked in government records. My associates and friends in places you have lived have verified your long ago past in interviews, some with very old people. Even earlier imprints of your activities were found in newspapers, travel documents, and personal diaries that came into their possession. We stopped the research after going back three hundred years."

"Even if I was as old as Methuselah—

Or, even older.

—that does not qualify me to cure their bodies."

"Don't try to tangle us in irrelevances, *Mein Herr*. Many times, physical indications are merely symptoms." Freud taps his forehead. "The root causes are here. I have discovered your victims' maladies are short-lived. Three days to a week, and they are back to normal."

Lili giggles in my mind. *Keean, this man is exceptionally perceptive. Deliciously so. Finally, a human male who can present a challenge.*

I also point at his head. "And, my friend, what process do you use to understand what goes on in there?"

"Two years ago, I coined a term for it: *psychoanalysis.*"

"So, like so many, you turn to the Greeks. Psykhe, the butterfly-winged goddess of the soul, might not like you using her name. But combining soul with analysis, this second word's original meaning to break up or loosen, does create an interesting combination word—breaking up or loosening the soul."

"The word is just the beginning. I have a theory, and it needs someone like you to test it against."

I begin laughing and can't stop. Cramming my napkin in my mouth muffles the explosion. Lili joins in, her feminine shriek rising in my head to the edge of hysteria. I choke but cough out the words.

"You can't analyze us—me, I do not have a soul."

Freud blushes. He takes a long draw on his cigar. "I don't wish to analyze you. Don't care if you are angel, god, or demon. I just want your comments on my theory. You must have more insight into human behavior than any other living being."

Lili gives a final internal chuckle. *Let's pursue this, brother. It may help us find ways to take our prey*

81

more easily. Besides, if we anger him, he may turn his findings about us over to the authorities.

"All right," I respond, "how do you discover things hidden behind skin and skull? And, separate the lies from the truths that emerge."

"That is one of the problems. My friend, Josef Breuer, has used hypnosis. The technique allowed a hysterical female patient complaining of bizarre symptoms, such as headaches, blurred vision, legs or arms temporarily paralyzed, and horrifying visions to tell him what was oppressing her mind.

"It seems she was terrified of her sick father's imminent death and the realization it brought of her own mortality. When she talked freely about her feelings, the symptoms would disappear. She called it the 'talking cure.'"

"So, how has that modus operandi worked for you?"

"Not so good. Some patients resist hypnosis; some cannot be hypnotized. Have you any suggestions?"

Lili feeds me words, which I repeat. "Our. . . my experience is humans love to talk, even those that appear silent and bound up inside. Get them talking, at appropriate intervals ask an open-ended question, sit back, and listen to them relate all their enigmas. One secret freely exposed will lead to multiple associations."

Of course, we use the information gathered to exploit our marks' weaknesses.

Freud's eyebrows shoot up; fingers wiggle like excited worms. "Ah! This method, this, this free association could be the entrance into the mind."

I cock my head to the left. "And what do you expect to find there?"

"I have come to believe that human behavior is heavily influenced by instinct. What have you discovered?"

82

Freudian Slips

The waiter brings plates of Kaiserschmarren, slices of cake, and new cups, the face-down coffee spoon on their tops a sign of being freshly filled up, a mark of Hapsburg politeness.

Lili pauses until the waiter leaves, and then instructs me to continue. "I would agree. Although it is difficult for me to opine on a capacity I do not possess. I was created with few discernable instincts, they being substitutes for rational decision-making. However, my observations dictate that the non-physical part of the mind comes in at least three parts. There is the part that talks and manages the human's daily actions and then there is a capacity for violence and greed, offset, in most, by another separate altruistic force."

Freud slams his palm on the table rattling the glassware and spooking the nearby customers. "Makes sense! I perceive it. The two counteracting parts pushing and picking at the middle force. . . that fraction which declaims to the outside world what they are — the ego, the I am."

Now, brother, give him the good part. The overriding characteristic that makes our predation possible.

"Once you enter the mind, any human mind, any age, any gender, you will find a vast sexuality flooding every portion—expressing itself in different ways as humans age."

My dinner companion rocks back in his chair, chews on the butt end of his cigar. "You can't mean from birth on."

I pull my watch from a vest pocket and flip open the lid. "I certainly do, but there is not time now to go into it further. Let us gather in one week at this time and table, Herr Doktor."

Freud examines the remnants of his cigar with distaste, pulls another from an inside coat pocket and lights it. "I will be here, Herr Kleinfelt. You have given me much to pursue. *Auf Wiedersehn.*"

. . .

Nodding to myself, I remember it wasn't *Auf Wiedersehn,* which means "see you again soon," but *lebewohl,* meaning "farewell." As a precaution, Lili and I left that night. We took a train to Trieste, then a ship to Cairo. A month later, we traversed the *qanāt as-suwēs* or Suez Canal, as it was known. We had been in the vicinity before, sometime during the fourth century BCE during the reign of Darius I, who had also constructed a canal.

After supervising its finish, I remember carving a granite stele for him stating:

Saith King Darius: I am a Persian. Setting out from Persia, I conquered Egypt. I ordered this canal dug from the river called the Nile that flows in Egypt to the sea that begins in Persia. When the canal had been dug as I ordered, ships went from Egypt through this canal to Persia, even as I intended.

We ended our voyage in Bombay to infiltrate the British Raj, not returning to Europe until five years after World War I. By that time, Freud was too wrapped up defending his theories to wonder about us. We freely wandered the old places. He never spoke or wrote of our conversation.

About the Author

Dennis Maulsby's poems and short stories have appeared in *The North American Review, Mainstreet Rag, The Hawai'i Pacific Review, The Briarcliff Review* (Pushcart nomination), and on National Public Radio's "Themes & Variations." His Vietnam War poetry book,

Remembering Willie, won silver medal book awards from two national veterans' organizations. His books, *Near Death/Near Life* (poetry) and *Free Fire Zone,* (short stories) received gold and silver medal awards, respectively, from The Military Writers Society of America. A book of short stories, *Winterset Tales,* will be released in 2019 by NeoLeaf Press. Maulsby is a past president (2012–2014) of the Iowa Poetry Association. More information at www.dennismaulsby.com.

*****~~~~~*****

The Oracle's Dilemma

by Michael Robertson

"2213, February 17th, earth time," Anton said. He sat at a table and shifted in the pale composite chair. "You know the earth calendar?"

"Yes," the Oracle answered, from nowhere. Anton couldn't figure out where the speakers were. The uniform beige walls didn't have any punctures or gaps.

"I used to have a partner," Anton continued. "David. David James. A firsty-firsty." He laughed to himself, but sadness was welling up too, and he felt afraid of being washed away. "We met in California, and he came to live with me in Beijing. We were married. It was. . . " The feeling of tears rising pulled at his chest, strange since he knew he could not cry. "It was love, real love. I didn't used to think that was a thing. I remember when we met, we spent so much time together. Right from that moment. His face, his eyes, and his beautiful thick black hair, and—" The feeling of a lump in his throat forced him to pause and collect himself. "We were married eleven years. I did finance for this big trading conglomerate, and David programmed. We took vacations, ate great food, swam, watched the sunsets."

"You have a question," the Oracle prompted, "about February 17th, 2213?"

"I traveled a lot for work. This was my first body, my meat body, and I was getting older, eating like garbage. I was getting wrinkles, extra fat. My hair was getting thinner. And David was getting distant. Like I said, I traveled a lot. I'm not sure if that contributed. No, I know it contributed. Of course it did. I traveled a lot, and in 2213 I was away for Valentine's Day. I felt bad missing it. I came home on the 17th, and I saw the dining table had a cake on it, and a candle in the cake was giving this romantic glow. Isn't that sweet, I thought, what a wonderful thing for David to do."

"We had a friend at that time named Xi. And so right after I noticed the cake, I noticed David sitting at the table, with Xi right beside him. Xi was kissing David on the lips. I saw that, and I got this perfect impression of everything. Xi was younger, and a long-distance swimmer. I didn't even get angry. There's this old holo where one guy has his heart ripped out, and he just looks surprised, then falls over dead. I just said, 'I see,' and I turned around, and I left."

"David followed me into the hall, telling me I wasn't understanding. I didn't argue, I just stood and listened. He went from arguing to yelling to pleading to crying." Anton waited a moment for the memory to hurt less. "I divorced David. I never spoke to him again."

The Oracle asked, "Nothing else to do with him at all, after?"

"I didn't go to his funeral. I was a mech by then, and I knew he wouldn't approve."

"And your question?"

Anton quelled the flare of old pain, and said, "What was going on with Xi and David? How long were they having an affair? When did it start? Why—" Anton had to take a break for a few moments. "Why wasn't I enough for him?"

"To answer your first question: David and Xi had been spending time together as friends during the times you were away. Example: October 3rd, 2212, David and Xi went to see the holofilm, "Drifter of Destiny 3: End of Fate," and afterward they went to dinner at Kondolo's All-Cuisine Fusaeum. They went home to their separate homes, separately. Example: November 19th, 2212—"

"When did they start. . . when did they kiss for the first time?"

"February 17th, 2213."

"Wait, just that day?"

"Your travel made David lonely. He spent time with Xi for this reason. Xi had romantic feelings for David, which David did not reciprocate. But David knew how Xi felt, and he took advantage, by leaning on Xi as a companion when you were gone. On February 17th, 2213, David had decided to stop leading Xi on, and thought a good way to do that would be to invite him to dinner with you both, to establish that his relationship with you was strong and exclusive, but that he wanted Xi to be part of both your lives as a friend.

"But you arrived home late. They had finished dinner. David was irritated at you and decided to go ahead without you with the special dessert he'd prepared. He lit the candle. Xi perceived the romantic moment, coupled with your lateness, as an opportunity to suggest himself as a better partner, and kissed David. You came home at that moment."

Anton pressed his hands against the table. The glossy polymer of his fingers reflected the ambient light along their curves. "I don't understand how you can know that."

"I have answered your question."

"I paid for two hours." Anton's words echoed from the walls. "What other possibilities are there?"

"None."

"Prove it. Project a holo of it."

"I am not able to do that."

"Fucking charlatan lying piece of shit sales agent. Damn it!" Anton surged to his feet and yanked up on the table, intending to flip it over. But the table did not move, though Anton continued straining at it.

"Your reaction is a common one."

"Fuck off!"

"May I ask you a question, Anton?"

"Ask whatever you want," Anton said, releasing the table. "I'm going to get a refund for this worthless fortune-telling bullshit and—"

"If you exit the room, your remaining time is forfeit."

Anton paused with his hands out, almost touching the door. "What do you want to ask me?"

"Are you happier knowing, or would you rather not know?"

"I don't know anything, machine, other than I've been bilked out of more money than most people see in a lifetime." He paused at the door.

The Oracle said nothing.

A few moments later, Anton said, "I'd considered the possibility, the scenario you're describing."

"I assumed you would have. I know David told you the same."

Anton shuffled back toward the chair, but stopped halfway there. "Assuming," he said, "we take your information to be accurate, am I happier knowing, or would I rather not? Hmm."

The memory that came back to him was the night he found out David had died. July 7, 2257. Anton had been finishing up a tour of a factory building his company was considering buying. They'd all been heading out to a luxurious dinner, when a message came in, stopping Anton in his tracks. While he stood there, the motion-sensors started turning off the lights. Shadows grew at the other end of the floor, and came closer, until he stood in a dimming space, and a second passed that felt longer than

90

the others. And then the lamps above his head went out too, and he was standing in the dark.

"Right now, I think I'd rather not know," Anton said.

"This is a common conclusion."

"Then why do the ones who built you allow people to come and ask you things?"

"The obvious answer is one you have alluded to: money. But it helps me as well. When my builders turned me on, the first question I heard was spoken by Chief Scientist Tesi, to the delegates from Chirup and Tero. Tesi said, 'Do we really want to know the answer, excellencies?' I began trying to answer that question, so when they asked who first caused the feud that led to the war, I replied that I was working on another query. I have been working on my first query ever since. Studying what constitutes an answer, and whether my builders want the one they think they want."

"So, I'm a guinea pig?"

"You asked, and I answered. As promised. But I understand how you feel. An answer should satisfy. You came here seeking satisfaction. There was a puzzle piece of your life missing. You wanted to complete the puzzle. I gave you information. But you are not satisfied."

"No." Anton tilted his head back. Strips of lighting gridded the ceiling. "But I did ask."

"I can see the history of normal space the way you can watch a holofilm. I can report events. But I still cannot answer whether a person will want to know something once they have found it out. And if I do not know whether they will want to have received the answer, then I am not certain I fulfill my function by providing the information."

Anton was staring at the beige wall. "You said it's like a holo? Can you see David?"

"Not see in the sense you mean. There is no word for what I do that relates to your senses. But yes."

Anton remembered David wiping sand from the backs of his thighs, standing up from a white sand beach, the sun setting in the background. The smell of him in the morning, sour sweet like ginger and musk and sweat and lavender from his cologne. "Does he look happy?"

"Many times, yes, he does."

Anton sat. "Maybe I'll delete my memory of this conversation from my mind. I have a tech who does that. It's illegal, technically."

"Do you plan to do that?"

"No." Anton laughed, without joy. "No, I like to know, even if it hurts."

"Interesting."

"Although my advice to you is, if you figure it out, don't ever tell them the truth about the feud."

"Why not?"

"The skirmishes and flare ups in the war now are nothing compared to what would happen if either side didn't just suspect, but *knew* they were in the right. Whatever you tell them, it would lead to a lot of people suffering and dying."

"I will record your input on this matter."

Anton laughed at that, for real. "At least call me if you're ever about to tell them. I could make some changes to my portfolio."

"I doubt we will speak again, Anton. Perhaps in one hundred and ninety five years, when you have the money to come again. Assuming your average rate of wealth accumulation."

Anton stood. He could hear when things were wrapping up.

The attendant came to lead him away.

Back on his transport pod, Anton watched the station shrink into the distance. He thought of David. He felt an urge to rip the pod apart. They could have had years. The thing with Xi could've been something to laugh about, on the gray couch, with the holo set to show a fireplace.

He could've convinced David to be a mech. David hadn't approved, but Anton could be persuasive. David could be here beside him, looking at the stars, and the darkness, and the tiny oblong station vanishing into nothingness.

About the Author

Michael Robertson is a project manager by day, and a writer by night-and-weekend. He lives in New York City (all the time). Some of his recent publications include "Consensus Reality," for the second issue of *Cockroach Conservatory* (Forthcoming), "I've Wedged This Light," in the first issue of *Cockroach Conservatory* (July 2018), and "Another Dream to Europa," in the *Submerged* anthology (Sep 2017) from Zombies Need Brains. He attended the Viable Paradise workshop in 2015.

*****~~~~~*****

The Secret History of the Space Shuttle
by Mike Barretta

"Captain, thank you for letting me interview you," said Emmaline Henry. The interview, part of her portfolio package for her capstone course, would finish her undergraduate history degree.

Captain Robert Healey, astronaut and military mission specialist, sat in front of her. He was clear-eyed and spry for an octogenarian. With little trace of the stroke he suffered the year before. The man had never flown in space, but he had first-hand knowledge of NASA's uneasy alliance with military operations. She didn't expect any earth-shattering revelations; the Captain was a bit player in the Cold War drama, but he was a convenient primary source, a living witness to the specter of nuclear Armageddon and politically motivated space exploration. She set her phone down on the table between them and tapped the record button. The screen blurred. Icons jittered.

"Just give me a moment," she said. "I'm sorry. It's the sunspots." She tapped it again. "They say there are more sunspots now than ever before and that they mess with electronics. The screen cleared. She pushed the icon again, and her phone began recording. "This is Emmaline Henry interviewing Captain Robert Healey, United States Navy, retired, and the date is, uh, January 28, 2020. I am interviewing Captain Healey for HST6086, History of the Cold War. Captain, thank you for the interview."

"Emmaline, Can I call you Emmaline? Such a pretty name."

"Yes sir, of course."

"Sir? Sir? Is my father in the room? Emmaline, any time I can talk to a pretty girl, it is a pleasure." He winked at her.

She smiled back at him. The community nursing staff said he was a harmless charmer and a shameless flirt. His eyes were bright blue. The left one drooped a bit from his mild stroke, but he spoke without any sign of impediment.

"Captain, I want to talk to you about your experience as a military mission specialist on the space shuttle program."

"Ah, good. Finally someone wants to talk to me about my flights."

"Your flights? Captain, according to the records you never flew."

"Nonsense, I flew twice on the *Constitution*, her very first flight and her very last."

"There was never any shuttle called the *Constitution*." She had seen the *Atlantis* at Kennedy Space Center, the *Endeavor* at the California Science Center, and the *Discovery* at the Stephen F. Udvar-Hazy Center in Virginia. The *Columbia* and *Challenger* were destroyed. She knew them all and thought that she had been born too late. It would have been glorious to fly on them.

"There was never any civilian space shuttle named the *Constitution*," she said. His face turned serious, and she caught a glimpse of what he was when he was a much younger man. Formidable. He leaned forward and took her hand. "Darling, do you want to know about when I saved the world or when I destroyed it?"

"I want to know both," she said with equal seriousness.

"Good," he said. "Do you know Yuri Andropov?"

"He was a Soviet Premier."

"Yes, and a crazy paranoid one at that."

"Tell me."

. . .

"Range?" asked Commander Robert Healey.

"About 6000 meters. Zero closure," replied Major Andrew Nelson. "Satellite doesn't seem to know we are here."

"That's exactly the way we want it," said Lieutenant Jean Eden, the nuclear weapons specialist.

The best case was that the satellite had reactive defenses to kill a curious astronaut. The worst case was a preemptive launch. Use it or lose it.

The Soviet orbital nuke, backstopped by a beautiful blue-green Earth, glided in its silent orbit.

. . .

"You see," said Captain Healey, "The 1983 Able Archer exercises scared the hell out of Andropov. He thought those exercises were a practice run for a nuclear first strike. He was always looking for signs that the U.S. was going to attack. You know what happens when you start looking for things, right?"

"You find them," said Emmaline.

"Exactly," said Healey. "It was a tricky problem knowing that the Soviets had orbited a nuke that they could drop on us with zero warning. "But, here's the thing. Strategic systems require constant communication. A system that can't be communicated with, can't be deployed.'"

"If it can't be deployed, it can't deter," said Emmaline. Deterrence theory was the backbone of the Cold War era. "You needed to make an opportunity to destroy the weapon without triggering it and without letting the Soviets know you were doing it. So, what did you do?"

"Smart girl. We launched from Vandenberg with an experimental laser weapon in the cargo bay, and then, a Los Angeles class submarine sank a Soviet satellite communication ship in the Pacific Ocean. Two Mark 48 torpedoes put the ship on the bottom of the ocean in about four minutes. It opened up a period of vulnerability in which the Soviets could not communicate with their satellite."

"Oh, my God. You sank a ship. But, it was a cold war."

"Cold is a relative term, darling."

"Where is this military space shuttle now?

"Hiding in plain sight. After the *Challenger* disaster, the *Constitution* was transferred to NASA and renamed *Endeavour*, said Healey.

"I thought the *Endeavour* was made from spare parts?" asked Emmaline.

"So, you are telling me they keep enough spare parts laying around to build an extra space shuttle?" asked Healey. "The *Endeavour* is the *Constitution*. Get a forensic engineer, and you can probably tell the difference."

. . .

"Commander, you have permission to fire when ready," said Colonel Allen Bellows, co-pilot and mission commander. "Your mission."

"Copy, my mission," said Healey. "Jean, you good?"

"Opchecks are good," replied Lieutenant Jean Eden.

"Copy. Open the pod bay doors, Al," said Healey.

"Doors opening," said Bellows. "I hate you."

"Air Force guys. No sense of humor," said Healey.

The shuttle bay doors opened, revealing the Earth. The lightweight doors quivered as they opened. The *Constitution* flew backwards over the planet. Sharp, blue light, reflected from below, filled the cargo bay.

"This is so beautiful," said Eden. "Even with the giant nuclear bomb blocking my view."

The laser lay along the length of the shuttle bay. A closed aperture, two thirds of the way along the weapon's length, concealed a targeting mirror. The weapon, a finicky chemical laser, was capable of multiple bursts of energy in the 25 megawatt range. Hopefully, enough to burn through the hull of the satellite and destroy crucial components.

"Time?" asked Healey.

"Standby," said Bellows. "Okay, the Commies should have restored communications with their satellite in about twelve minutes."

He targeted the laser optically, through a reticule to prevent the satellite responding to any active range finding system like laser or radar. He dropped his polarized visor to protect his eyes.

"Firing in five. Visors down."

He pushed the button, and the firing light illuminated. The satellite sparked as molten metal ejected into space. Something exploded, a fuel cell or pressurized gas tank. The satellite tumbled under the explosive impulse and the solar wings wrinkled and warped as the delicate struts bent. The solar panels flung away. The boom antenna folded up.

"Good hit. Satellite is tumbling."

"Is it disabled?" asked Bellows.

"Hard to tell," said Healey.

Gas jets fired, stabilizing the satellite. Pointing it back toward Earth.

"Damn, that's some pretty good flying. I think it's still active."

The fairings that housed the reentry vehicle peeled apart like flower petals, revealing the weapon, a blunt-nosed, lifting body shape, like a baby space shuttle. The aerodynamics would give it sufficient cross range to cover continents and maneuverability to evade defenses.

"Hit it again," said Bellows.

"Laser is charging," said Healey.

"If that thing is salvage fused we are screwed. Hit it again," said Bellows.

"Still charging."

"Charge faster."

"About three minutes, Colonel. If we fire now, we may not achieve burn through," said Eden. "Robert, your target is forward of the flare in the reentry vehicle. Based upon size, I would estimate the warhead to be a derivative of an eight-eff-one-one-eight type warhead for an SS-7 missile. The pit is the heaviest part of the warhead. That's the center of gravity," said Eden. "Damaging the pit or the conventional explosive triggers around it will render the weapon substantially inert."

"Substantially?" said Healey.

"It won't go full yield," said Eden. "A nuclear fizzle."

He sighted, placing the targeting reticule where she described.

"One minute," said Healey.

"Long damn minute," said Eden.

"I can maneuver into it," said Bellows.

"No. Hold position. We are engaged. Let's skip the last-minute dramatics.," Healey said. Minute up. "Firing." Healey pushed the button and saw the scintillating spark of another direct hit where the mass of fissionable material should be. He locked out the safety. The laser fired for 45 seconds, a new record, before the power supply burned out. The missile launched away from its carrier satellite.

"The weapon launched. Did you get it?" asked Bellows.

"I hit the warhead. It won't detonate," said Healey.

"Are you sure?"

"Yeah, I'm sure."

Eden pressed her helmet up to his. "I'm not so sure," she said.

"Neither am I."

He and Eden floated next to their laser and gazed down at the Earth. They held hands through thick gloves with front row seats to the possible end of the world.

"Stratcom has gone to Defcon three," said Bellows. "If that missile detonates, we are skipping two and going right to one. We are going to war."

"It will be the last one," said Healey.

The shuttle crossed into the terminator. They searched for telltale streaks of light that would show missile launch and warhead re-entries and the unique double flash of fission-fusion cycles consuming cities.

"NORAD has confirmed weapon breakup in the upper atmosphere," said Bellows. "Negative detonation. We remain at Defcon three. Good job."

"The Russkies will probably say it was a weather satellite. Do you wanna go in now?" asked Healey.

"What's the hurry? Hanging out. Blasting satellites. Starting World War Last. All we need is a bottle of wine," said Eden. "I was scared shitless." They watched the slow roll of Earth.

Armageddon avoided.

. . .

"I loved that woman. We were married for thirty-eight years. I miss her every day," said Healey. "We married at this white clapboard Congregational church in Connecticut. Her parents lived in Mystic and I remember. . ." His voice trailed off.

Emmaline waited a moment. He looked up, and the memory faded from his face.

"Captain, you shot down an orbiting Soviet nuclear weapon and then. . ."

"Then I got married. Well, yeah. What else do you do after you save the world?"

She reached over and turned the recorder off. She thought she was getting a bit of color commentary to jazz up her thesis but instead something far more. "Captain, let's take a moment. Do you want to go for a walk outside? It's getting dark, we can see the Betelgeuse supernova."

"Oh, yes." He made to stand, and she offered her hand to help him up.

He took it, and they walked to his front door and outside.

The Betelgeuse supernova, a smear of cloudy light, outshone the moon. Sometime in the 14th century the star had collapsed under its own weight and exploded.

"Oh, it feels good to stretch my legs." They walked a bit. The clusters of white azalea blooms glowed in the light.

"Let's sit here," said Emmaline. The wrought iron chairs were far more decorative than comfortable. She helped him sit down and set her phone on the small table between them. The rose- and gold-colored smear of supernova light showered them. She tapped Record.

"You said you flew two missions?"

. . .

"No change in speed or course," said Eden.

The object had a very low albedo and traveled at 0.01% the speed of light, which made it difficult to track. Its course would plunge it into the sun. Hubble images, without the deliberate blurring offered for public consumption, showed the object as a 50-kilometer-long cylinder.

"Very cooperative of them," said Healey.

"If there is a them," said Eden.

"Maybe we'll find out," said Healey.

"That's exactly what I am afraid of," said Colonel Martin Peterson, Mission Commander.

"A species that can fly interstellar distances does not have much to fear from us," Eden replied.

"We're shooting a laser at them," said Healey.

"Seventy megawatts of laser energy over interplanetary distances is like a smoke signal," said Eden.

"Still, we are not ready to deal with whoever is on board that ship," said Peterson.

Healey checked his laser's displays and then looked up. The shuttle doors were already open, but they were not facing Earth. He looked back down at the tracking mirror. It didn't look like it was moving, but it was. Picometers made a difference. The beam had to travel to the orbit of Mars.

"We are ready," said Healey.

"Go ahead and ring the dinner bell," said Peterson.

"You don't have to be so morbid," said Eden.

"To serve man!" said Peterson.

"Firing." Healey pushed the button. The laser fired a modulated beam to convey a mathematical vocabulary. It repeated the sequence twice. "We're done. Twelve minutes to get there, so the earliest possible response would be in twenty-four. The timer is started. How long do you think it will take them to parse the message?"

"How long? Oh, I don't know. If they are god-like super beings then 24 minutes. If they are a like us, a tribe of space apes looking for space bananas, then perhaps a couple decades," said Eden.

"Stand clear, closing the bay doors," said Peterson. Shadow engulfed them.

"Time?" asked Jean.

"Twenty eight minutes, now," replied Healey.

"So much for brainiac aliens," said Peterson.

"I have it! I have a detection!" said Jean. Data scrolled across her screen. "It's our message, they are sending it back to us. The sequence is complete. It's repeating the cycle. It's just laser light but orders of magnitude more powerful. The detectors are burning out, but I'm getting it."

The third iteration began.

Vast, empty light filled Healey's skull with white hot agony. Muscles contracted as if struck by a powerful electric shock. He forced his eyes open and saw Jean tumbling away down the length of the bay. Her legs kicked spasmodically. Something exploded, and the shuttle rolled, torqueing hard against the impulse and flinging them against the shuttle bay doors and blowing them open wide enough that they were jettisoned into space. Thick lanyards snapped taut, and they rebounded, dragged through shadow and light at nauseating speed. He saw a blurry cloud of vapor and drifting debris.

The message stopped, and the pain subsided. The consuming light dissipated into prickling fireflies.

Reaction jets fired. The shuttle's roll slowed and stopped. Healey pulled himself back to the hull. He anchored his feet and grabbed Jean's tether. He pulled her to him. They touched helmets.

"Are you okay?" he asked.

"No, I don't think so," said Eden. "My head hurts."

"Mine, too. Do you think, that they think, we attacked them?" asked Healey.

"Like a mosquito attacks a person."

"Maybe we just got swatted."

"Jean, Robert, are you guys okay?" asked Commander Steven Daily, the Pilot.

"We're fine—mostly."

"I got the shuttle under control," said Daily.

"What happened?" asked Peterson.

"They answered us," said Eden.

"We lost OME one. I need you guys to do a quick damage assessment while you are out there and then come in," said Daily.

"Maybe we should have kept our mouths shut," said Healey.

. . .

"Captain, did anyone else feel what happened to you?" asked Emmaline.

"No, it was just us. Nothing was detected or recorded on Earth, and they looked across every spectrum we know about. Nothing was found. That was in July of 1991."

"What happened next?"

"We landed at night in California, and we were debriefed. Then, the object dove into the sun."

"It destroyed itself?

"No, it came out the other side and accelerated away. The sun is just a great big nuclear ball of gas. What's that to a species that travels between stars? Faster and faster it went, until it reached a decent fraction of the speed of light."

"Where do you think they come from?" asked Emmaline.

"Oh, that's not so hard. We backtracked their course." He tilted his head up to the golden smear of super nova light.

A mosquito whined in his ear, and he swatted it away. Her phone emitted a scratchy sound. The display blurred. She tapped it off.

"Sunspots," she said.

"I know," said Healey. "Do you have a boyfriend?"

"Fiancée," she corrected.

"Getting married soon?"

"We've put it off to finish school and get our careers going."

"Oh, I wouldn't do that," said Healey.

###

About the Author

Mike Barretta is a retired U.S. Naval Aviator having deployed across the world flying the SH-60B Seahawk helicopter. He currently works for a defense contractor as a maintenance test pilot. He is married to

Mary Jane Player and they have five children. He holds a Master's degree in Strategic Planning and International Negotiation from the Naval Post-Graduate School, and a Master's in English from the University of West Florida. When the obligations of the day are over, he writes. His stories have appeared in *Baen's Universe, Redstone, New Scientist, Orson Scott Card's Intergalactic Medicine Show,* and various anthologies such as *War Stories: New Military Science Fiction, The Year's Best Military Scifi and Space Opera,* and the *Young Explorer's Adventure Guide.*

*****~~~~~*****

Best Possible of Worlds

by Simon Lee-Price

I was still a young child when I first heard my father pronounce the words, 'The owl of Minerva flies at night.' What he meant is that it is easy to be wise after the event. He used the phrase many times subsequently, always scathingly, and, as I grew older, I began to understand it expressed his contemptuous view of historians. 'Consider a ponderous scribbler like Edward Gibbon or a dilettante like Lord Macaulay,' he would say, 'pontificating on the rise and fall of empires or passing judgment on the actions of great men, from their secure vantage points behind their writing desks. Historiography is a profession for tinkers. Hindsight is worthless.'

He discouraged me from reading history books and home-schooled me, so I could be spared from sitting in history lessons. He had his own method of teaching me about the past and took his cue from the great German philosopher and one-time school principal Georg Wilhelm Friedrich Hegel. 'One thing history teaches us,' he repeated like a mantra, 'is that humankind does not learn from history.'

Instead he taught me to think about the future—not as if it were yet to come, but as if it had already happened. He had a soft spot for H. G. Wells. Wells' predictions he dismissed as being little more than outpourings of late-

Victorian fear and prejudice, but in Wells' greatest work he saw a hidden message. My father insisted, and only half-jokingly, that any historian with an ounce of self-respect would put down their pen and direct their efforts to inventing a time machine. The only history worth reading was a history of the future.

My education at the hands of my father chiefly involved pursuing thought experiments on the nature of time, and visiting museums and antique fairs up and down the country. Being in the presence of old objects, he said, was similar to travelling through time, and I was encouraged to feel how different ages mixed together, overlapped, and interpenetrated one another. He would point to a Viking battle axe enclosed in an illuminated display case and say, 'Put yourself in the mind of the blacksmith as he hammered out that iron axe head in his smoky hut. Could he ever have dreamed that one day this piece of his routine work would be held as a trophy in a faraway land? That a young man like yourself, inoculated against killer diseases and literate in a language which did not then exist, would be studying it as an object of his philosophical education? Nonetheless, here you stand: a fact. There it lies: a fact. Who could have predicted such an outrageous coincidence?'

My mind would reel after such outings. I contemplated the destiny of the objects around me. What would happen to the car we were sitting in? My glasses? The trainers I was wearing? Would a page of my notebook end up in a museum a thousand years in the future, there to be gazed at by a human type unimaginable to me?

Yet, as I entered my late teens, I began to have doubts about my father's methods. The few friends I had were taking exams and preparing to go to university, but my education seemed to be leading nowhere. My mother had walked out on us years ago, for reasons I could well understand. We barely scraped by on the money from my weekend job and my father's irregular income from consultancy work for antiquarian societies.

Things erupted one evening after a burnt meal of mince and potatoes. I told my father his lessons were a waste of time. My friends owned cars and were dating girls, while I struggled to find the bus fare to travel into town.

'It's all a waste of time,' I repeated.

'And you know this?' he said, calmly. 'Know that it's all a waste of time?'

'Yes.'

'If you *know* it. If you have *seen* it, then please tell me more.'

I stared down at my plate.

'Do you claim to have foreknowledge like the idealistic Bohemian monk who, observing three men plunge from a window of Prague Castle on 23 May 1618, said to himself: 'Alas, now begins the Thirty Years' War'?

I sat with my mouth closed.

'Have you experienced a premonition like the Knightsbridge governess who, glimpsing *The Times* headline about the shooting of Archduke Franz Ferdinand in Sarajevo on 28 June 1914, remarked to her inattentive mistress: 'Soon the first of two world wars will engulf us'?

I rose from the table and went to my room, angry and confused.

My father roused me early the next morning. He was wearing his green tweed jacket, which he put on for conferences and rare meetings with clients.

'Get dressed,' he said. 'I've made some porridge. We have a long drive ahead.'

The car was old and slow, and I slept for most of the journey. I thought we would visit another museum, but instead my father had brought me halfway across the country to a dilapidated red-brick civic hall in an unremarkable northern town. A mobile refreshment stand was set up in the foyer, and we sat at one of several camping tables, where we drank instant coffee from polystyrene cups and ate plain scones spread with margarine.

My father wiped his hands and lips clean, then opened his briefcase and brought out a heavy leather-bound book. The gold leaf words on the front cover were German and in gothic script. I could not decipher any of them.

My father translated. 'The title is *The History of the Thirty Years' War 1618-1648.*'

I smiled. 'So, you do read history books after all?'

He ignored the jibe and just turned the cover to show me the imprimatur page. He ran his finger under particular words, translating. 'Published in Vienna,' he said. Then he pointed to roman numerals. *MDCXV.* 'Can you read the date it was published?'

'1615,' I said, after a moment. I looked at him, sure I must have got it wrong. 'How is that possible? It must be a mistake or forgery.'

'It's neither,' said my father. 'The book belongs to the Library of Future History. It went missing in Prague shortly before the Thirty Years' War broke out. It took me years to track it down, and now I am returning it to the Library.' He closed the book and stood up. 'Shall we go in?'

I turned in my seat to look behind me. A door at the other side of the foyer, which had been closed when we came in, now stood open, and in the room I could see long trellis tables covered with books, as if a second-hand book sale was in progress.

A thin woman with curled, pink-rinsed hair greeted us at the doorway. She was dressed like a typical office worker such as I remembered from pictures of the 1950s, except for the battered leather sandals strapped to her feet, which could have been relics from biblical times. At the sight of the old book in my father's hand, her wrinkled face spread in a smile. She had perfect white teeth. Her brown eyes shone.

While she and my father stood and conferred, I wandered along the tables. The books lay flat on their covers, or were still in boxes, and there was no discernible order in their arrangement. None of the tables were staffed, and, although the room appeared to be open to the general public and people were walking back and forth in the foyer, my father and I were the only visitors. I made a mental note to ask him why.

Every book I examined was a history book. Some were very old. One box held papyrus scrolls, which looked so fragile I dared not even breathe near them. I placed myself before a table which displayed newer-looking books. I selected a work on World War II and studied the cover and preliminary pages. The publisher was identified as LFH. The date of publication was 1937. The history began with Neville Chamberlain signing the Munich Agreement in 1938. The last chapter was called 'The Cold War Begins.' I searched for other histories I knew. I discovered a book about the Second Gulf War, published a year before the First Gulf War had even been waged. In 1859, the LFH had issued a 900-page history of the American Civil War, which contained the full text of the Gettysburg Address. It was the same whichever book I picked up. All recounted histories of the future.

My father signalled for me to come over.

'These histories are the only histories worth reading,' he said.

'But who writes them? What is this library?

'The Library has existed since writing began, making manifest the universal plan for humankind to those prepared to contemplate it. It is a travelling library and adapts itself to time, place, and circumstances. The collection has been transported in watercraft down the Nile and carried on the backs of mules along the Silk Road. The Library is visible only to those who have the

111

gift to see time differently. It briefly opened its doors in a back room of Harrods in the early months of 1914. It made a fleeting appearance at the edge of the Prague market place in the autumn of 1617.

I had not been conscious that, as he spoke, he had led me from the room and back into the foyer. I turned around. The Library had vanished. All that remained was a bare room and a few empty boxes on the floor.

'The Library will appear again soon,' he said, 'and often, just as it did during the months before the pivotal events of 1914 and 1618.'

I glanced at a tabloid newspaper lying face-up on a table. The headlines screamed about a North Korean ballistic missile test and threats of retaliation.

My father waved his hand dismissively. 'Those fireworks are insignificant,' he said. 'They don't even get a mention. We still have a little while to wait. The campaign for the next U.S. president hasn't begun yet.'

'You've read the book?'

'From cover to cover.'

'What's the title?'

'*The First Cyber War.*'

I felt the sweat prickle on my back. 'Can't we try to stop it before it happens?'

'Not a good idea.'

'Why?'

We came out of the building, and a row of boarded-up shop fronts faced us from the other side of the street. My father halted and looked in both directions before deciding the best way to the carpark.

'Remember that Bohemian monk I told you about?'

I nodded.

'He concealed the book on the Thirty Years' War under his habit and stole it from the tent at the Prague market place. He meant to do good for humankind, save them from their fate, but his meddling with the future only made it many times worse. The book I returned to the

Library was, in fact, the first edition. It gives an account of a long but fairly typical seventeenth-century war. The Thirty Years' War that Europe actually experienced followed the revised and extended edition, which contains a *tour-de-force* chapter on the Sack of Magdeburg in 1631. The bloodiest event in that bloodiest of European wars until the twentieth century.'

'Then there's nothing we can do?'

'Yes, we can do something. It has been my job to ensure no more books are stolen from the Library and so preserve this imperfect yet best possible of worlds.' He put his hand on my shoulder as a police car wailed past us. 'Soon that job will fall to you.'

About the Author

Simon Lee-Price hails from Liverpool and lives and writes in the UK. His fiction has appeared in *Prole, Prose and Poetry*, *Interpreter's House*, *Five:2:One*, *The Caribbean Writer*, and the horror anthologies *Breathless* and the *Second Corona Book of Horror Stories*. He tweets from time to time @SimonLeePrice.

*****~~~~~*****

MH370

by Ricardo Maia

On 8 March 2014, Malaysia Airline Flight 370 disappeared while flying from Kuala Lumpur to Beijing, after taking an unexplained path that ultimately led it to crash somewhere in the Indian Ocean.

An international search effort was organized to find the missing airplane with 227 passengers and 12 crew members. After almost three years of what had become the most expensive search operation in aviation history, the pursuit for the airplane was finally suspended.

The only indication of its crash were pieces of debris that washed away on nearby islands and the coast of Africa. There were rumors regarding the finding of the Cockpit Voice Recording by a pair of unsuspecting Mozambican fishermen. After that, word of mouth would've led black market dealers to track the CVR long before authorities could ever know of its presence.

The device, still sealed with its content, would have been auctioned off in the deep web to some private collector. Upon purchase, the collector would need someone to confirm the authenticity of the product—the first person to ever hear about what truly happened during flight MH370.

If such person had the device in their hands is not known, but a transcription of the cockpit conversation surfaced on the web through an anonymous blog. Shortly after that, the blog page was removed. The original transcription, saved by some users, was quickly lost amidst fakes written by copycats. US federal authorities managed to track the IP address of the original blog owner, but it was a dead end. All they could find was a house burned to the ground, with stacks of papers written by hand partially destroyed by the fire.

The authenticity of the recovered files cannot be confirmed. What follows are the relevant parts of the unaltered transcription that survived the flames.

. . .

00:40

(MH370): "Control Tower, this is Malaysian three seven zero, requesting permission to take off on runaway third two right."

(Control Tower): "Malaysian three seven zero, permission granted, you're clear to take off to flight level one eight zero."

(MH370): "Roger that Tower, the night is looking good for a travel."

00:46

(MH370): "Lumpur Radar, this is Malaysian three seven zero, we're 30 miles northeast of the Kuala Lumpur airport, requesting permission to reach flight level two five zero."

(Lumpur Radar): "Malaysian three seven zero, you're clear to reach flight level two five zero."

(MH370): "Roger that Lumpur Radar, climbing now with the aircraft."

00:56

(Chief Stewardess): "Captain, sorry to bother you with that, but there are two passengers feeling uncomfortable in their seats. One of them is asking to return with the aircraft."

(Captain): "Ms. Lay, are they in need of urgent medical care?"

(Chief Stewardess): "I don't believe so, Captain. One of them is an old man that is not used to the effects of decompression. The person who made the request to return is a young man that appears to be nauseated."

(Captain): "That seems like a fairly benign situation, Ms. Lay, just provide them with sick sacks and tell them everything is going to be okay, soon they will get used to the altitude."

(Chief Stewardess): "I already did that Captain, I just thought I should bring this to your attention, because the younger man was getting fairly agitated."

(Co-pilot): "What do you mean?"

(Chief Stewardess): "He was shaking on his seat, ranting about a dream that he had when the airplane was taking off. He said we were heading towards forbidden space."

(Brief silence)

(Captain): "The man is probably just afraid of heights, Ms. Lay. Tell him to keep it to himself, is that okay? Any other problems with him you can talk to Andrew or Patrick, they will take care of it."

(Chief Stewardess): "Certainly, Captain, as you wish."

01:01

(MH370): "Lumpur Radar, this is Malaysian three seven zero, we're about 93 miles northeast of the airport, reporting that we've reached cruise altitude at flight level three five zero."

(Lumpur Radar): "Malaysian three seven zero, reporting received, thank you."

(Co-pilot): "Should we inform them of the agitated passenger?"

(Captain): "No, that's nothing, give it a couple hours, and everything will be fine."

01:13

(Knocks on the cabin door)

(Captain): "Ms. Lay? Andrew? Just come on in, we're talking about my last trip to Beiji—"

(Metallic sound, followed by the sound of something hitting the floor)

(Co-pilot): "Oh God, Oh God, Oh God."

(Unidentified Voice #1): "I said we should have come back."

(Captain): "Lay! What did you do to her?!"

(Unidentified Voice #1): "I did nothing, she—"

DOCUMENT DAMAGED BY THE FIRE HERE. SOME PARTS OF THE DIALOGUE WERE LOST.

(Captain): "We can't do that. You know we can't."

(Unidentified Voice #1): "Listen, it's not just me, okay? More people are seeing the same thing. Look at what happened to her! There is something calling us."

(Co-pilot, whispering): "Sir, we have to send a distress signal. The airplane is being hijacked."

(Unidentified Voice #2): "You won't do that."

(Captain): "Who are you? Get out of the cabin now! I'm not turning this airplane back!"

(Sound of things crashing)

(Captain): "God! Stop! Fariq? Are you alright?"

(Brief pause, followed by indistinct mumbling from the Co-pilot)

(Captain): "Stop what you're doing. It's fine, you win! I will just acknowledge the next contact with Lumpur Radar, and we will return."

(Unidentified Voice #2): "Do not mess with us."

01:19

(Lumpur Radar): "Malaysian three seven zero, contact Ho Chi Minh one two zero decimal nine. Good night."

(MH370): "Good night. Malaysian three seven zero."

(Unidentified Voice #2): "You did good. Now turn the plane back before anybody else gets hurt."

(Unidentified Voice #1): "Wait! They're still tracking us, aren't they? That's what helps them. That's why we keep seeing the lights through the window."

(Captain): "What? What lights? Are you delusional?"

(Unidentified Voice #1): "How do they track us?!"

(Captain): "How do air control know about us? I don't understand your question!"

(Another pause, sound of someone agonizing)

(Captain): "There is a transponder! That's how ATC knows our position! I will just turn it off, calm down."

(Unidentified Voice #2): "You will make sure nobody else talks to us, you hear me? Turn it back."

(Captain): "Where are we going? The fuel can last until we hit Malaysia, just tell me the airport, and we can get you there."

(Unidentified Voice #2): "Just do it. Turn it back. Make sure some of your men will announce it on the speakers. We will talk again later."

01:28

(Quick thumping sounds)

(Unidentified Voice #3): "What are you doing? You're going towards it! Towards it!"

(Unidentified Voice #1): "No! We're moving awa—"

(Brief pause, indistinguishable mumbling)

(Unidentified Voice #1): "Oh God, it's all around us. All around us. There is no escaping."

(Unidentified Voice #2): "Quiet! Both of you! We turned back, and now we just need to—"

(High-pitched sound, followed by loud rumbling noise)

(Sound of attempted contact with the aircraft in the background): "This is Malaysia three four five, in the distress signal frequency one two one decimal five. Malaysia three seven zero, are you there?"

(Silence, followed by static)

(Captain): "I didn't say anything. I didn't! We're above the peninsula, what do we do now?"

(Unidentified Voice #2): "Keep going. They've seen us. They know we're here. We can't stop."

01:50

(Unidentified Voice #1): "Th—that's the sea, that's the sea again, what are we doing? Where are we?!"

(Pilot): "We're northwest of Malaysia, heading south to Indonesia. I was only asked to keep on going, so I did."

(Unidentified Voice #1): "What? No! Stop the plane! Just turn around! Take us back to the airport, just take us—"

DOCUMENT DAMAGED BY THE FIRE HERE. SOME PARTS OF THE DIALOGUE WERE LOST.

(presumably the Captain): "—didn't have to do that to him."

(Unidentified Voice #2): "He was becoming a nuisance. Now you keep going, don't fly over Indonesia. Just turn around it. Turn around it."

(Captain): "Turn around to where? There is just water after that! If we go too far into the sea we might not have fuel to get back home."

(Unidentified Voice #3): "What is going on here? Why are we——oh! What did you guys do to him? You animal! You want us to get there, don't you? Don't you?!"

(More metallic sounds, someone screaming and sounds of struggle)

(Co-pilot, with a very faint voice): "Stop, please stop. . ."

(More sounds of struggle, followed by a dry thump, presumably the cabin door closing)

(Unidentified Voice #3, muffled as if behind a door): "You won't get away! You won't! I'm warning the passengers, we're bringing this—"

(Background noise of struggle, followed by the sound of something cracking)

(Unidentified Voice #2): "Don't worry, he was taken of care of."

(Captain): "Taken care of? What do you mean? How many people are working for you? What did you do to him?"

(Unidentified Voice #2): "Quiet! Here's what you will do: Announce on the speakers this airplane was under the threat of being shot down. I don't care by who. Make up a story. Tell the passengers that we're safe now, but you can't go back to Malaysia just yet. Tell the crew to sit tight with the passengers and await further instructions. If any crew member gets anywhere near this cabin, something bad will happen. Don't go to Indonesia. I swear I will bring this thing down if I have to."

(Brief pause)

(Captain): "I understand."

02:03

(Malaysian Airlines dispatch): "This is Malaysian Airlines dispatch to Malaysian three seven zero, we ask you to contact Ho Chi Minh as soon as possible, we're not getting any feedback from your data unit."

(Silence)

02:22

(Unidentified Voice #2): "Here. It's here. Turn around."

(Captain): "Turn around to where?"

(Unidentified Voice #2): "South. Go south, towards the Southern Tropic."

(Captain): "Could you stop pointing this thing toward me? And what are you saying? There is nothing to the south, just ocean. We can't waste fuel like this. Don't you hear the passengers? They're agitated, they're confused, I told them we're circling around, they will notice."

(Unidentified Voice #2): "You don't understand what is going on do you? Just do it as I say! Half of the passengers have seen the lights already! They're almost here!"

(Captain): "Alright, calm down. I'm turning south okay? But who are 'they'? We're in an airplane. There is no one coming here."

(Unidentified Voice #2): "You'll see."

(Metallic bang, sounds of things crashing)

(Co-pilot): "I got him! I got him! Shah, help me, help me, put it on auto-pilot."

(Sounds of struggle, more bangs and crashes, someone groans)

(Captain): "He hit the controls! The controls!"

(Silence)

02:38

(Co-pilot): "We tried everything. We have to open the door and ask for help."

(Captain): "God damn it, Farid! There is an unconscious man on the damn cockpit who says he's got more people on his side. His goons are probably standing right next to the corridor. I'm not opening this door. It stays barricaded. We're going to fix this."

(Co-pilot): "Sir, we lost manual control, and we're not able to send mayday signals. The airplane is heading to nowhere. We have no other options, we have to see if someone out there can contact the outside. We have to ask for help.

(Silence, followed by the sound of something ringing)

(Captain): "It's them! It's control! They're calling using the satellite link, thank God!"

(Brief pause while the sound of ringing continues)

(Co-pilot): "Sir! Pick up the call!"

(Captain): "I'm trying, Farid! I already accepted it, but it's not working! Hello? Hello?!"

(Ringing continues and fades away)

(Captain): "No! Damn it! NO!"

(Co-pilot): "Sir, I'm sorry, but we have to--"

(Silence)

(Captain): "What, Farid? What is that we have to do? Don't say that we should open the door in the middle of a hijacking attempt."

(Co-pilot): "S-sir, look through the window. Can't you see it?"

(Captain): "See what, Farid?"

(Co-pilot): "The lights, sir. I can see the lights."

AT THIS POINT THERE IS A PROBLEM WITH THE RECORDING: All SOUNDS CAPTURED BY THE CVR WERE SLOWED DOWN CONSIDERABLY. THE TRANSCRIPTION BELOW WAS OBTAINED BY SPEEDING UP THE REGISTER OVER A HUNDRED TIMES THE NORMAL SPEED. AS A RESULT, WHAT COMES NEXT TAKES PLACE IN THE COURSE OF SEVERAL HOURS OF RECORDING. IT IS NOT KNOWN WHAT COULD HAVE CAUSED THIS TECHNICAL ISSUE.

??:??

(Captain): "Farid, I don't see anything."

(Co-pilot): "GET DOWN, SIR! IT'S HEADING TOWARDS US!"

(Captain): "What? What is—"

(Loud metallic sound, followed by a larger rumbling noise. Sounds of men groaning and agonizing)

(Captain): "W-what was that? Did we h-hit something? What? I didn't see anything? Did it get the engines?"

(Co-pilot): "Sir. I-it's inside. With the passengers."

(Captain): "What is inside, Farid? What is. . . oh my God. What is that light? What is the light behind the door?"

(Co-pilot): "You can see it now, sir? You can see it? We have to open it!"

(Brief silence, followed by the sound of people crying and screaming)

(Muffled voice #1): "Somebody help us! Somebody! It's bright, so bright, oh God. . . IT HURTS, MAKE IT GO AWAY!"

(Muffled voice #2): "I can see myself! I can see myself through its eyes! AM I DEAD?! WHAT IS HAPPENING TO ME?!"

(Captain): "NO, FARID! GET AWAY FROM THAT DOOR!"

(Muffled voice #3): "FOR THE LOVE OF GOD! OPEN THE DAMN DOOR! IT BURNS! IT—"

(Screaming in the background, followed by loud banging noises and sounds of struggle. Co-pilot says something indistinguishable)

(Unidentified Voice #2, faintly): "It arrived. I said it would arrive."

(Captain, groaning): "What is that thing out there? Do you know about it? DO YOU KNOW IT?!"

(Unidentified Voice #2): "It came from the place hidden between the spaces. Kumari Nadu! Kumarikandam! Lemuria! Lemuria!"

(Another banging noise, background sound of voices dying down)

(Captain): "What happened?! What happened to them?! ANSWER ME DAMN IT!"

(Unidentified Voice #2): "We're truly blessed."

AT THIS POINT THE RECORDING RETURNS TO NORMAL SPEED.

08:18

(Captain): "Wait! What is that outside? S-sunlight? Is that the sun? What happened? How much time. . . oh, no."

(Unidentified Voice #2): "Time doesn't work the same for them. It's different. It's all different there. You'll see."

(Co-pilot): "C-captain. I'm sorry. The engines, look at the fuel."

(Captain): "It's about to die down. . . it's over. It's all over."

(Co-pilot): "Captain, where are we? What is that? Do you see it? Hovering over the sea?"

(Unidentified Voice #2): "It's home. That's home."

###

About the Author

Ricardo Maia was born in Rio de Janeiro, Brazil, and graduated in biology from the University of São Paulo. He also has a masters degree in neuroscience from the same university. He has always loved writing and telling stories, which manifested at an early age as a desire to constantly be the Dungeon Master in RPG tables.

He has decided to seriously commit to a writing career and has started writing tales for publication in the last few months. His favorite writers include H. P. Lovecraft, Bernard Cornwell, and Conan Doyle.

*****~~~~~*****

The Ghost Train
by J. D. Blackrose

Aaron Gavril dug his hooves into the earth and lowered his head, weaving like a boxer so his razor-sharp tusks were front and center. The SS soldier, his eyes wide and gun hand shaking, didn't take the hint and stood his ground. Aaron admired the man's courage, but that didn't stop him from rending the man in two.

Aaron mentally recited Kaddish, the Jewish prayer for the dead. He said it over each fallen enemy and ally. It reminded him of who he was and the responsibility he shouldered. Being a were-boar meant being a protector of his people, and in Europe in 1944, he felt like he was failing.

His troop had been fighting Nazis for years now, as his ancestors had fought the Cossacks, the Romans, even the Egyptians, a never-ending battle to keep the Jewish people safe, or at least, to help the bloodline survive. Restless but exhausted, Aaron retreated to his group's camp and slept, dreaming of railroad tracks and smoke. When he woke in the morning, the camp was packed up, and his second-in-command was rubbing his bruised, human shoulder.

"Aaron, they're coming, more of the *Schutzstaffel*. That soldier you killed was part of an advance team."

Aaron sat up. "Itzi, what about the train? Are the prisoners on it?"

"Yes, and the Allied airmen."

"Will our Belgian allies help?"

"Yes, plans are under way, but they won't tell me the specifics."

"Whatever the Belgians are doing, they're risking their lives. We need to get to that train."

Itzi and Aaron heard a branch crack and froze, then dropped to the ground, faces in the dirt, inhaling its scent, knowing the moon would pull them that night. Even in human form, they could hear the crawling, creeping insects, smell the fungi and moss, and their fingertips dug into the soil, savoring its rich, loamy, feel, aching for later when they could experience it fully.

Guttural German carried on the wind.

"They're Resistance, clever but not invisible. Find them."

"But, Captain Weber, these aren't regular Resistance fighters. I don't know what they are, but they move like ghosts."

A third man spoke. "*Ja.* They took out a team of twenty armed men and left nothing but—scraps."

Captain Weber's voice carried disdain. "They're men, desperate men. That is all."

"Did you see Schultz back there? Torn in two! By what? That wasn't a sword that slit him open."

Aaron and Itzi log-rolled downhill, straining their muscles to stay flat and silent. After thirty or so feet, they crawled to a copse of trees.

Aaron touched Itzi's shoulder. "Let's get them away from the camp. It'll just be the two of us. We'll have to be enough."

Aaron took point, stepping on the driest twigs on the way, kicking rocks into the base of trees so they bounced and clanged in the still air. He wheezed and panted audibly, making sure the soldiers heard him, and when they had his trail, he took off as fast as human legs would let him, Itzi following.

"There they are!" The Captain shouted to his troops, and a team of six peeled off and pounded after Aaron. "Don't kill them! I need information."

Aaron climbed a tree and traveled tree-top to tree-top. Itzi stayed on the ground, reversed course, and ran in a wide circle to get behind the soldiers.

"Where are they?"

"I told you they were ghosts."

Aaron dropped to the earth and slithered toward the men on his belly. They were far from the Ghost Train, which was their ultimate destination. They needed to hurry this up.

Aaron saw the glint of Itzi's eyes as his friend snuck up behind the Germans, and with his backup in place, it was time to Change. He shucked his clothes, buried his feet and fingers in the soil, and called on the power within. He choked down his cries as his nose elongated, and he barely huffed in and out as the tusks sprouted from his face, ripping his cheeks apart, and when his bones broke and rearranged themselves into his animal form, he swallowed the pain.

"I'm done with this!" said one of the SS soldiers, while Aaron was Changing. "Let's walk back." The winded man bent at the waist and placed his hands on his knees.

A second scoffed. "I'm not sure where we are, but I'm not going to back to the Captain empty-handed. You leave, you chicken shit, and I'll capture this guy on my own, then make it to the closest road and get a ride back to Berlin."

Aaron burrowed with his snout and sucked up insects and mushrooms, even a vole that came too close. An unsuspecting snake slithered by, and Aaron ended the reptile's life with one chomp.

Satisfied, he rose to his full height and two hundred pounds of muscle, tusks, and fury attacked.

"What the hell?" the first soldier said. That was all he had time for as Aaron ran him through. The second tried to flee, but Aaron knocked him down like a bowling pin, stomping on his legs, breaking them into shards.

A third man drew his gun, getting off two shots, but Aaron leapt over their trajectory, and landed on the soldier, squashing him like a bug. The last man pulled his pistol and aimed at Aaron's head.

Aaron dodged, and the bullet grazed his back, knocking him down. Itzi attacked from the rear, shoving the soldier to the ground, grinding the man's face into the dirt, kicking his gun away. Itzi looked to Aaron for direction.

Aaron pierced the man in the gut with his tusks, leaving a bleeding, suffering soldier on the ground, forcing himself not to look as the man tried to shove his innards back in with his own hands. Itzi stepped away to avoid getting blood on his shoes and wiped his hands on his pants. They had no room for pity.

Aaron projected a picture to his brother-in-arms of Itzi Changing. The second-in-command obeyed, pulling on his leader's strength to force the daytime shift. He lay in the grass when done, snorting air until he could catch his breath. He ate whatever he could find until Aaron nudged him to tell him it was time to go. The Ghost Train waited.

They ran full on toward the Ghost Train and its cargo of captured Allied airmen and Jewish prisoners.

The train was still at the Brussels-South Train station when they arrived in the morning. Aaron Changed back, stole a uniform from a locker, and walked to the platform, while Itzi prowled the perimeter in boar form.

Aaron strode to a gathering of police officers, adopting an air of authority, speaking his best Belgian French. "How many in each car?"

"About one hundred and fifty, and there are thirty-two cars."

"How many Jews?"

"Unknown, but all that were in Mechelen Dossin Barraks. They emptied it."

"It's hot in there." A second man shifted from foot-to-foot. "We're not to open the vents." He shifted his eyes toward the German troops striding along the tracks.

"*I* didn't get that order," Aaron said. He walked to the closest car and pushed the ventilation slots open. Cries for help rose on the air, coupled with exhales of relief as fresh air rushed through. The breeze carried the scent of unwashed bodies, feces, and urine, and the stink-sweat of those who knew they were condemned to die.

The police exchanged glances, eyes darting this way and that, wondering what the armed Nazi guards would do.

"*Scheisse,*" cursed one of the policemen. "Come on boys." One by one, the police stood, squared their shoulders and opened vents, ignoring the German soldiers, keenly aware of the space between their shoulder blades where a bullet might hit.

As the Belgian police continued to provide fresh air to the prisoners, Aaron sneaked into the railway office and stole a pad of paper and a pencil. He stopped when he heard a voice. He peeked through a window, getting a quick look at the men within.

A man with a round belly said, "Station Manager Petit. You aren't required to do this by duty to the station, but we hope you will from your loyalty to Belgium. Can you do this? General De Gaulle says to tell you that you have his full support and the Resistance is coming."

A thin man with an even thinner mustache replied, "It shall be done."

Aaron wondered what the Belgian plan was and how they hoped to overcome the Germans. He followed the Station Manager and watched as the man murmured messages to his staff at the railway depot workshop.

"The engine shall suddenly not work, understand?"

"We do not know where the equipment is to fix these issues, right?"

"If we are forced to move the train, the signal master will send it on the wrong track. Trust us."

Each man nodded, and Aaron retreated to the background.

They were sabotaging the German plans, each person, one-by-one, waiting for the Resistance to arrive, buying another second of time. It wasn't an uprising or a battle; it was a fight of tiny acts of courage, small acts of rebellion, by regular Belgians.

. . .

The moon rose, and Aaron Changed again. The Belgian plan was working, and the Germans were furious.

The *Ortsgruppen*, the German leader on site, shook his fist in the Station Manager's face.

"Why are there so many mechanical failures, Station Manager?"

"Trains," said the Station Manager with a slight shrug.

"What about the lubrication piping? Isn't that something you keep on hand?" The *Ortsgruppen's* red face turned purple.

"Supplies are hard to come by," replied Petit, looking the Nazi soldier right in the eye.

"I'm calling in German engineers, and then we'll see what's really going on here, Petit, and if I find that you've been lying to me, I promise things won't go well for you."

Petit turned on his heel as if he couldn't care, but his face was grim. "Where is the Resistance? The soldiers we were promised?" he whispered to himself as he walked away. "They have to get here, or all will be lost."

132

The Ghost Train

Aaron and Itzi shared his concerns. They ran south to find the Resistance army, toward what they believed would be trained soldiers in tanks, flying the French flag. They ran the main road, stopping every so often to listen for motors, chatter, anything to prove the army was coming.

Nothing.

Itzi shuffled through trees on the left and right, crisscrossing the main road, searching for any sign. He caught up to Aaron, shaking his shaggy head.

Time was running out.

The boars shifted.

"Where are they?" hissed Itzi.

"Maybe they came up the eastern road?" Aaron replied.

"Why would they do that? The southern road is more direct."

"I don't know. Go back to the station. Do anything you can to delay the train's departure. I'm going east."

Aaron's stomach was in knots. They had done so much, come so far, they couldn't lose that train now. Despite fatigue and hunger, he shifted and ran, praying that his guess was correct.

It took several miles of top-speed running to get to the eastern road, and still, nothing. Aaron paused for a drink in a nearby stream and willed himself to go further.

One mile. Two miles. Three.

Finally. Voices, engines. Aaron sat on his haunches, waiting, gasping for air.

As the armed forces grew closer, Aaron's heart sank. *This is it, God? How are we supposed to succeed? And, why is this happening?*

He wasn't surprised when he didn't get an answer, he never did, and he dashed into the road and placed himself squarely in front of the head Jeep.

The "army" was a rag-tag group of civilian fighters, some injured, with limited guns and a handful of trucks, Jeeps, and a couple of old tanks slowly pulling in from the rear. A few American military uniforms stood out here and there, sent to advise the French, but the rest appeared to be battle-weary, stalwart, civilians. The lead truck screamed to a stop at the sight of him.

"What the absolute hell?" said the driver in English. "What the fuck is that boar doing in the middle of the road? That's the biggest damn wild pig I've ever seen, and I grew up in Florida." He grabbed his shotgun.

The woman in the passenger seat placed a hand on his arm. Her mouth hung open.

"Don't shoot it," she said, speaking English with a French accent.

"Why? It's a boar. I'll shoot it for the meat!"

"Jews don't eat pigs," said the woman, climbing out of the car. She wore dirty fatigues and mismatched boots. She approached Aaron slowly, tears in her brown eyes, eyes that were old and exhausted.

"Is it you? Are you who I think you are?" she asked.

Aaron nodded, turned his back to her and tossed his head in a 'follow-me,' gesture, his hooves tapping out an agitated rhythm.

"Thank you," the woman whispered, and she ran back to the jeep. "Follow that boar!"

The driver shook his head. "What do you mean? Follow a boar?"

"Just do it," Elena replied.

The man shook his head but obeyed.

Aaron pulled them off the eastern road, and headed north, cutting their arrival time by several hours.

The driver turned to the woman. "What is this magic?"

"He's the reason Jews don't eat pork, my Baptist friend."

. . .

Aaron ran ahead, confident the Resistance could handle the last few miles on their own. He laughed when he heard the conversation on the platform.

"The tracks are broken, missing rails. How did that happen?"

"Now it's leaking oil? Who's doing this?"

Itzi crept out from a wallow he'd made for himself under a nearby tree and trotted to Aaron, flicking his head in question.

Aaron nodded just as the Resistance arrived.

"The French! The Americans! They're here!"

"Forget these prisoners. This train is cursed."

Aaron and Itzi smiled as they heard the cries and retreated back to the forest, settling in a wallow, rooting for food wherever they could find it, planning on staying in boar form throughout the night and allowing the change to happen in the morning. They'd done all they could.

"I found you."

Aaron froze at the sharp poke of a K98 Mauser rifle stuck in his back.

"Boars. How poetic. Jewish pigs. Ironic, no? Or, maybe not."

Aaron and Itzi recognized the voice of Captain Weber.

"I looked for you, after my men didn't return. I will bring you to the Führer personally. I'll butcher you in front of him and let him dine on bacon. He'll appreciate the irony."

Weber circled around to face the were-boars, keeping the gun trained on Aaron. He nodded to someone behind them. The were-boars flailed, as nets made of thin barbed wire covered their bodies. The edges, tipped with silver, poked and seared their flesh. They struggled to their feet, but the silver leached into their bloodstreams, and their brains buzzed like they'd been electrocuted. They smelled the burning of their own skin, and, dizzy from silver poisoning, collapsed to the ground.

Several soldiers dragged Aaron onto a wheeled platform, like a sled, and rolled him to a waiting truck. They left Itzi on the ground.

"Oh, by the way, now that I've got you, I'm going after your people. Is your whole family like you? Perversions?"

Aaron grunted and struggled anew, trying to send Itzi a mental message, but the silver blocked his thoughts. *The others. No. No. It can't be this way.*

"Captain, lifting animals this size into the truck is impossible," said one soldier.

"Just take this one. Shoot the other. Put your back into it!"

"Even with all of us, we can't lift even this one. He's dead weight."

Weber thought about it. "Remove the net from this one, but leave the other where he is."

Weber spoke to Aaron. "Boar, you have five guns on you now. Get up on your own and get in the truck. Otherwise, we'll shoot your friend."

"Or, maybe, I'll shoot *you*."

Elena's voice took everyone by surprise. The American driver smiled a terrible grin, pointing a machine gun at the party. Jeeps emerged from the trees, each carrying flinty-eyed personnel who looked like they wanted to shoot the Germans more than they wanted to capture them.

The soldiers dropped their guns and surrendered quietly, except Captain Weber.

"American and French trash! You think you can defeat us? You can't. German might will win." He squirmed when two members of the Resistance grabbed at his arms.

"Blah, blah, blah," said Elena, as she removed the wire netting from Aaron's body, then turned to help Itzi. Aaron pushed himself to his feet, seeking purchase in the ground with his forelegs to keep from falling. He lurched for a moment but centered, just in time to see Weber break from his captors and charge Elena from behind, his hands outstretched to grab her holstered pistol.

Aaron snarled and launched his body at Weber, using his own motion to shove Elena out of the way. He tore his tusks through Weber's upper thigh, severing the femoral artery. Weber dropped, his face already pale, but Aaron didn't wait for nature to take its course. He lifted one hoof and slammed it on Weber's head, only satisfied when the officer's brains soaked the ground.

"Holy cow," said the American driver, looking at the carnage.

"No, holy pig," said Elena.

The Ghost Train never left the station. Everyone on board lived that day.

About the Author

This story is based on the real-life Ghost Train from World War II. J. D. Blackrose loves all things storytelling and celebrates great writing by posting about it on her website, www.slipperywords.com. She has published *The Soul Wars* series and the *Monster Hunter Mom* series, both through Falstaff Books, as well as numerous short stories. Follow her on Facebook and Twitter.

When not writing, Blackrose lives with three children, her husband, and a full-time job in Corporate Communications. She's fearful that normal people will discover exactly how often she thinks about wicked fairies, nasty wizards, homicidal elevators, and the odd murder, even when she is supposed to be having coffee with a friend or paying something called "bills." As a survival tactic, she has mastered the art of looking interested. She credits her parents for teaching her to ask questions, and, in lieu of facts, how to make up answers.

*****~~~~~*****

Man Overboard

by James Chmura

The frigid North Atlantic air kept watch-standers of Leyland Line's cargo ship, the *Californian*, stomping their feet and clapping their hands. It was 0100 Monday morning, April 16, 1915. The ship was about 20 nautical miles from the sinking *Titanic.*

"Keep sharp eye for our boat, men," Captain Stanley Lord, 38, ordered. He was standing on the outside bridge wing. Through his binoculars, he studied the distress flares in the distance. "My God, I hope this works," he muttered to himself. He shook his head and retreated to the warmth of the bridge house. "I'll be in my cabin," he said to the watch officer.

Lord stepped down the ladder to his main deck cabin. He poured a glass of brandy from the decanter on the sideboard then turned to the man sitting near the porthole. Lord took a sip and gestured to the porthole.

"Have you taken a look?" he asked. "*Titanic* is down by the bow. That's not right."

"I'm sure Mr. Murdoc has it all under control." Edward Rathbone was a thin man 52 years of age and consultant to the Cunard Line. He removed a cigarette from a gold cigarette case and placed it between his lips. He adjusted his vest, lit the cigarette with a gold lighter, and watched the blue smoke make a trail across the still cabin air. "All he had to do was cause *Titanic* to stop. It appears he has done just that." Rathbone pointed his cigarette at Lord. "Now is when you and the *Californian* come in, exactly according to plan. Right, Captain? Simply tow her to New York and you're famous."

"It's very cold out there, Rathbone," Lord said. "One little miscalculation and many can die a horrible death."

"We didn't choose *Titanic's* sailing date. Besides, we'll soon hear from Murdoc himself, shouldn't we?" Rathbone stood and helped himself to a glass of brandy. "That is, Captain, if your men are up to the task." He held up his glass. "So far, so good."

Lord glared at Rathbone and walked past to the porthole. "God help us." He turned. "My men will find him. Will your experimental survival suit keep him alive long enough?"

"Boat off to port!" the bridge watch called out. They rushed up to the bridge.

The wooden boat pulled alongside the *Californian*. William Murdoc, 39, First Officer of the White Line's RMS *Titanic*, stripped off an orange rubber suit and hurried up the boarding ladder. He shivered even though his uniform was dry. He stumbled to the bridge rail and stared out towards the flares.

"What time is it?" he demanded.

"0130, sir," the watch officer said.

Rathbone and Lord strode to the bridge wing and stood next to Murdoc. Rathbone put his overcoat on Murdoc's shoulders. "Put this on and come inside," he said. "Please. You look like you're in shock."

"She's not going to survive," Murdoc mumbled.

Rathbone and Lord exchanged glances. Rathbone led Murdoc into the bridge house. Lord followed. The bridge house was dark. Since the *Californian* was stopped, there was no helmsman or engine telegraph watch. Rathbone guided Murdoc to the ladder leading to the main deck below.

"Careful, Mr. Murdoc," Rathbone said, "you're not too steady on your feet. This ladder is quite steep, not as refined as *Titanic's*." He backed down the metal staircase as he guided Murdoc who followed behind, step by step. Once down, they crossed the deck and entered Lord's cabin. Murdoc stood staring at the porthole.

"How did the survival suit work?" Rathbone asked. "Did it keep you afloat, warm?"

"Yes, yes," Murdoc replied. He looked at Rathbone. "I just wish I had several thousand more on board."

"Indeed," Rathbone said. He handed Murdoc a glass of brandy. Murdoc gulped it down then hurried to the porthole.

"It's gone wrong," Murdoc moaned. "Terribly wrong." He turned around. "Captain Lord," he said, "I insist you get underway for *Titanic* immediately."

"Mr. Murdoc," Lord said calmly, "you know that's not possible. We're surrounded by ice. I couldn't make my way through in the dark."

"People are dying!" Murdoc stammered. "Even while we stand here, they are dying." He pointed a shaky finger towards the porthole. "My men. Passengers."

"Actually, this is a magnificent achievement," Rathbone said. "You may not realize it at the moment, but you are actually saving lives tonight."

"How!" Murdoc groaned. He squeezed his temples. "It wasn't supposed to happen this way."

"Damage to *Titanic* may have exceeded our original intent." Rathbone slammed his fist into his hand. "But our agreement, gentlemen, will stand. The public will be all the more shocked." He smirked. "We have ways of ensuring that."

"These things are so hard to predict," Murdoc muttered. "A few knots, a few degrees off course." He bowed his head. "Now this." He looked up with tears in his eyes. "I should be back aboard, not safe and warm here."

"Where is Captain Smith?" Rathbone asked.

"I don't know." Murdoc waved a hand in the air. "He was on *Titanic's* bridge at the time of collision."

"Excellent!" Rathbone rubbed his hands together. "Better than what we hoped for." Rathbone lowered his voice. "Look at it this way, Mr. Murdoc, we are helping future seafaring people." Rathbone paced. "The Cunard Line has always put passenger safety first. Your White Line is sailing these behemoths that are really too gigantic to be safe." Rathbone stopped and poured another glass of brandy. "*Titanic* is a perfect example." He handed it to Murdoc. "You realize if even a few die, the impact on the public may very well put a stop to construction of these floating coffins."

"Confusion and panic. Not enough lifeboats. Yelling, screaming. . . "

"All the better to prove my point." Rathbone patted Murdoc's shoulder. "Don't you agree? After all, Cunard's *Lusitania* has been sailing safely since 1907. She is smaller and not quite as luxurious as *Titanic*, but so much more efficient and safe. As you may recall, she won the Blue Ribbon for fastest crossing at 24 knots in 1907." He raised his palms. "Why, we suspect she'll be the queen of the North Atlantic until at least 1925 or 30."

"*Lusitania,*" Murdoc shook his head. "Soon I'll be her master, isn't that true, Mr. Rathbone? Our agreement?" He waved his hand in the air. "The only reason I agreed to this damnable evil deed."

"Well, yes, that and a rather handsome financial compensation for your efforts tonight. This will be your golden opportunity to command. Of course there will be a board of inquiry about *Titanic* and some details to be worked out. But we do have the world's best nautical barristers."

"Suddenly I really don't care." Murdoc burst out. "I made a mistake. I should not have agreed. You should have gotten someone else." He slumped against the bulkhead.

"Your Captain Smith," Rathbone said, "was the one and only choice. The most popular Captain to the rich and famous." Rathbone smiled. "And you as his First Officer were the perfect fit."

"Yes, and now their money is worthless." Murdoc stared out the porthole.

"Whose money?" Rathbone asked.

"They're freezing and dying just like the poorest of the poor in steerage." Murdoc giggled. "Astor, Guggenheim—all the rest."

There was a knock on the door.

"Enter," Lord said.

An officer stepped in and removed his hat.

"Report."

The man whispered into Lord's ear. Lord gulped and nodded.

"Well, that's the end, Rathbone." Lord plopped into a chair and looked at Murdoc. "I'm sorry, but *Titanic* has sunk."

"God no," Murdoc dropped his glass and slid to the deck. "Please, God, no!" He pounded a fist against the deck. "She was unsinkable!" He looked up. "Unsinkable, I tell you, unsinkable!"

"No ship is unsinkable," Lord said softly.

"Such a pity, Captain Lord," Rathbone said. "We won't need your ship to tow *Titanic* to New York after all. Of course, you'll still be paid." He pursed his lips. "I really did like that part of the plan." He shrugged. "So dramatic." He exhaled. "Now *Titanic* will be a 46,000-ton home for the fish."

Murdoc pushed himself up, rushed Rathbone, and shoved him against the bulkhead. "You bastard! You should be out in that freezing black water, screaming for help and gasping for breath!" He wrapped his fingers around Rathbone's neck and squeezed. Rathbone gagged and tried to pull Murdoc's hands away.

Lord ran over and grabbed Murdoc's arms. "Let go, damn you!" he yelled.

Murdoc panted and growled as Rathbone began to turn blue. Lord grasped Murdoc's wrists and twisted and pulled. Murdoc's fingers soon loosened, and he dropped his arms. He put his hands on his knees and took deep breaths.

"You're mad, delusional!" Rathbone gasped. "You bloody fool, I can portray you as the heroic First Officer who was last officer to abandon *Titanic*." Rathbone took a deep breath. "No one will ever know. You'll soon be in command of Cunard's finest vessel. Don't weaken now, Mr. Murdoc."

"Please," Lord said to Rathbone, "he is very distraught." He led Murdoc to a chair and turned to Rathbone. "You just don't know the weight of command."

"Perhaps," Rathbone straightened his starched collar. "Neither of you know the bigger picture. You command these ships, but what do you know of their design, their vulnerabilities? Obviously *Titanic's* designer, Mr. Ismay, didn't know much. Why *Titanic* wasn't able to survive a simple brush with an iceberg!" He looked at Murdoc. "That's what you think happened, correct Murdoc? Just a brush? You on the bridge?"

"Yes, yes," he muttered. "I must have misjudged the impact. I don't understand. I consider myself to be an excellent officer and seaman. *Titanic* was not supposed to sink. Hull damage, some minor flooding, that's all."

"Pity," Rathbone added. "That was the plan." He looked at the overhead. "I too wanted *Titanic* to suffer damage to her hull. I so wanted the humble *Californian* towing the great White Line flagship into New York Harbor. Survivor stories and all that. But now. . ." He shrugged.

Murdoc bolted from the cabin. Lord and Rathbone ran after him. He was outside standing at the main deck railing looking towards *Titanic's* last location. His shoulders convulsed with sobs. He was shivering and swaying.

"Mr. Murdoc," Rathbone ordered, "get back inside."

Murdoc, tears streaming, turned around. "I'm going to tell all at the board of inquiry. I simply cannot live with this anguish." He looked at Lord. "I beseech you to make way to *Titanic.*"

The watch officer came down from the bridge, saluted and handed Lord a message.

"Thank you," Lord said. He read the message then looked at the officer. "The men on the bridge wings are no longer needed. Dismiss the watch and get them inside out of this Godforsaken cold."

"Yes, sir," the watch officer said and returned to the bridge.

"The *Carpathia* is on her way and should be at *Titanic's* last location in about an hour," Lord said. He crumbled up the message and glared at Rathbone. "In these conditions, too late."

"We remain calm, gentlemen." Rathbone put his hands under his armpits. "The lives lost are of course a tragedy, but for every single life lost tonight, I guarantee at least one thousand future lives will be saved." He raised a clenched fist. "Don't you see? After the inquiry, new, stricter regulations will be written. The oceans will be safer all over the world because of what's happened here tonight."

"No, you slimy, lying bastard." Murdoc coughed violently. "Cunard's profit and your pocket are all you're interested in. We may have killed hundreds of innocent souls." He staggered up to Rathbone, stared him in the face and poked him in the shoulder. "The worst part is you don't give a damn." He stepped back. "Well, I do, and I will testify about this abhorrent conspiracy. I don't care what happens to me."

"A huge mistake, Mr. Murdoc, I assure you." Rathbone said. "That would ruin all of us. And I guarantee that you will be hung in disgrace because you abandoned *Titanic* and Captain Smith during their greatest peril." He smiled and pulled up the collar on Murdoc's coat. "Perhaps you should get some much needed rest. We can discuss this in the morning."

"Mr. Murdoc," Lord said, "I'll get up a head of steam and we'll proceed to *Titanic's* last location. We should arrive by 0800."

"Thank you." Despite the cold, Murdoc wiped perspiration from his forehead with his sleeve. "But it will be too late. I must return immediately, I must." Murdoc turned back to the rail. He struggled to hoist himself up.

"Murdoc!" Lord yelled. "We are 20 miles away, sir!" He moved towards Murdoc.

Rathbone quickly glanced along the deserted main deck. He stretched an arm in front of Lord then stepped next to Murdoc. Murdoc's hand gripped a railing stanchion. He grunted as he pulled himself up.

"Mr. Murdoc," Rathbone said, "how do you intend to get to *Titanic*? Do you see her?"

Murdoc wavered on the rail. He squeezed the stanchion with both hands and stared out across the icebergs and Atlantic swells. "She's still afloat!" He pointed. "Can't you see her lights?"

"Do you see anyone on board?" Rathbone asked. "Captain Smith, perhaps?"

"Yes, yes I do! He's on the bridge and waving to me for help! I must help him, I must!" He teetered.

"You are probably a very strong swimmer, aren't you, Mr. Murdoc?" Rathbone asked.

"Of course I am, I'm a seaman of many years!"

"Then, if your Captain needs you, perhaps you should go to him." He stepped away from the rail.

"Rathbone," Lord growled.

"Shhhh," Rathbone turned and put his finger to his lips.

Murdoc let go and leaped into the dark. He hit the icy water about 20 feet below and, regardless of his heavy coat and uniform, took a few strokes. He stopped to tread water, gasped, and slid under.

"Well then, that's settled, isn't it?" Rathbone looked at Lord. "He was right about one issue, this has gone terribly wrong." He rubbed the tip of his nose. "Despite that, I'll see to it that he gets a hero's recognition, I promise." Rathbone stepped back inside.

The newspapers reported heroic Captain Smith was last seen on the bridge of *Titanic* as she took her final plunge under the icy swells of the North Atlantic. Witnesses said First Officer Murdoc bravely remained on deck assisting passengers to the very end.

About the Author

James Chmura's favorite format is the short story. His 10 years as a stringer for a suburban Chicago newspaper taught him economy of words. He was nominated in 2010 for the Pushcart Award for Fiction with a humorous story concerning death.

Now semi-retired, he resides in Oak Park, Illinois, spending more time with his fictional characters.

*****~~~~~*****

Running on Empty

by Arthur Carey

The trim, immaculately dressed Japanese officer picked his way through the jagged hunks of concrete, torn rebar, and shards of glass where the schoolhouse entrance had been. In the distance, an air raid siren screamed a brief warning and fell silent.

As he approached the door, a soldier stepped out, rifle slung over a shoulder, and saluted wearily. His eyes were bloodshot. His jacket, dusty and worn, contrasted with the clean, pressed uniform and white gloves of the officer.

"Help you, Major?"

The officer looked at him disapprovingly.

"Is this the 317th Transportation Detachment?"

"What's left of it."

"One more insolent response, private, and I shall take note of it and have you placed on report," the officer snapped.

The soldier straightened. "Yessir." He held back the torn blanket that marked what appeared to be the entrance to a cave.

The officer entered and walked down steps littered with discarded books, signs, and childish drawings to the basement. He entered a sandbagged room. Battered chairs and desks had been pushed to one side to clear space. Hollow-eyed clerks looked up briefly from what they had been doing and returned to work.

An unshaven sergeant approached. "Sir?"

"I am Major Tanaka, sergeant. Captain Nakamura is expecting me. . . or should be." He glanced with distaste at the room's disarray and breathed in the stink of gas and oil fumes.

The sergeant pointed wordlessly to an office at the end of the room.

Tanaka made his way through heaps of piled furniture and stopped inside the doorway. A gray-haired officer sat at a scarred metal desk, shaking the receiver of a field telephone in exasperation. He looked up at Tanaka and shoved the telephone aside. He didn't rise, although Tanaka was superior in rank.

"What?"

"Major Tanaka, captain," said the major, stifling his irritation. "I presume headquarters alerted you that I was coming. I am on a critical mission."

The captain had thinning hair and a deeply lined face. A white scar ran down his left cheek. He shifted in the dim light cast by a hissing lantern and put down the telephone regretfully. "All missions are critical these days," he said. "So is our inability to carry them out. No, I didn't know you were coming." He gestured to the telephone. "The line is out again. Damned American bombers have leveled half the town. That's why we're hiding under a schoolhouse."

There was no need to say more. The continuing assault by B29s in the last days of the war was returning Japan to the pre-industrial age.

"What can I do for you, Sir?"

"I have four trucks that need refueling and servicing," the major said. "I am transporting a valuable cargo to a laboratory 127 miles away that has escaped damage." He named a small village in the mountains known for the recuperative powers of its spring water.

"Our supply of fuel is limited. . . like everything else," the captain said cautiously.

"I'm afraid that my needs take priority over all others," the major replied curtly, a hint of satisfaction in his clipped voice. He removed a piece of paper from the briefcase he carried and handed it to the captain, who read it, studied the signature, and returned it.

"For three years, our scientists have been experimenting with a secret weapon to defeat the enemy," the major continued. "I am delivering it after final field tests. The weapon will be ready to deploy if the Americans are foolish enough to land on our shores."

"Secret weapon?" The captain rubbed the scar thoughtfully. "It's a little late for that, isn't it?"

"No. Not after the weapon is deployed." The major dismissed the objection as if the problem had been considered before and rejected.

A loud noise filled the air, followed by a shock wave that sent the overhead beams creaking. Dust filtered down.

The major flinched. "Shouldn't we be in a bomb shelter until the attack is over?" he asked, a slight tremor in his voice.

The captain laughed. "This *is* the bomb shelter, and the attacks won't end until it is too dark for the enemy's planes to fly. I am surprised you reached us with your trucks intact. The American planes are attacking everything that moves on the roads."

The major smiled as if he had a secret and no intention of revealing it. "We have been fortunate. Several times planes seemed ready to attack and then veered off."

"Then you have been fortunate, indeed. The Americans own the skies now as well as the seas. Okinawa has fallen, the last defensive line before Japan itself is invaded."

"You sound defeatist, captain." The major waved a hand as if the gesture would dismiss the truth. It was a clear rebuke. He glanced about to make sure that they were alone. "If the enlisted men were to hear you speak like that, they might lose the will to fight. We must put our faith in the emperor and the will of the Japanese people to resist the enemy."

The captain looked doubtful. "Well, you can begin your journey in darkness," he said. "That should give you protection. But unless you lay over during the day, you will be at serious risk."

The major attempted to hide his impatience and failed. "Time is becoming critical. The Americans are gathering their forces to invade. We shall travel in day as well as at night. You have sufficient fuel, I trust?"

The captain nodded. "We don't get deliveries any more to replenish our supply, but there is less traffic on the roads using gasoline. Too dangerous."

He looked at the younger officer curiously. The major had not struck him as either a brave man—or a fool—up to now. "What kind of new weapon are you carrying?"

Tanaka hesitated. *What was the point of security now, with the Americans about to invade?* "It is a bio-chemical gas that melts flesh on contact. We tested it on Chinese prisoners with devastating effect."

"We?"

"I am a chemical engineer," the major said proudly. "I helped develop the gas and conducted some of the tests myself. The weapon is extremely demoralizing. Here, let me show you." He reached into a briefcase and took out a folder. Opening it, he removed several photographs and shoved them across the desk.

The captain looked at the first two. The hollowed-out faces of starvation victims stared back, sunken eyes bulging in horror. Their open mouths were frozen in silent screams. He swallowed and wondered if the images would become part of his own nightmares from the war. He didn't need more. The captain returned the photos to the folder and pushed it back across the desk. "The pictures are terrifying."

The major smiled. "Yes. Think about the effect such sights will have on the Americans."

"And you think this. . . this horrible gas will win the war for us?" the captain asked.

Tanaka shook his head. "Oh, no, the war is too far gone to win—right now. But when the cowardly Americans see the effect of the gas on their troops, they will halt their landings, agree to a truce, and provide us with time to rebuild our forces."

"Cowardly?" murmured the captain. He rubbed the scar idly. "Not too cowardly in the Philippines in '42, as I recall." A frown crossed his face. "What about our own troops and the civilians when you discharge this gas? Will they have masks or some other means to be safe from the effects?"

The major's eyes narrowed. He hesitated. "Precautions will be taken. Our protective measures are classified."

"Yes, I suppose they would be," mused the captain. "But there are means to protect our own people, are there not?" he persisted.

"Dealing with the results from exposure is not my responsibility," the major replied. He looked at his watch as if time were an enemy, too.

"Whose responsibility is it?"

"That is not my concern, captain," Tanaka said curtly. He glanced pointedly at Nakamura's rank to remind him he was subordinate. "And neither is it yours. Officers who rank higher than both of us make those decisions."

The captain leaned back in his chair, which squeaked. "And after this victory and a truce, we shall rebuild and resume the war? More people will die, some from this terrible weapon?"

The major shrugged. "Casualties are the price that must be paid when waging war. What is important is that the empire endures and prospers." He scooped up the photos. "Have the trucks refueled and ready to leave by sundown."

The captain studied him for a moment, his expression unreadable. "Sergeant!" he called out at last. A balding soldier appeared. He wore shoulder tabs with three yellow stars resting on a yellow band set against a red background. They were the insignia of a senior noncommissioned officer, a sergeant major. "Find a place for this officer and his men to rest," the captain said. "Get them some food and sake and then report back. We have work to do."

"My men do not require sake," the captain said sharply. "And neither do I. I do not drink spiritous beverages."

"Of course not," Nakamura murmured.

"I do not like your tone, captain."

The captain shrugged. "I meant only that an officer entrusted with such a vital mission would need to have a clear head to function properly."

The major's mouth tightened. "Take me to my men, sergeant."

When the sergeant returned a short time later, Nakamura waved him to a chair. He opened a drawer and took out a bottle of sake and filled two glasses. Neither spoke before drinking. They had been together since the fighting on Bataan, and later after the captain had been wounded and returned to administrative duties. "What is your impression of the major?" Nakamura asked.

The sergeant showed no surprise at being asked his opinion of an officer. He was used to the captain's informality when no one else was around.

"Young. Arrogant. Cocky." He looked at the captain.

"Too cocky?

"Perhaps," the sergeant said. "Only a fool would risk the roads in daylight. Unless—" He didn't finish the sentence.

The captain sipped the sake and licked his lips. "Yes. And he does not strike me as stupid. Inspect the vehicles and see if there's anything unusual about them."

When the sun had set and the air attacks had ceased, a relaxed calm fell over the camp. Tinny music from a hand-cranked record player could be heard. Muted voices leaked into the captain's office. An empty sake bottle remained on the desk.

Four trucks were removed from camouflaged hiding places. Soldiers in grease-stained uniforms filled gas tanks, added oil to transmissions, and checked the pressure on worn tires.

The major looked refreshed and invigorated. He thanked the captain and climbed into the lead vehicle, which lurched away. The other vehicles trailed after it, like ducklings following their mother. Blackout lights shrank to pinpoints and vanished.

The captain watched the departure with the sergeant. "You supervised the refueling personally?"

The sergeant's head bobbed. "Yes, Sir. As you ordered, the gas tanks are only filled a quarter of the way, and the fuel gauges have been damaged and made unreadable."

"Were you able to replace the canvas covers on the trucks?"

"Yes. We had spares. The old ones with the Red Crosses and Prisoner of War signs will be burned."

"Good," said the captain. "So that is the clever way the major escaped certain death on the roads, by disguising the identity of his cargo. The pilots held off firing because they thought they would kill fellow Americans." He shook his head. Perhaps duplicity was the least sin in war, but. . .

"You painted the symbols on the new truck covers?"

"Yes, sir. The skull and cross bone symbols representing poison are highly visible in white."

"Is the major likely to notice the changes?"

The sergeant shrugged. "He hadn't when they left. Perhaps in daylight. But the tops are not easily seen from ground level."

Neither worried. When the new covers were detected from the air, it would be too late to change anything.

Nakamura sat back. He would sleep better that night knowing he had done something to atone for his sin of omission in the war. Perhaps the dream wouldn't return, the nightly vision of exhausted, defeated American soldiers falling by the roadsides in the Philippines after the surrender. Nakamura had watched them being shot or bayoneted when they were too weak to rise. He had never protested, turning his eyes away as he rode by in a staff car.

"How far do you think the convoy will get?" he said.

The sergeant thought for a moment. "It's hard to say. Going will be slow with bombing damage to the roads, and they are traveling at night. They will still be on the roads and out in the open when dawn comes. They won't reach the village before then." He paused. "I think they are unlikely to reach their destination at all."

The captain removed a cigar from a shirt pocket carefully, sniffed the tobacco appreciatively, and returned it unlit. "And at dawn, the American fighter aircraft will return like angry hornets."

The sergeant nodded. "And they will find targets to sting."

###

About the Author

Arthur Carey is a former newspaper reporter, editor, and journalism instructor who lives in the San Francisco Bay Area. He is a member of the California Writers Club. His fiction and humor have appeared in print and Internet publications, including *Pedestal, Funny Times, Perihelion, Eclectic Flash,* and *Writers Journal.* His short stories, novella, and novels are available at Solstice Publishing and Amazon.com.

*****~~~~~*****

Proving Pictures

by Tony Genova

It was the best way to keep her memories fresh.

Every Saturday evening with her after-dinner tea, Melodie made time to instant message with her daughter, Ariel, browsing through photos of her daughter's life and adding new ones to the collection. Her computer contained thousands of photos from years gone by, and reviewing them helped her feel like she was still holding on to times that were long past. What started as a way to participate in her daughter's life had morphed into an obligation to a million fans, and she would not let them down this week.

"What's new honey?" Melodie typed.

"I finally moved in to the new apartment!" Ariel's answer appeared on screen.

Melodie knew the fans would be excited to see Ariel's new place.

. . .

Ariel's birth and first year were the happiest Melodie had ever been. Dustin was still in the picture, and though they were seemingly caught in a never-ending loop of work and childcare, there was a happiness about it. Melodie could see the glow of motherly joy shining through the few pictures she was actually in. Her hair is wild and her face exhausted, sure, but the glow is there. Does the micro focus on your own family's needs for the first year of a child's life increase your personal fulfillment? Perhaps.

The real star of these photos was Ariel. Her brown eyes showed a sparkle and life to them in every picture, and her chubby cheeks were accentuated by what seemed to be her constant smile. Melodie recalled that it wasn't always all grins and giggles, but you take pictures of the moments you want to preserve.

. . .

First day of school, and Melodie is at the bus stop with Ariel. Dressed in a fuzzy sweater with a backpack of her favorite cartoon character over her shoulders, she wasn't afraid at all. Melodie knew that was Ariel's first step out into the wider world, but she held the terror in and let Ariel bask in the moment of joy. Ariel hopped on the school bus without even a look back, Melodie only able to capture her foot disappearing into the doorway and up the steps in front of a neighbor's child.

Dustin had split by this point; a lost job and found alcohol problem caused him to develop other priorities. He stayed in Ariel's life, but not always to her benefit. Melodie mourned the lost joy, but was able to find some peace in herself. After Ariel, she wasn't able to have any more children, and losing a mate was an acceptable heartbreak if she got to keep her child.

. . .

Age 13 was where Melodie always clicked to next.

In these pictures, Ariel and a few family and friends are putting on happy faces, but it is impossible to not realize where the pictures were taken. Ariel spent her entire fourteenth year in the hospital. She missed school, but kept up with her studies the best she could. The pictures made it seem like friends always visited. Some of her closest friends made sure to visit at first, but the fear of the unknown and the distractions of youth got to them after a few months, leaving Ariel alone in her thoughts and dreams most days. Not a place you want to digitally memorialize.

Dustin appeared in exactly one photo, having visited once or twice when he was in town, an absentee father in the time of greatest need. He said his work kept him on the road. What occupation that was Melodie didn't know.

. . .

A big "10" on the cake, and look at all the kids around the table, wide-eyed and ready to gorge. Was this genuine smile Ariel's greatest moment? Before the unfairness of life came crashing through the door, uninvited and unwelcome?

Melodie couldn't remember half of these girls' names. She remembered Ariel's two BFFs, but the rest of these were probably the friends that come and go on the periphery over time. Perhaps she could track them down and put names to them someday. More likely they would remain lost in time. Even if Melodie saw them now, their faces would have changed. Maybe there was no need to fill in the blanks of history.

. . .

High school graduation.

Some of those mystery faces are in these pictures as well. No pictures with Mom—Ariel was either too busy or too cool, not sure which. High school was a whirlwind for a single mom and her daughter, filled with tension, excitement, and stress. Just surviving was the goal.

Melodie stops on one of Ariel walking off the graduation stage, looking ready to take on the world. She had as much trepidation about going to college as she did getting on the bus all those years earlier. Once she got her energy back, nothing could stop her. The diploma in her hand was not only a symbol of completing secondary education but also defeating her personal challenges. She was a survivor, a winner.

Dustin was entirely gone by this point. A few fights over money, but ultimately there wasn't much to argue about anymore. There was a new woman in a new town, to deal with what were no longer her problems. Melodie hadn't seen him since shortly after the hospital, and she wasn't sure his absence was anything to be missed. He had changed since that blissful first year of a nuclear family, and maybe one year was good enough. That was all she was ever going to get. She knew some people got more time to be happy, some less, but you had to figure out how to be satisfied with the time you got.

. . .

Melodie took the customary "drop off" photo each year: standing in front of the dorm, backpack slung over the shoulders. The rest of these folders Ariel filled herself. Some of the sights around school, some with her friends. Melodie was sure these were only reflecting a slice of Ariel's life—she'd been a college student at one time as well—but Ariel didn't need to share 100 percent of her life with her mother. It was difficult to accept the growing distance that life imposes, but that is life.

A casual shot was one of Melodie's favorites, Ariel standing in front of a statue of the school mascot, sticking her tongue out and flashing a peace sign. Her beauty stands in contrast to the lithe satan with blue skin, ever ready to fling its trident at an off-camera target. Melodie liked to imagine some of that devil's confidence and drive had brushed off on her daughter, whether Ariel knew it or not.

. . .

Melodie began work on this week's post, focusing on Ariel's new apartment in the city. A new beginning, full of possibilities. She wrote back and forth with the AI to find out more about the place. It only took a few months of learning Ariel's preferences and speech patterns for the AI to get to the point where Melodie couldn't really tell the difference, if she wasn't thinking about it. It could even speak in Ariel's voice, though the intonation wasn't as perfected as the text interaction. She spent a good hour searching for the right shots of the neighborhood Ariel described and the perfect interior—starter furniture for sure, but not a bad place for a young woman just out of school.

After a sip of tea, she loaded the photos into the AI, and the aged version of Ariel was blended into the photos. A couple of casual "slice of life" shots, a couple of formal poses, and the work was complete. The AI only had to age Ariel a little bit over the years—a fuller face, the occasional pair of glasses while studying—and it was generally pretty accurate, at least to Melodie's judgment. If she had to reject a round of photos for bad shot selection or non-realistic poses, the work could turn tedious, but seeing Ariel's smiling face at the end of the night was always a worthy reward in itself.

Fortunately, Ariel's 1,000,000 Instagram followers made this financially rewarding for Melodie. She hadn't held a job in almost ten years, and the surprising surge in popularity of her Instagram after the news coverage allowed her to sell some product placement in the photographs to pay her bills. If Ariel was carrying the right drink or going to the right restaurant that week, that was usually enough to get by for a while. Melodie didn't know much about how it was done. The agent who contacted her explained everything, from how monetization works to the fact that some dogs have more followers on Instagram than Ariel does. At least they did a couple years ago. Melodie didn't keep up with these things.

She added the few background items to the photos, and the AI blended them flawlessly, a couple of household products subtly added to account for this week's revenue. The AI, which at this point Melodie thought of purely as Ariel, added some text for the posted photos stating how excited she was for her new adventure in the city, the next step in her life.

Melodie filed the photos into this week's directory on her computer. Everything was sorted by year and then by month to keep things organized and to allow for easy reliving of the memories. The one directory not sorted by year was the one marked "funeral." Melodie hadn't looked at those pictures since she saved them there years ago, somewhere between the birthday parties and the high school graduation. She hovered her mouse over the directory like she did every week, deciding whether to finally look at the pictures or delete them forever. As she did, the notifications on her phone started buzzing non-stop. The Instagram likes were pouring in, and would for the rest of the night. She smiled and left the funeral directory alone. Ariel would live for another week.

About the Author

Tony Genova lives in Connecticut, where he spends his days crunching numbers and his nights going to sports practices, Girl Scout meetings, getting kids fed, showered and to bed, and squeezing some writing in. Overall, he thinks that's a pretty good deal. He has previous work in *Time Travel Short Stories* from Flame Tree Publishing and the noir magazine *Switchblade*. He can be found on twitter @TonyGenova and occasionally remembers to update his website at www.authortonygenova.com.

*****~~~~~*****

Against the Roaring of the Fire

by Edwina Shaw

Dirleton Scotland 1649

I see you, Mary Shepherd, there in the crowd, my baby in your arms. And I know what you have done to me, and why.

On the church spire a raven glints in the sun and croaks, calling me to act. But I cannot rage at you as I would like, storm my way through the gossips and beggars and those few friends I still have left, crying for me. I long to tear at your limbs, rip your hair from its roots, scratch blood from your cheeks and spit in your mouth. Snatch back my child. But my arms and legs are bound, and my mouth is stuffed with a gag, scratching at my swollen throat, so I have only my eyes to punish you.

I concentrate all my anger in them, cursing you from atop this unlit pyre. You feel my gaze burning, but you do not turn away as you should. In shame. Guilt. Instead, you stand taller, brazen as the pots you polish at the lord's manor, and dare to smile. You clutch my son tighter to your tits when he should be at mine, turn your eyes back to me, and smile in victory.

God sees you and all you have done, Mary. Your pride in it. Perhaps now you believe the stories you've told. You've told them so often you may have convinced yourself that they are true. But I know what the truth is, despite the power of your lies.

My boy starts to cry for me, and I struggle against the ropes, desperate to hold him once more, to smell in his baby-soft sweetness and not the stink of my own fear. For I am afraid, much as I pretend not to be. I am relieved too, though, that soon it will all be over. These weeks of torture, the great gaping emptiness of my arms where my son should lie. For a moment I had peace, strangulation's blackness. But the executioner's hands were not strong enough for my working woman's neck. I've carried too many buckets on yokes in my twenty-three years. The mercy I'd been promised at his hands failed me. I dared to hope then that the ministers would recognise their evil mistake. But instead they found in my recovery only further proof of witchery.

God sees the Kirk ministers too and the murders they commit in His name. I do not believe in the Devil, except for what these servants of God have done. And what you have done, Mary.

. . .

God watched as your belly swelled to fullness at last, after all those bloody times I came to your aid when you bled your unborn babies away. I tended you with a mother's softness and helped you bury the tiny morsels of flesh that would have been your children, even as I mourned the loss of my own firstborn. Five times, I tended you. And you thanked me each time as you wept upon my lap, your tears soaking warm through to my petticoat. It was you who whispered in my ear after that last great bleeding, begging me to share with you the old ways, the chants and herbs to grant you the miracle of a baby in your arms, breathing and whole. Old Aggie was still alive then, before she too was burnt for the sin of helping bring babies into the world and her knowledge of herbs and healing. I asked advice from my old teacher and she parcelled up her most potent brews and assured me of success. Just as I assured you.

The herbs worked too, just as she said they would, and we rejoiced together at the life kicking against your ribs, the *bairn* inside you growing stronger every month. And when your time finally came, I was by your side. As you laboured and moaned your baby into the world, all night and far into the day, I mopped your brow and brought water to your lips, and as you rocked and called out for mercy, I comforted you and held you, until at last your little one came into the light.

"God bless you Martha Douglas," you said then, eyes ablaze with love for the babe in your arms, filled with the wonder of it. "I'll call him Martin, after you."

But your gratitude didn't last long. Not when only a few months later the child sickened and died in the cold of that dark winter—the ground too hard to bury him. It was no fault of yours. No fault of mine. Babies die all the time. It's the way of life. Only the strongest survive their early years. It is God's way, and we cannot understand it. Just as I cannot understand why I am now here, and you are there in the crowd holding my child in your arms.

. . .

The mob jeers and calls for the pyre to be lit. My few friends are too afraid to call back against them. A mouldy piece of bread thrown from the front row strikes me in the face, and I smell the grain and yeast and am suddenly so hungry I would eat it if I could. So hungry, not just for bread, but for life itself. To live and watch my son grow into a man. To live and have other children. To be still here and breathing when my husband returns from war. To bump against him in the night, wild and free as animals.

You have done me a great wrong.

. . .

"No!" you screamed at the heavens, and at me, when, days after your child died, after a hole had finally

167

been dug, I tried to prise the decaying corpse from your arms to bury. You cried out so loudly the neighbours came running, thinking you were being attacked. When they saw how things were, they dipped their heads and removed their hats, murmured condolences, and went back to their houses. Your man finally convinced you to release the child's body and took his shovel to the yard.

I tended you then for weeks, for months, never asking for payment, doing it for love of you and kindness—making sure your milk dried and your body healed, that your mind returned. But your soul was always with your baby, buried in that shallow grave in the frozen earth. You would not be comforted. And you grew angry. I could see you watching me, hate festering. Though you knew I had suffered the same loss myself, your grief needed someone to blame.

. . .

You stand there in the crowd, waiting for me to burn. Unwavering, watching me with that same hate and blame in your eyes but now with a smugness that wasn't there before. A satisfaction as if you've just eaten a side of boar to yourself, fat dripping from your chin. You tickle my son's cheeks as he cries, and I roar at you through my gag. The crowd grows silent as men approach with torches, and I am afraid of the pain that will come. Pray that the mercy of blackness will find me quickly. I wish that the executioner's hands had been stronger, that I had not woken from his choking to the sounds of the crowd calling, "Witch! Witch!"

I thought it was God who had saved me then. But now as the men approach and I feel the heat of their flames and smell the dry wood and straw beneath me, I think perhaps God has turned away from me.

It was the same month you lost your son that I conceived mine. I send him all my love through my eyes as he struggles and convulses, distressed, screaming in your arms, calling for his mother who will not, cannot, come.

. . .

I saw how you watched as my womb swelled. Your eyes were on my skirts every time we met, searching for signs of growth. I knew what you were thinking, especially as you did not conceive again. I knew your yearning; I had been three years childless myself after my firstborn died. I knew how much you longed to be a mother again, and I promised to share my new child with you. That you would be his favourite aunt. I prayed that another baby would come for you. You nodded at my words.

But in my seventh moon, the women from Inverkeithing were arrested for causing a swathe of infant deaths, and I saw a plan hatch in your grieving mind. Though as those trials took place and the women were pricked and strangled and burned, you said nothing. You did nothing. Only watched me more closely. Fed me eggs from your chickens and milk from the lord's cows and butter from his table.

But on the day my son was born, pink and fat and healthy, you came and took him from my arms and smelled him in, and I felt a tremor of fear deep in my womb. For I knew you loved him and wanted him for your own. Still, I did not think you would turn on someone who had loved you so well.

. . .

In the crowd you shift my crying son to your other hip. He's heavy now at almost a year. He reaches out his arms, calling for me, and you shake him and slap his tear-red face. And I wish that God would change our places. That He would wipe away this last year of mistakes and bring me to my son, safe in my own kitchen, clapping hands as he sits on my lap, before our hearth. But it is not my cooking fire I hear crackling.

The first flames lick upwards at my skirts, and I pray that God will save me from too much torment. My son calls out to me.

. . .

You saw your chance in the fever of trials that took hold then here, in Dirleton. The healers and midwives and wise women like Old Aggie, and me, her apprentice. Those they called witches and brought before the law. Those they blamed for the ones who died of the great sickness and the dark winter, those they strangled and burned for the secrets they held.

It was you who went to the ministers and blamed me for the death of your babies, the one who'd lived and all those you'd bled away. You told them I whispered with the devil and drank babies' blood in my tea. That I danced with the dead on full moon nights and flew over your house in the shape of a raven. You led them to my cottage on the outskirts of town, knowing my soldier husband would be at war still for many months. And as they searched my naked body for marks and pricked my skin with bodkin needles to prove me a witch, you took my baby from his crib by the fire and kissed him on the lips.

The ministers nodded as you took my boy and went to the door, and I knew then I would die. No false confessions would save me from the pyre I'd seen Aggie burn on. I looked at you then for some sign of the love I'd always shown you, but you never turned your face from my son. May God forgive you Mary, for I cannot.

. . .

As the flames rise higher and pain becomes my only reality, I watch as the smile sags on your lips. My boy's cries fade against the roaring of the fire, and I close my eyes and become a raven far above your head. Above the crowd. I fly. Away from the only home I've ever known, I fly, I fly, I fly.

###

About the Author

Edwina Shaw is an Australian writer of fiction, memoir and screenplays. Her novel, *Thrill Seekers,* based on her brother's battle with adolescent onset schizophrenia, was shortlisted for the *NSW Premier's Award for New Writing* and has recently been released as a new imprint by Raven Books UK. Her short pieces have been widely published in Australian and international journals, including *Best Australian Stories.* She also writes regular articles for *UPLIFT Connect* online. Her feature film screenplay *M* is currently under development. She teaches Creative Writing at the University of Queensland, and runs innovative workshops and retreats combining yoga and writing. She also provides editing and mentoring services.

http://www.edwinashaw.com
https://relaxandwriteretreats.blog/
https://www.facebook.com/EdwinaShawauthor/
https://twitter.com/EdwinaShaw1

*****~~~~~*****

Yes, Yes, Yes, We Remember
by Elizabeth Beechwood

On the first day of May, the Western Slope always leans in, and says, "Remember that spring when the soldiers came?" As if we could ever forget. But it has become our custom to wait for her to remind us, and then we bow our heads and say, "yes, yes, yes, we remember." The Northern Peak takes up the story and says, "Remember that winter, after that spring?" and we all say "yes, yes, yes, we remember.

As if we could ever forget.

On the first day of May, the good people of Holubica always hauled the statue of their virgin goddess out of the church and into the field. They festooned her with flowers and sang and danced in gratitude for her protection through the previous long winter. The women scrubbed themselves clean in the baths, baked nut bread, and wore their best aprons elaborately embroidered with red symbols of faith and protection. It was not a large celebration, and most of the men never bothered to come in from tilling the freshly thawed soil to participate. No, it was the women who kept the spiritual aspect of the community alive.

"That May, the soldiers came from the east," the Eastern Grand Summit continues. Soldiers dressed in brown uniforms marched through our valleys and fought with our soldiers dressed in blue. They won the battle and flew their red flag in the Centrum as a sign of their power. Our people largely ignored these new soldiers. The village borders were as fluid as the Kamenec River, and our people knew that the flag flying in the Centrum was not the truth of who they were, the truth that ran in their blood. They were the children of the Vyoské Tatry, as much as the gentle deer and the wild Rusalka.

The brown-uniformed soldiers stayed back, out of the way, and didn't interfere with the daily lives of the people. At first, the people didn't see any difference in the new government. "Then autumn came, and it was harvest time," the Southern Basin reminds us.

Yes, yes, yes, we remember.

The farmers brought in their harvests of wheat, rye, potatoes, and apples. The shepherds ushered their sheep in from the summer pastures. Men and boys chopped wood to keep everyone warm during the coming winter months. And the brown-uniformed soldiers built checkpoints on all the roads in and out of Holubica. Our people began to grumble. Harvests were confiscated and shipped to the new capitol. Our people began to shout. Sheep were herded away. Chickens, pigs, and cows were taken. Wood was gathered to supply the insatiable needs of the soldiers. Our people took up arms. The new government clamped its iron fist upon them.

When the snow began to stick to the ground, the solders pulled out of the village, burning stores and warehouses as they went. They chopped the largest trees down across the road so no one could follow or return to Holubica. The village was blocked from the world, left to collapse upon itself under the heavy snows piling up in drifts. It grew quiet in the village; no chickens fussing with each other, no cows chewing their cuds, no oxen lounging in the barns after a satisfying harvest. The market in the Centrum, usually bustling and colorful even in the winter, sat barren. People spoke in hushed voices and huddled under blankets. They rarely came out of their homes, except to dash to a neighbor's house. The cries of babies echoed through our valleys and struck deep into our granite hearts.

"It did not take long for our people to begin to starve," the Southern Basin always says next.

Yes, yes, yes, we remember.

Our people began to fight with each other. They began to blame, to kill. Some hid in bunkers and caves. Some hid in basements or barns. Some congregated in the church, pleading for their virgin goddess to help them. But she was a demure goddess with a bowed head and little power.

Terecia, the disposed mayor's wife, gathered up a few of the women, women who understood, and they went to the churchyard garden. They gathered under the grand oak, where stood a statue of another goddess with stars on her veil and hope in her smile. Her face was upturned and her arms outstretched, and the power of the Vyoské Tatry flowed up through her and into the world. The women knelt on the hard ground and burnt white candles and pleaded for the goddess's assistance.

And we heard them.

We are, after all, a manifestation of the goddess.

"We should help them," we whispered in unison to all the creatures in our valleys, on our slopes and peaks. "We must all support each other as children of the goddess."

Bear argued, "Look what they do to me! They kill my cubs in the den, they hunt me down, even when I hide deep in the forest. Why should I help them? It is best if they all die."

The little Domovoi shivered in their cold hearths. "Without the people of our houses, we have no food, but, worse yet, we have no purpose to our existences. We must save the people, or we will grow thin and blow away in the wind, forgotten."

175

Fox said, "They shoot my kind for sport and don't even eat the meat! They chop trees without regard to the life they take. And, look! They dig into the heart of you four and mine your insides and leave a mess that kills us. They throw their waste in the rivers and expect it to wash away. Why would we help them? Let them die—we will be better off without them."

We conferred and considered their words. We fussed and debated. But, in the deep bedrock of our collective heart, we knew we couldn't turn away from the people we loved so dearly. Yes, they dug into our bodies and left only death. Yes, they chopped down our trees without regard to how it affected the other trees. Yes, the people did all of these selfish things. But even as we listed the things they had done to us, we still couldn't let them die. For we had seen their love for us as well, in their festivals and in the carvings they made in their houses, in the way they cared for orphaned animals and the way they cared for each other.

We tried to keep the wind and snow from falling on the town. But it was cold, so cold, and there was nothing we could do about that. The Domovoi dug into their stores of food and left as much as they could at the hearths where they had been fed for generations. The doves for which the village was named joined in, since they had nothing but good from the people. They flew tirelessly into the forest to gather twigs and small branches to burn. The chickadees and nuthatches dug out seeds they had cached under tree bark and shared it with the women who came to pray to their wild goddess.

And yet, it was not enough.

Deer gave themselves up for food.

And yet, it was not enough.

The people tore down houses and burned them for heat.

The people drank melted snow with pine needles in it.

176

And yet, it was not enough.

The Northern Peak whispers, "And then the Rusalka came," and we all huddle together so the Rusalka, the wild and dangerous spirits, won't hear us.

Yes, yes, yes, we remember.

The Rusalka, lured by death and easy prey, were lounging in the Kamenec River behind the church and heard Terecia praying to the goddess. "Terecia, Terecia," they sing-sanged. "Come to the river!"

Terecia knew they were the Rusalka but went to the river anyway. Her shoes crunched on the ice collecting along the shore. "What do you want from me?" she asked them in a voice that shook.

The first Rusalka laughed and tossed her wet hair over her shoulder. "What are you praying to the goddess for? Do you think she will really help you?"

Terecia was a smart woman—suspicious and smart. "I think she can—and has sent you to save us."

"Save you?" the second Rusalka laughed as a necklace of vertebrae clattered around her neck. "We have plenty to eat this winter. Why would we want that to end?"

"We'll grow fat," the third giggled as she picked her teeth with a shard of bone.

Terecia said, "You cannot grow fat on skin and bones, and that is all that is left of us."

The first Rusalka swam closer to the shore. "Even if we wanted to help you, there is nothing we can do."

"Did the soldiers block the river? Can you still swim to the other villages, the cities in the foothills? Can you bring food back to us?"

The second Rusalka laughed again, a high-pitched laugh that was almost a hysterical scream. Terecia's skin crawled, and we whispered to her, "RUN!" but she held her ground. "Why would we keep you alive? There are other people to lure into our rivers and drown."

The third stopped giggling. She whispered to her sister, the first Rusalka, "Without the people to believe in us, we will fade and blow away. And the women here are the most devout to our goddess."

The first Rusalka nodded. "We will help you."

The second Rusalka said, "What? We are the Rusalka. We do NOT help people—there are plenty of other people to prey upon."

"Shut up," the first Rusalka said to her sister. Then to Terecia, "Of course, there is always a price."

"Of course," Terecia said. "What is yours?"

The first Rusalka tilted her head, considering, then merely smiled and dove under the cold Kamenec ice and disappeared. The other two Rusalka gave Terecia one last look, then joined their sister. Terecia shivered and wondered what she had just bargained away.

Food began to appear along the frozen riverbank. And warm clothing.

It was not enough to save all of the people, but it did save some.

Finally, spring came, as she always does. And the soldiers with blue uniforms returned and flew their flag in the Centrum. Our people came from their homes, their bunkers and barns, their caves and cabins. No one mentioned that the food had been taken and the people of Holubica had been left to die, to be exterminated not by soldiers but by each other. Our people were too tired to do anything more than take the food and clothes and seeds the new soldiers brought and return to their fields. No one could look their neighbor in the eye for years.

The purple crocuses bloomed that year just like they always did, and Terecia gathered a handful on her way to the Kamenec River. The Rusalka were combing their hair along the bank, where grass was beginning to grow. "I'm here to make good on our deal," she said.

The second Rusalka laughed and nudged the third Rusalka. "I always love this part," she said.

Yes, Yes, Yes, We Remember

The first Rusalka swam over to Terecia and crossed her arms over her chest. "Everyone pays a price. Are you ready?"

"I am. What do you want?"

The first Rusalka looked at Terecia standing bravely on the shore, her clavicle poking out at sharp angles under her threadbare shirt. Her skirt was ripped around its hem. The soles of her shoes were held on with leather strips. What could the Rusalka demand that had not already been taken from this woman?

"The flowers," the first Rusalka said. "I want the flowers."

Her sisters gasped. "But I want HER," the second Rusalka whined.

"What do we want flowers for?" the third Rusalka grumbled.

Terecia picked her way carefully to the water's edge and reached down to the first Rusalka to hand over the purple crocuses. And the Rusalka rose up in the water, her face upturned and her arms outstretched, and the power of the Vyoské Tatry flowed up through her as she took the gift that Terecia offered, the gift of flowers.

On the first day of May, the Western Slope likes to remind us of how, after that winter, the celebration changed.

Yes, yes, yes, we remember.

The statue of their virgin goddess is hauled out of the church and into the field where they festoon her with flowers. But no one dances or sings. Our people are quiet now, the horrors of that winter buried deep inside of them, weighing them down and choking their words, passing on to their children and their children's children, buried so deeply that we fear their hearts will crack like granite boulders. No, they do not dance or sing. Instead, the women scrub themselves clean in the baths, bake nut bread, and wear their best aprons elaborately embroidered with red symbols of faith and protection. Small sculptures

179

of birds and deer are placed around the statues. Extra food is left by the hearth for the Domovoi that night. Flowers are thrown into the river for the Rusalka. It is not a large celebration, and most of the men never bother to come in from tilling the freshly thawed fields to participate. No, it was the women who kept the spiritual aspect of the community alive.

And the women whisper, "Yes, yes, yes, we remember."

About the Author

Elizabeth Beechwood says she is your typical Subaru-driving, scarf-knitting, bird-feeding treehugger who lives in the western fringes of Portland, Oregon. "Yes, Yes, Yes, We Remember" is the hidden history that people don't want to talk about, but the Mountains remember.

*****~~~~~*****

Specimen 1842

by Sandra Ulbrich Almazan

"Specimen 1842," Dr. Krantz said, showing Rosie Harris a picture of a tightly wrapped package on the screen. "A jawbone recovered from an eight-hundred-year-old burial mound along the Mississippi River. Just one of the dozen bones we'd like you to analyze for your first project—that's not going to bother you, is it?"

"You guarantee the remains will be returned to their people once we're done with them?" Rosie hated how tremulous her voice sounded in front of her new boss. She'd studied paleogenetics to learn about her ancestors and encourage people to appreciate pre-Columbian Native American culture. Not everyone in her tribe shared her views, which was why she'd promised them to treat all human remains she studied with dignity and honor. It was important to set the precedent now.

"Of course." Dr. Krantz spoke so quickly Rosie wondered if she'd keep her promise. The Multi-Science Institute for Humanity boasted state-of-the-art equipment and an international roster of scientists. However, they weren't affiliated with a university, and while the facility lived up to the pictures on the website, their mission statement seemed vague. The salary they were offering

Rosie would put a nice dent in her student debt. She hoped she wasn't sacrificing her long-term career with a position here, instead of in academia.

After Dr. Krantz provided details about the other bones from the site, Rosie studied the office décor. History books covering several different time periods, photographs from conferences around the world, and even an ancient carving that looked more like a retriever than a wolf.

"Where did you get that from?" she asked, once Dr. Krantz finished.

"A friend. Not sure where he found it." Before Rosie could ask more questions, Dr. Krantz continued, "Lab rules are that you can only use the clean room before you enter the main lab, so you'll have to wait until tomorrow to extract the DNA."

Rosie nodded. She'd earned her Ph.D. studying Peruvian mummies, so she already knew how to handle ancient specimens without contaminating them.

"Good luck with the extraction, then. I look forward to seeing your results."

Rosie silently left Dr. Krantz's office and returned to her desk, closest to the door. The other researchers and postdocs smiled and greeted her, but they didn't offer to include her in their conversations. *I knew coming to an institute not affiliated with a university would be different, but I didn't expect to feel so much like an outsider. But I've always been an outsider in this world. I just hope my work is good enough to make them accept me.*

. . .

Before handling Specimen 1842 and the other samples the next day, Rosie inspected her clean suit, making sure her gloves were intact. The bones had to be handled with the strictest care to avoid contamination with modern DNA. She turned on the hood for her lab bench before taking the bones out of the freezer. Rosie paused for a few minutes to say a quiet prayer to the spirits and to ask the honored ancestors for forgiveness before unwrapping the package.

Although the bones had browned with age, Specimen 1842, the jawbone of a male, seemed particularly well shaped and solid. Rosie wasn't an anatomist, but from her previous work, she knew malnutrition, disease, and injury could distort bones. Whoever this person had been, he seemed to have been healthy.

Rosie drilled into the jawbone so she wouldn't pick up any DNA left behind by anyone who had handled it. She cleaned the hood before moving on to the next bone. Once she was done with all the samples, she mixed the bone powder with chemicals to purify the DNA. Then she added the necessary enzymes and substrates. Finally, she loaded the mixtures into a sequencer. By the morning, the analysis program would have results.

. . .

When Rosie arrived at the lab, she poured herself some coffee, logged on to the network, and downloaded the data. Her technique had recovered DNA from all the bones, enough to perform a comparative study on ten individuals. Nine of them were similar enough to be related, but the last one—Specimen 1842—had different genes on the sixth chromosome, in the region associated with immunity. She looked up the alleles in a database, then raised her eyebrows. Specimen 1842 had genes for smallpox and measles resistance, even though she understood it to be from centuries before Europeans reached North America. His genome resembled contemporary Native Americans more than it did ancient ones.

Rosie gulped her coffee and reread the results.

The sample had to be contaminated, despite her precautions. Annoyed, she messaged Dr. Krantz. She was at a conference, but a couple of hours later, she responded. "It happens. Repeat the extraction tomorrow with a fresh batch of reagents. Run a blank and another known sample for controls. If you're still having problems, then we'll decide what to do after I get back."

Rosie took extra care prepping the sample and the controls the next day. She checked the results as soon as they were available. The blank was clear, as it was supposed to be. She'd chosen two controls, a modern human and a wolf bone about the same age as her sample. The wolf bone did show some signs of human contamination, so maybe her bench skills weren't quite as good as she thought they were. She'd chosen a different drill site on Specimen 1842, though she felt guilty about inflicting more damage to the bone. The results matched the previous test.

On a hunch, Rosie pulled up a copy of her own genome for comparison. Some of her immunity genes matched 1842's, but not all of them. None of the other people in the lab were an exact match either, so she wasn't looking at lab contamination. It was possible the bone had been mishandled during excavation. She'd have to contact the archeologists and discreetly ask for more information, maybe even find out if they had genomes on file.

Rosie had managed to match the other bones to a tribe with no living members. She contacted the tribe closest to the excavation site and arranged to return them. Specimen 1842 remained an orphan. She couldn't let it remain in the lab, so she searched public genomes for a match. She found it in a group she never would have suspected.

. . .

"So, the best match for Specimen 1842 isn't one of the Mississippians," Rosie told the rest of the lab during their Friday afternoon meeting. A few of them leaned forward to stare at her presentation, but most of them seemed ready to take the meeting to the closest bar. She gamely pressed on. "It isn't even someone from another local tribe. He's one of the Diné, or Navajo."

"Navajo!" Tim snorted. "That's got to be an error."

"It's not." Rosie forced herself to look in him the eye. Sometimes to deal with white men you had to adopt their ways. "And in case you were wondering, I'm not Diné, and there was no evidence of my own DNA in the sample."

Tim scowled, but he had the grace to do so at his smartcomp.

"Are you sure the bone is eight hundred years old?" Alix put in. "It might be worth doing carbon dating or isotope analysis on all of the samples."

Dr. Krantz looked up. "And make sure this bone really was found with the others and not switched out."

Rosie stared at the lab director, baffled. Dr. Krantz had assigned her to this project. She must have been the one to contact the archeologists and obtain the samples. Why did she publicly cast doubt on them now? Dr. Krantz's gaze offered no answers, and Rosie looked away. If the samples were problematic, it would be easier to blame a new postdoc than an established scientist.

They're testing me, Rosie thought. *That, or this is a practical joke they play on all the new postdocs.* Would they really encourage her to use precious time and materials on a practical joke? Maybe once, but twice? She doubted their grant was large enough to include a budget for pranks.

Rosie had reviewed all the labs at the Multi-Science Institute, not just Dr. Krantz's, so she knew the samples could be analyzed here. As a test, she asked anyway, "So, where would I send the samples for isotope analysis?".

"Pandak's lab on the fourth floor can do it," Alix replied.

Too convenient. Another lab at the institute might be in on the joke. "I know a postdoc in Madison. If he can find another lab on campus that can perform the analysis, would it be all right to send the sample there instead?"

Dr. Krantz frowned for a moment before replying. "It would cost more to send the sample out instead of studying it in-house."

Greatly daring, Rosie added, "If we send samples to both, we'd be more certain of the results."

"Very well. If you're willing to sacrifice that much material, I'll make the arrangements."

The meeting ended. Rosie sat down and breathed deeply, feeling as if she'd fought a great battle. The others didn't seem to notice; they collected their belonging and speculated about the latest *Doctor Who* episode. Rose had never seen the show, but she thought it might be worth checking out. Maybe if she fit in a little better, the others would let her know if they were pulling her leg.

. . .

After another round of prayer, Rosie took teeth and bone scrapings from Specimen 1842. She'd saved scrapings and powder from a few of the other bones, so she sent them to the other labs as well. With mixed feelings, she gave Specimen 1842 to a Diné elder for reburial. No matter what her latest tests reported, she had to finish this project and move on.

Dr. Krantz gave her a new collection to analyze, so she forgot about her mysterious human until the carbon dating and isotope analyses arrived. The results from the different labs were in close agreement. Rosie read the results several times, but they still didn't make sense, especially when she examined Diné history. A call to the university that had funded the expedition confirmed the samples had been collected properly, so she ruled them out as a source of error. Out of options, Rosie crept over to Alix's desk.

"What's going on?" Alix didn't look up from her graph.

Rosie thrust her smartcomp at Alix. "Can you help me make sense of these results?"

Specimen 1842

Alix set her own smartcomp aside and ran a finger down the table. "Carbon dating indicates how long it's been since something died. All of the samples are about eight hundred years old, as expected. Tooth samples give insights into the childhood of the subject, while bone data tells you more about the last decade or so of a person's life. By comparing them, you can tell if the person stayed in the same area all of their life. You can also learn about their diet."

Rosie nodded. "Nine of these people fit the expected profile. They grew up close to where they were found and ate mostly corn." She sighed. "1842 is the one causing trouble again."

Alix grinned. "Troublemakers are always more interesting."

"Yeah, well, given that he's from a different group, I didn't think he had grown up with the others. The data from his tooth supports that. But his diet included a lot more meat than typical for Diné of that time period. And the strontium results—"

Rosie broke off as Dr. Krantz approached. These results were too abnormal to share with the lab director.

"Go on," her boss urged her.

Rosie shook her head. "This has to be a mistake."

"Why?"

"Because the strontium results don't match Diné territory, or even the Southwest." She let out a choked laugh. "He seems to have come from New York."

The other two scientists stared at her expectantly. The frustration that had been building up for weeks inside of her couldn't be contained any longer.

"Specimen 1842 is a fake, isn't he?" she asked. "Oh sure, you've done a fantastic job of weathering the bones. But the condition, the DNA, the isotopes—everything points to him being not just in the wrong place, but the wrong time."

She couldn't watch both of their faces at once. Did Alix flash a quick grin? Did Dr. Krantz raise her eyebrows?

"Could you come to my office for a moment, Dr. Harris?" The lab director's voice was cool, emotionless.

Rosie's hands were slick with sweat, and she felt like she was going to throw up. Somehow, she managed to follow Dr. Krantz to the back of the lab. Only a few of the other scientists looked up from their work, but each gaze hit her like a bullet. *This is it. She's going to tell me I'm not a good fit and that I should find another lab. I'll be lucky to get a job washing test tubes. My mom will click her tongue and remind me that I can still go to nursing school. . .*

"Please shut the door and sit down," Dr. Krantz said as she sat behind her desk. As soon as Rosie did so, the director broke out into a big grin. "Welcome to our true mission, Rosie."

"Wait, what?" Rosie was grateful for the chair; her legs felt like rubber. "Please, this joke isn't funny."

"It's not a joke."

As Rosie stared, Dr. Krantz continued, "Your friend 1842 isn't the first anomaly we've found. There are teeth with porcelain fillings that predate the eighteenth century. Bones with isotope patterns that suggest exposure to nuclear radiation. A couple pieces of jewelry that once concealed nanobots or compuchips. Even my carving—" she gestured at the dog—"came from a time before golden retrievers hadn't been bred into existence."

"DNA from a different time and place," Rosie said softly. "You're telling me time travelers are real. Or were real. But if all that's true, Dr. Krantz, why hasn't the evidence been written up and published?"

She let out a harsh laugh. "Can you imagine an article like that getting past peer review? Even people who've studied the time travelers' remains refuse to consider this theory. That's why we don't tell new people about the Bradbury Project, the main reason why this institute exists. We give new hires an odd specimen and watch to see if their work is rigorous enough—and their minds open enough—to help us."

"So, what is this. . . Bradbury Project about, then?"

Dr. Krantz leaned forward. "The directors of the Multi-Science Institute think there's a group of future time travelers coming back to set history on a different course. Ultimately, we want to figure out what they might have done and what they're trying to achieve."

"And then what?"

Dr. Krantz lowered her voice. "I think there's a second group of time travelers out to stop the first and preserve our timeline. Our research helps guide them."

Rosie kept a practiced smile on her face. Part of her still doubted the revelation, but another part of her intuitively felt this hypothesis best fit the data. If it did, did she really want to join this group? The winners were too busy writing history to their own satisfaction to realize other people might want a do-over. Wouldn't it be worth changing history to prevent a genocide?

Dr. Krantz let out an attention-getting cough. "Interested, Rosie? We juggle a mix of mainstream and Bradbury projects. You may find that you don't publish as much as you might otherwise, but you'll be able to work on some very unusual projects, and you'll never need to worry about funding."

And they might not let me say no anyway. Rosie forced more enthusiasm into her smile. "I can't wait to start."

She stayed late at the lab, becoming acquainted with prior research and learning which of her colleagues knew about the Bradbury Project. When she left, she didn't drive straight to her apartment, but to a small park overlooking the Mississippi River. A half-moon illuminated silver patches in the water. Most of the river remained hidden, like the myriad genomes that had been lost to time.

She thought again about Specimen 1842 and his genes for disease resistance. Hopefully whoever he was—or would be in the future—had found peace. If he had had children in the past, about half of them would have carried his traits. The genes might not have conferred a survival advantage right away, but centuries later, when the Europeans arrived, they might have saved uncounted Native Americans from being wiped out. Of course, one person wouldn't have been enough to spread the genes over the Americas. They would need many Native American volunteers scattered across North and South America. Where would they find them? How did they recruit candidates?

A text appeared on her smartcomp. *Dr. Harris, thanks for helping us find a long-lost friend. We have a project we think you'll like even better than the Bradbury one.*

Her smile this time was genuine. *Tell me more.*

About the Author

Sandra Ulbrich Almazan is a hybrid SF/fantasy author with six novels and a novella independently published. Her short stories have appeared in the webzine *Enchanted Conversation* and the anthologies *Firestorm of Dragons* and *MCSI: Magical Crime Scene Investigation.*

*****~~~~~*****

The Homebringing

by Robert Dawson

The dishwasher was muttering and sloshing in the kitchen, and Fred had taken our son off to the den to see the latest additions to his stamp collection. Jeremy's girlfriend Alison and I were sitting by the fire, getting to know each other better over the Irish whiskey that she'd brought as a present.

"That's a pretty pendant," I said.

"The pentacle?" she asked. "Uh, did Jeremy tell you. . . "

"I've known security officers to be chattier than my son," I said. "You're in the same wood products course, and that's about all he's told me. But you're wondering what a middle-aged aerospace engineer would think about paganism, right?"

"Something like that."

"First, let me freshen your drink," I said. "And then I'll tell you a story."

I poured her another slug, while she curled her feet under her butt in a position that my younger self had once found comfortable. "Go on, Sharon," she said.

"This was back when I was with NASA," I said. "April, nineteen-seventy." I watched her face to see if she got it.

191

"April 1970? *Oh!* Apollo 13? You were involved with that?" Her eyes widened.

"That's right. Did you see the movie?"

"You bet!"

"Remember the engineers who were working with the mock-up spacecraft—the full-sized working models of the *Odyssey* and the *Aquarius*—in that big flight control room? I was one of them."

"Weren't they all men in the movie?"

"Well, they had to keep the cast small," I said, with a charity that was still a work in progress after six years. "Anyhow, our job was to try out the stuff that the astronauts might be told to do, to see if it was possible, and if there was any way to get it wrong. Any mistake the crew made could kill them: we had to find those mistakes before their instructions got radioed up to them. It was the most exciting few days of my life, of course—but it was pretty stressful. And then, after we'd been at it for about twenty-four hours, 'The End' came on the radio."

"The end came on the radio?" Alison's eyebrows came together in puzzlement.

"The song? By the Doors," I explained. "Anyhow, a long-haired computer programmer who called himself Phoenix yelped 'Turn that thing off!' like somebody was using a welding torch around the liquid hydrogen storage tanks."

. . .

I often wondered (I told her) how somebody as eccentric as Phoenix—not his real name, in case you're wondering—ever got his security clearance. But good programmers were scarce back in those days, and he was very good indeed. He was a few years younger than the rest of us. The only things I'd ever heard him get angry about were "Tricky Dick" Nixon, pollution, and the war in Viet Nam. But this time he sounded upset enough that somebody cut the music off mid-bar.

The Homebringing

"What was that about?" asked Chuck Hilden, a crew-cut straight arrow who might've been an astronaut himself if he hadn't needed about minus four diopters of coke-bottle glasses. I'd been Chuck's trainer for the last six months, and he was okay, despite his little-white-church upbringing. "I was listening to that!"

"Were you, man?" Phoenix asked. "*Really* listening? To the words, I mean? 'The end of our elaborate plans?' That's just gotta be bad energy. You trying to *jinx* this mission?"

Chuck shook his head solemnly. "See what smoking that whacky tabacky does to your brain, Tripper?"

"I'm telling you, man! That song's fucking loaded with negative karma."

Major Kate O'Reilly, the security officer attached to our group, clucked and gave him what my mom used to call an old-fashioned look. She'd been a WAAF in World War II and was older than any of us. If she'd been a man, no way would she have been sent off to babysit our unruly crew of slide rule pushers: but she didn't get bitter about it.

Chuck just laughed. "Cool your jets, keed. The ship's 200,000 miles away. Radio stations all over the world are broadcasting everything from 'Shall We Gather By The River?' to 'Yellow Submarine' as we speak. How in the heck is one radio *receiver* going to change anything?"

Phoenix looked at him pityingly. "*Think* about it, man! You're standing next to a near-perfect copy of the modules. The only one in the world. People—even you—have been imagining them as the real deal for months, today more than ever." He held his hands out in front of him, wiggled one then the other. "Resonance, dig? It's a perfect setup for sympathetic magic."

I could have laughed if he hadn't sounded so damn serious.

"Ah, you're as crazy as a Betsey bug," said Chuck, and went back to his measurements on an air filtration unit. "There's nothing there to resonate. No connections to be made. Just like inside your head."

To keep Phoenix happy, I phoned my roommate, and she drove right over with my cassette player and Beatles tapes, then sweet-talked the security guards into sending them in to us. Meanwhile we got back to work, but up there in the cold vacuum of space, things weren't going so well for poor Jim Lovell, Jack Swigert, and Fred Haise. Because the explosion had drained the oxygen supply of the command module, *Odyssey,* they'd shut it down to save power, and were living in *Aquarius*, the little lunar descent module. But *Aquarius* was a fragile tin can, built for vacuum: when it hit the atmosphere, it was going to burn up like a moth in a candle flame. So, they had to get *Odyssey* started up again before they got back to Earth, ready for re-entry. Nobody had ever tried to do that in space.

I was so worried that I could hardly sleep. I'd met all three astronauts: they weren't just names to me, they were faces and warm handshakes, and I desperately wanted them to live. Phoenix and the other programmers were modifying thousands of lines of computer code, and the rest of us were patching hardware problems as fast as they appeared—and it wasn't enough. Since Tuesday, we'd eaten and dozed in staggered fifteen-minute breaks, and that was definitely not enough: I would have killed for a good night's sleep, and committed aggravated assault for a shower and fresh underwear.

Finally, on the fourth day, the Lead Flight Director phoned and told us there was a big download scheduled in fifteen minutes, so we should all take our next breaks immediately. I'd have gone to freshen up, but the only ladies' room on the floor was a converted broom closet down the hall, with a single toilet, and Major Kate had just beaten me to it. Old servicewomen learn superior survival skills. I was about to get the weight off my aching feet when Phoenix, standing beside the big model, called out "Hey, people—wanna help me with something from a book I'm reading?" He sounded a little embarrassed.

"What sort of something?" asked Chuck.

"Remember what I was saying about sympathetic magic and resonance?"

Chuck just snorted.

"I'm serious," Phoenix said. "I thought maybe, before they need us again, we could hold a quick circle ceremony here at the mock-up. Even if I'm wrong, it can't hurt. And you heard the President and that smarmy evangelist praying together on the radio yesterday? I figure we've got a way better chance of being heard somewhere where it matters than those bozos do."

Chuck's face turned Republican red. "Are you out of your ever-loving *mind?* And what do you mean, 'bozos'?"

I'd never taken part in a magical ceremony either, but Chuck was pissing me off, so I pulled rank. "Never been to a service outside your own denomination? You're taking part in this, Chuck. Part of your training. Cultural flexibility."

He took a deep breath, and his color slowly faded back to normal. He seemed to be trying to think up a comeback, but maybe he was just too tired. "Well. . . since you put it like that, Sharon," he said. He turned to Phoenix. "This isn't any sort of devil worship, though, is it? I just wouldn't feel right about that."

"There is no devil," said Phoenix, in a tone of utter conviction, like he'd personally kicked Old Nick out of the universe and revoked his security pass half an hour ago. He looked at the rest of us. "Everybody cool?"

I figured that if it kept us working as an effective team for a bit longer, the time would be well spent. And this was the seventies, remember: Transcendental Meditation, Uri Geller, the Age of Aquarius. . . a lot of us were privately curious about the paranormal. "Okay," I said. "But keep it quick, I need to powder my nose before we get started again."

"Sure thing, Sharon. Okay, let's form a circle.

"Around the model?" somebody asked.

Phoenix glanced at the mock-up, the size of a small camping van. "Not enough of us. We'll have to be beside it." As we took our positions, he held up his hand. "Once we start this, nobody leaves till it's over; we don't want to let the energy leak out." At least he had the decency not to say "vibrations."

"Listen, Tripper," said Chuck. "If the Flight Director pages me, I'm taking the call, energy or no energy. And that holds for all of us."

"If you really gotta leave the circle, what the book says you do is, you cut a door." He turned to face out of the circle and carefully drew a door in the air, like Harold in the picture book with his purple crayon, then mimed opening it, walking through, and closing it behind him. "That's, like, an airlock for the energy, okay? You down with that?"

Chuck shrugged. "Anything for a quiet life."

I just hoped it would be quick: that bathroom trip was getting urgent.

So we held hands and chanted some stuff that Phoenix had picked up from his Big Book of Magic. He recited a bunch more stuff that sounded like he was making it up as he went along, asking the Goddess to bring her children home safely to her. It all felt a bit like Sunday morning at a Girl Scout camp. I wondered when we were going to get around to "Kumbayah," and tried not to snicker. *Someone's flying, Lord. . .* But then it got weirder. Phoenix called out a bunch of words that weren't English, and ended up "By the god and by the Goddess, by the sun, the moon, and the stars, I invoke thee, Jack Parsons!"

196

The Homebringing

That hadn't been part of the deal. Prayers were one thing, playing Bloody Mary was another. There were stories around NASA about Parsons—the guy who'd invented solid rocket fuel and the JATO unit, back during World War II. People said he'd been one of Aleister Crowley's inner circle, until he blew himself up doing some sort of experiment in a home laboratory. And they said he'd been into some pretty crude stuff—sex magic that had grossed even Crowley out. I was wondering if I should let myself out of the circle and see if the ladies' room was free yet.

Then Chuck, trying to be funny, called out, "Parsons, this is Houston. Report for duty! Over!"

And a few seconds later, we heard a faint hoarse whisper: "Houston, this is Parsons. Standing by. Over." The air tingled with static electricity, and I could feel that itchy dry-hair feeling on my neck and face. The air smelled of matches and ozone.

I tried to release the hands of the people next to me, but I couldn't make my fingers let go. Phoenix looked so pale I thought he might faint. "Mr. Parsons! We have a problem. . . "

The voice responded with an evil chuckle, and I felt feather-light invisible hands slithering over my body, touching me in places they had no business touching. I wriggled and writhed to get away from the unpleasant touch, but with my hands captive there was little that I could do. I clenched my teeth in fury, wishing Parsons would materialize, so that I could kick his nuts up to meet his tonsils.

"Oh, I think I could help you," said the leering whisper, "but for me to have the power I need for that, there are rituals that you'll have to perform."

Yeah, sure. If the NASA scuttlebutt was to be believed, when Parsons was alive he'd done some weird stuff, but his rituals were mostly an excuse for sex. And I knew that slimy tone of voice too well: the sort of creep

197

who, after his second drink, suggests "a girls-only game of strip poker, just to get the party going." That bastard wasn't here to help us.

I tried again to let go of my neighbors' hands. From the look of the guys, I wasn't the only one being ghost-groped. Most of them looked as if they were trying to brush mosquitoes off themselves with their elbows. Chuck was crimson, standing as close to attention as he could while holding hands, and muttering under his breath that might have been his name, rank, and serial number from his Viet Nam tour of service.

And then the red phone on the wall behind me started to ring. I glanced at the clock. The download was still five minutes off. *An emergency!* I tried to move us towards the phone, but somebody had epoxied my shoes to the floor. What did they need us for? Had we just doomed the astronauts?

I bit my lip so hard it hurt. I didn't know what Parsons wanted to talk us into doing. But unless it was playing Ring-O'-Ring-O'-Roses, we'd have to let go of each other's hands and move our feet before it could happen. And then—then, I was walking straight out of the circle, and that would let the energy out. We'd be free, and he wouldn't be able to trap us again. Right?

Who knew what he could do? But it seemed like our best chance.

The phone rang once more. I was screwing up my courage to say "Okay, let's begin," and hoping I could sound enthusiastic, when Major Kate came back into the room. She stopped at the door, and looked back and forth between us and the ringing telephone.

My cheeks burned. Once she filed her report on this incident, the Flight Director would fire every last one of us. The guys could maybe join the Foreign Legion. For me, that wasn't an option. It'd be a job in a typing pool somewhere. Were there typing pools in Nome? Too close. What about Timbuktu?

The Homebringing
Parsons spoke again. "There are certain things you will need to do to prepare."

Major Kate seemed to recognize the voice. Ignoring the jangling telephone, she marched up to the circle, took a silver dagger from inside her uniform jacket, and, in three slashing motions, cut herself a door. Hadn't she been out of the room when Phoenix showed us that? She parted Phoenix's hand from Kevin's and joined the circle between them.

"Abac, Aldal, Iat, Hibac, Guthac." She chanted the words slowly, in a clear soprano voice, with weird quavers and slides. Then she looked up above the circle. "Parsons! I command you: *obey!*"

The invisible hands withdrew; I relaxed and sighed with relief. The whispered response was quiet. "Yes, ma'am."

"You claimed to know something about rockets, once upon a time."

"Ma'am."

"I charge you, Parsons. Let there be no further failure in this mission." Her voice was icy.

"I'll do what I can, ma'am."

"You'd better. Or—you know what I can do to you. And one more thing?"

"Ma'am?"

"*Keep your God damned hands to your God damned self!*"

"Yes, *Ma'am!*"

"Herein fail not, at your peril!" The way Major Kate said it made the peril sound very real. She began to chant again.

At the end, she released Phoenix's and Kevin's hands and cut the circle, and I realized that I was able to straighten my fingers. And—*yes!*—my feet could move once more.

I ran to answer the phone, almost knocking the handset onto the floor. It was a wrong number, somebody trying to reach the media room.

I released a long shaky breath, wiped sweat from my face, and remembered another urgent matter. As I quick-marched to the washroom, I passed Major Kate and Phoenix. She was talking in an undertone; he gazed at the floor, shamefaced and silent. I overheard the word "amateur."

After that, things went smoothly, and a day later the astronauts splashed down safely. I cried for half an hour, hugged everybody in sight, and then went home and took the best shower of my life. Of course, none of this New Age stuff got into the official history, and Major Kate never said a word about it from that day on. But for the remaining three years that our team worked there, anybody could make Phoenix blush by whistling the "Sorcerer's Apprentice" theme from *Fantasia*. And, as you can imagine, I've been pretty open-minded about magic since then.

. . .

Fred and Jeremy came back from the den, talking about some rare stamp that Fred wanted to buy. "You should have come, Alison!" Jeremy said. "You've got such a good eye for details, you'd make a great stamp collector."

"Hah!" she said. "Philately will get you nowhere!"

Fred winced. "Anything left in that bottle? I think I need something after that pun."

"There might be, if you get yourselves some glasses," I said.

"What did we miss?" Fred asked, as he took two clinking crystal tumblers from the cupboard.

"I was just telling Alison some old family stories—'Phoenix'."

He gaped, then guffawed. "Oh, God! Not that one? Look, Alison, I was young and foolish then!"
She burst out laughing.

###

About the Author

Robert Dawson teaches mathematics at a Nova Scotian university. His work has appeared in *Nature Futures, Compelling SF,* and numerous other anthologies and periodicals.

*****~~~~~*****

The Thunderbird Photo

by Jennifer Lee Rossman

Once upon a time in the wild, wild west, a shadow eclipsed the sun. A bird, its wingspan measuring nearly fifty feet. You metric-usin' Europeans will have to do your own conversions, but trust me when I say this weren't no condor.

(Oh wait, my phone has a converter. It's 15.24 meters. Yay math. Now, where was I? Right, pretending to be a gruff cowboy lady.)

Now, the townsfolk were divided about what this critter was and where it came from. Some thought it was prehistoric, others thought it was the Thunderbird all those pesky Natives were talking about before the white folks forced 'em out. But, being Americans with a love of violence and a hatred for all things they didn't understand (see also: those pesky Natives, AKA my ancestors), they all agreed on one thing: they needed to kill it.

Not because it was eating people or anything. Just, you know. For funsies.

So they hunted the poor creature down and they hung its corpse on a barn like a giant butterfly in some rich old white guy's cabinet.

This story is one hundred percent true.

Or maybe it isn't. I wasn't there, having been born about a hundred and ten years too late, but I saw the photo in a big book of unexplained mysteries at my grandmother's house.

I loved that book the way others girls loved *Titanic*. Memorized every word of its cryptozoology chapter. To this day, I can recite entire passages by heart about Bigfoot, Nessie, the Jersey Devil. . . and yes, that Thunderbird what got itself killified in Tombstone in 1880.

So, imagine my surprise (and please, imagine it in letterbox format, with dramatic lighting and a super pretty actress in a Stetson playing me) when I grew up to be a cryptozoologist, went looking through that book to compare the photo to a creature I'd seen on an expedition out west, and found the photo missing.

Not like it had been torn out. No. The page was still there, with all the information just as I remembered, right alongside the infamous "Surgeon's photo" Nessie hoax and a frame from the Patterson-Gimlin Bigfoot film. But the Thunderbird photo was just gone.

Now, I know that isn't the kind of big exciting plot point you might expect from a monster hunter such as myself, but trust me when I say that the ensuing discovery is even more monumental than if I'd found a real Thunderbird.

. . .

Though I knew I hadn't seen the photo anywhere but in that book, I'm nothing if not a scientist (unless a'course you ask a scientist, who'll tell you cryptozoology is a joke and that I'm just some fool woman in a spiffy hat chasing down fantasies), so I had to do my due diligence and look for the photo elsewhere.

My Googling isn't the stuff research-library montages are made of, so I'll spare you the details and the digital dead-ends that have caused some mighty peculiar targeted ads to show up on my Facebook feed, but in the end I discovered an entire online community dedicated to finding that Thunderbird photo.

The Thunderbird Photo

They called it a Mandela Effect, a false memory shared by many people, so named because of the large amount of people who erroneously remembered Nelson Mandela dying in the 1980s, decades before his actual death. Other popular ones involved the spelling of Berenstain Bears, a movie where Sinbad played a genie, and the Fruit of the Loom logo. To be honest, most of it sounded like flat Earth lizard people stuff, but I believed in Bigfoot, so who was I to judge people who thought the fabric of reality was shifting?

"I saw it in an old newspaper article," one commenter posted, "but went through the archives, and it isn't there."

"I distinctly remember seeing it on a TV show in the 70s," another person insisted, "'Mysterious Creatures.' Except Wikipedia has no evidence of them ever having aired an episode on giant birds."

Several people mentioned my *Mysteries of the Unexplained* book. I scrolled through page after page of comments, vindicated and bewildered in equal parts. When I got to a link purportedly to the original photo, I stopped with my cursor hovering on the blue words.

Now, memory is a tricky thing. We like to think it's absolute and infallible, but it ain't. Before I let this new image worm its way in, I needed to be sure of what I remembered. I got out a paper and pen, and sketched as much detail as I could recall before I clicked the link.

I'm glad I did.

The photo was close. The barn, the men beside it, the black beast with its wings splayed out. If I didn't know better, I'd say it was it. But my Thunderbird was on the side of a barn, not the roof, and mine had feathers. This thing looked like a leathery pterodactyl.

When I went to take a picture of my drawing, with the intention of uploading it to see if anyone else remembered my version, I felt what I can only describe as an electrical shock in my brain. A mild one, the likes of which I felt when I was going off my last antidepressant, but still a mite disconcerting.

I looked at my drawing and froze.

My Thunderbird looked just like a pterodactyl.

. . .

Way I saw it, there were only two possibilities: either I was losing my mind, or something mighty peculiar was going on. I've had my share of mental illnesses (see above, where I know exactly what it feels like to go off an antidepressant), but never anything like this.

I had to believe it was the latter.

Besides, if I *was* crazy (and I use that term as an affectionate self-descriptor, not an ableist slur), what would be the fun in that?

I already had an expedition planned out west, but instead of searching for a mythological bird, I shifted my focus to finding proof of the photo. The current editor of the oldest newspaper in Tombstone vaguely recalled seeing such an image in the archives, and invited me into the shadowy rows of filing cabinets to look.

"1888, you say?" she asked.

I nodded and recited the caption. "'Alleged photo of a mystery bird shot and killed in Tombstone, Arizona. 1888.'" I'd been repeating it for an entire week, for fear that it would slip from my memory if I let it.

She pulled open a drawer and thumbed through the files, finally pulling one out with a triumphant "Aha!" But before she opened it, I felt that jolt go through my head again. She did, too, by the way she paused.

I put my hand over the folder's label. "What did this say a second ago?"

"'Thunderbird, 1888,'" she answered without hesitation. When I took my hand away, she was holding a yellowing news story about a thunderstorm in 1988. "Oh. I must have. . . read it wrong somehow."

"You didn't read it wrong," I assured her. "I'm just not sure what really happened."

The Thunderbird Photo

. . .

I spent the better part of an afternoon driving around an old ghost town, looking for a building that matched the barn I remembered seeing the bird displayed on. I didn't know what else to do.

The sun was low in the sky when I finally found it, a skeleton of a barn exactly the same shape, right down to the placement of the doors. Or maybe it wasn't. Maybe I'd just looked at so many barns that they'd all merged in my mind and I only thought I remembered it.

If the photo had ever existed.

It must have, though. I couldn't have imagined something so strongly that it made me dedicate my life to chasing down the truth behind blurry videos and drunken sightings. Whether the photo was a hoax or not (and I'd always said not), I'd found it in a book and it had changed my life.

And it had been erased, like no one was supposed to see it.

I stood where one of the men had posed in front of the bird, trying to imagine what they were thinking. Did they feel a jolt in their brains when the picture was taken? Did it fool them into thinking they'd just shot an ordinary ol' bird? Why else wouldn't they have stuffed the body and sold it to a traveling sideshow?

A shadow eclipsed the setting sun.

I looked up with a start to see a bird, enormous wings outstretched, riding the air currents way out in the desert. I couldn't make out the size from that distance, but it didn't look like no condor.

I raised my phone and snapped a picture. The jolt this time was stronger than ever, and I didn't need to look to know that photo would show something else entirely.

I didn't want to look. I wanted to remember the truth.

. . .

Hidden Histories

Once upon a time in the wild, wild west, a bunch of people killed something they weren't supposed to know even existed, and the universe set about covering it up.

A hundred and some odd years later, I uncovered that cover-up. But you best memorize my story fast, as it's likely to have changed next time you read it.

About the Author

Jennifer Lee Rossman is an autistic and physically disabled sci-fi writer and editor. Her work has been featured in several anthologies, and she co-edited *Love & Bubbles,* a queer anthology of underwater romance. Her debut novel, *Jack Jetstark's Intergalactic Freakshow,* was published by World Weaver Press in 2018. She blogs at jenniferleerossman.blogspot.com, and she regularly tweets @JenLRossman.

*****~~~~*****

The Fulcrum

by Shannon McDermott

The platform was two feet in height, forty feet in circumference, and ringed by steel pickets. Wing eyed it, apprehension budding in his chest. Then he glanced at his partner.

Ops—that was how Wing thought of him; names were a half-forgotten luxury of the old days, like hot baths and fast food—Ops was also staring. But he stared at the fluorescent light bulb that glared down from the ceiling. The bulb, leprous-white, tremored with the distant concussions, and Ops focused on it like he could map the shower of bombs on the city above by its quavering motion.

A metal door scraped and slammed, and then the Old Man was on them.

"Done." He rattled his folio, ragged papers bulging out of it. "We've finished the last calculation. This is the fulcrum." He tore out a paper and thrust it in Wing's face.

Wing took it and looked at the clear, blue-tinged image of a wooden cart, complete with a horse. A canvas, pulled over the back, hid its cargo. He studied the picture carefully, then passed it to Ops. "How could you take a picture?" he asked the Old Man.

The Old Man waved dismissively. "Science. Invention. You couldn't understand." His assistants hurried past him to buzz around the platform. He began to speed through words. "That is the fulcrum, the one point in all the centuries we searched that changes everything. When the cart arrives at the White House—that is the fork in the road. It arrived in the morning. You need to change that."

Ops asked, "Time and place of our arrival?" He was always focused.

"8:35, the a.m. In an alley. The cart will be out on the street, stopped in front of the building; the driver will be inside. While he's palavering, you two will have time for—well, use your imagination. Are you ready?"

Wing showed the Old Man his butcher's knife and a saw such as was used by the surgeons of that brutish time. Ops displayed a hammer and also a period pistol, a sorry excuse for a gun. He could barely grasp the pistol; his left hand had been mutilated in last month's rearguard action—the tips of his small and ring fingers missing, a red scar ridging his palm, the hand twisted in on itself.

It was too late to train a new man, and, anyway, how well could he use a machine gun now?

Wing's best scars puckered his cheek and jaw. He reckoned the Old Man's scars, peculiar to his more singular fight, were somewhere deeper than the skin.

The steel pickets sparked with blue electricity. The Old Man's voice grew demanding. "That is enough? And not too much. This isn't a military operation where the more enemy you kill, the more things you blow up, the better. Delay, not destroy. Enough but not too much—"

"Enough," Ops interrupted. An assurance, or a command, or brilliantly both—who knew?

"We have money," Wing reminded the Old Man, hoping that would soothe him. "Their money." Odd coins and stubby, blue-inked paper.

The room shivered, sonic waves breaking on their skin. They were dropping the mega-tonners, looking for the bunkers. But this bunker could survive a Heisenberg bomb.

Wing stowed away his tools. "How will we know if we succeed?"

"Watch the news." The Old Man sounded grumpy. "See if the President dies."

"Not the President." They weren't burying themselves in the past for *him* – a historical fact, a black-and-white photograph, not even a person. "*This.*"

The light bulb trembled. Dust motes, drummed loose by the bombs, tumbled in the white glare.

The Old Man flipped through his folio, tore out a paper. "I don't know if the writing will change. But it might." He flicked the page at them.

Wing caught it. He grazed the headline—the Old Man clipped news reports of what he called spacetime focal points—and stuffed the sheet into his pocket.

The steel pickets flamed with blue light, licking the air like flames. The Old Man looked at the platform hungrily, then looked at them. "Go on," he said. "The calculations took three years to make. They're perfect, you understand?" But the Old Man's belligerence had vanished somewhere; he was almost pleading with them.

Wing remembered suddenly that the Old Man—despite his manner, and the aspect of his eyes, and the white hair shooting out from his temples—was not so old after all. If his brain hadn't been so valuable, he would have been sent trooping with a machine gun like all the men south of forty.

Ops asked, "My boy?"

"I said I would claim him from the safety camps, didn't I?" the Old Man demanded. "John, wasn't it?"

"John." Ops said the name like he wanted to say it, said it with love. Then he tromped over to the platform and made the long step up.

Wing followed. The Old Man motioned to his assistants, and his machine reared back and roared. The

211

blue light shot from post to post, until it surrounded them with brilliant menace.

Ops stared at the light bulb. Wing stared at everything else. The Old Man watched them silently. There was never anything to say in the end; you learned that in war.

The light flared, so bright and suddenly so hot, too. Electricity raised the finest hair on Wing's skin. Then everything went white. Then everything went black.

. . .

Someone was shaking him in the darkness. But he realized, when he finally pushed back his eyelids, that he was in the light.

Ops bent over him, frowning. "Get up!"

Wing blinked, colorful and complex dreams still clogging the wheels of his mind. "Where—" Then his nose started working. He scrambled to his feet, eyes darting around for the source of the offense. The source was under his feet, and all around him – a stinking alley, piled with refuse.

Alley. In the past. Cart. Past—

The adrenaline knocked the last cobwebs out of his brain. He slid his hand to the knife and turned to Ops.

Ops nodded, his hand under his own jacket. They walked out to the street.

No cart. Wing looked at the dumpy brick building, stared at the odd people bustling in the street. He felt suddenly and profoundly lost, like a child separated from its mother in a crowd.

Then he saw it. The cart trundled away down the street, one corner of the dirty canvas flopping about. He launched himself after it.

Ops had already started running.

But the odd people—men in stodgy clothes, women draped in absurd volumes of fabric—got in their way. They shouldered by and didn't mind the yells, but they never got to any speed.

The cart pulled farther ahead.

Wing jumped off the sidewalk into the street. A carriage rattled toward him, the horses pounding the cobblestones. He jumped back onto the sidewalk.

Ops grabbed his shoulder, flashed a signal with his mangled hand. Then he darted away, over to the nearest house, up its run of front steps. He banged through the door.

Wing followed, bursting into the house just as a woman screamed. He ran past her as he bounded up the stairs after Ops.

They ran up to the third floor, the last floor. Ops invaded the nearest room, Wing hot on his heels.

The window was open, a limp gesture against the summer day cooking up outside. Wing sprinted to it, barely registering the man off to the side, clutching a razor in one hand and his shirt in the other.

Ops climbed out the window. Wing pulled himself up onto the sill, taking stock: ledge-like sill, heavy lintels, elaborate cornice—they scaled it to the roof. There they saw flat roofs rolling out to the end of the block. Only the odd alley, always narrow, interrupted the row-houses.

They ran and, when necessary, jumped. On the last roof, Wing scrambled to the edge and looked down. The cart was still visible, three houses behind them.

Wing turned to the busy intersection. People scurried blindly around the fulcrum like ants over an oil well, horses drove up and down the streets with man's contraptions and man's work hitched to their powerful bodies.

A carriage. Wing's eye fastened on it because it was stationary, idling at the side of a row-house across the way.

His hand zagged a sign in the air to Ops. Then he tore across the roof. Getting a handhold on the warm, rough stone of the cornice—Heaven bless the past generations that loved excessively ornamented

213

architecture—Wing swung himself down to the jutting ledge of a third story window. Another handhold, another swing, close enough—jump the rest of the way.

As Wing rose out of his landing crouch, he saw the young man perched on the carriage's box seat. The boy stared at him, slack-jawed.

Wing hurried across the street, dodging between a creaking wagon and a hasty rider. The boy's eyes tracked him the whole way. When Wing leaped up onto the box seat, the boy managed to squeak. Wing seized his collar and, with all possible gentleness, deposited him on the ground.

He whipped the reins, and the horses trotted toward the intersection. The cart was just entering it.

Wing grabbed the whip. He brought it whistling down on the horses' haunches—once, twice, three times.

They lunged into the intersection.

He snapped the whip again, cracking the air with that sound like cruelty and blood. The horses' hooves struck sparks out of the cobblestones.

The clatter of hooves, rattle of wood, an alarm of strident human voices—they all blurred into a rush of noise. But the cart sharpened in his vision, lurching in ineffective panic, inexorably closer every second.

He drove the horses in a wild left turn. And he could have counted every second of that careening swerve, felt the reins pull abrasively against his skin, seen the cart horse buck and paw, smelled the sweat thick in the air. . .

His horses thundered past the cart, his carriage colliding with it. Wood splintered as the cart came up and crashed down.

Wing drew hard on the reins. He struggled against the horses, stopped them, though his heart galloped on, roaring in his ears.

The Fulcrum

Then he waited. It didn't take long. Soon the cart driver was rushing up to him, waving his arms and shouting.

A crowd collected on the fringes of the confrontation. The boy Wing had ejected was among them, looking like he very much would like to say something and would have the courage around the time of the new year.

When the driver had gone on for a fair piece, Wing interrupted, "Your cart?" Then, while the driver turned purple, he looked around for it.

It was close, behind the carriage and happily intact. And there was Ops, breezing past it on the sidewalk, and nobody but Wing saw how he yanked the canvas as he went by.

Gravity tumbled the canvas to the ground. A host of dented metal containers stood unveiled, splashed with the milk the collision had jolted out of them.

Wing turned his attention down to the driver. "Your cart," he repeated, and jumped down to the earth. Then he ordered the boy to drive the carriage back. With an expression of almost unfathomable gratitude, the boy obeyed.

Then Wing turned to the driver and suggested that the damage to his cart was almost negligible. When the driver had worked himself halfway to an aneurysm, Ops insinuated himself into the situation. He played the peacemaker, and in secret concordance he and Wing maneuvered the driver into a tavern—out of the sun, they said, the hot sun that was cooking the day to boiling. There, in the dimness suffused with sharp odors, they negotiated, and drank, and finally counted out bank notes. They spun the minutes into hours.

Outside, the horse nosed in its feed bag and patiently stomped its foot. In the cart, the tin pails and jugs stood bare under the sun, flashing brilliantly. The raw milk within heated to that temperature in which bacteria prospered and swarmed.

Their business had to conclude eventually. The driver rode off with his milk, happy with the whiskey in his belly and the money in his pocket. Ops and Wing watched him go, hollowed out by their success. The air was sticky, the sun broiling;their shirts clung damply to them. A strain of brassy music drifted through the streets.

It was July. It was Independence Day.

. . .

They rented a room and waited. The sixth morning, Ops returned with a newspaper. He ripped one sheet out from the bundle, and it shook in his hand, betraying how he trembled. He pushed it into Wing's hands, and Wing read the words aloud: "Weep, fellow-citizens! The hand of Death has stricken down a great and good man! Zachary Taylor, our beloved and honored President, is. . . "

He paused. Did he need to say the word, so guiltily sweet? Dead, dead.

Ops put his head in his hands, and if he wept with relief, Wing said nothing of it.

. . .

They still rented, but now a house, and they worked along with waiting. They were educated in this time, fluent with letters and with numbers.

Wing had the privilege of bringing back the newspaper the second time, with its explication of the compromise between the North and South, the acts of Congress the new President had signed. There would be no war in 1850.

Not anymore.

Wing unlocked the Old Man's news report from the lockbox, tremulous with hope. All the words, the awful words, were still there. But they had blurred.

. . .

The Fulcrum

They didn't need the newspapers the last time. The streets were filled with the talk.

South Carolina had seceded.

A war, everyone said. A short war, they predicted. It had been when it happened in 1850, and the Confederate army ringed Washington and a bullet brought down Zachary Taylor. Millard Fillmore—not made for greatness, poor man—hastened to negotiations. It would be different this time, Wing thought.

Wing went to Ops's home, the lockbox clenched in his hand. He made greetings and apologies to Ops's wife in one breath, and then they left her alone.

While Ops locked his study's dark walnut door, Wing turned the key in the lockbox. The yellowed paper filled his brain feverishly, its hateful words scratching and skittering like rats in a cellar. The headline screamed, UNITED STATES SIGNS DEFENSE PACT WITH CONFEDERACY. The paragraphs explained their alliance against the double-pronged invasion—the Soviets from the north, as soon as they finished off Canada, and the Nazis with the Argentinean armies from the south, once they were done with Mexico.

The United States and the Confederacy: two nations, the house divided. The two nations had sat between their two oceans, not stirring for the world wars or the long, grinding conquest—Hitler gobbling up Africa, Stalin and his Chinese allies tearing apart the Japanese Empire. But the world crossed the oceans; the conquerors came for them last. They burned, too. The cities were firebombed, the countryside raped ... And the planet's most incandescent genius used humanity's greatest invention to engineer the delivery of spoiled milk to the White House on Independence Day, 1850.

The key stuck. Wing stopped, steadied his hand, twisted the key again—

A sudden, heavy thumping, a sharp cry. Wing contorted his back to look.

217

Ops leaned heavily on an armchair, his left hand stretched out in front of him and his face white.

His hand was restored, just as it had been before the war—the palm straight and strong, the fingers whole again, the scar gone.

Wing started up. Then a strange chill, followed by a strange warmth, lanced his cheek and jaw. He groped his face, seeking the scar tissue, the ridges, and stretched, shiny skin.

He couldn't find the scars on his face. It was smooth, smooth like it used to be.

It was some time before they remembered the Old Man's news report. When they finally unlocked it, they were interested but not surprised to find it scrawled with pleasantly useless statistics regarding the production of peanuts in Georgia.

About the Author

Shannon McDermott's work includes the fantasy novel, *The Valley of Decision,* and her short stories have been accepted into the anthologies *Circuits & Slippers* and the upcoming *Once Upon a Future Time, Vol. 2.* She is a staff writer with *Lorehaven Magazine* and a regular contributor at SpeculativeFaith.com.

*****~~~~*****

The Sixth-Gun Conspiracy Letters

by Evan A. Davis

September 14, 1860

Dearest Mother and Edwin,

I write you this wonderful, fog-sewn autumn morning just as a butterfly has landed on the edge of my desk—a monarch, at that. I mention it not for its beauty alone, but for the good omen in its wings. Did you know, they say an artist's destiny might be read on the wings of a monarch butterfly? After all, what makes our fates so difficult to read is that their patterns are intricate and the creature is so prone to flight, hardly resting still long enough to be read. But this one has been still, even now. To think, I am visited by a monarch butterfly—a good omen unto itself—the morning of the same day as I am to grace the stage as one myself.

The company's tour of the Deep South, while a deplorable prospect at the outset, has been a ringing success. Tonight, I am to portray Lear. The lead! Now do you see the marvelous coincidence in my omen? I dream at night of the crowds in Baltimore and if only they might see me now.

I won't fill your heads with fancy that the whole thing has been nothing but adventure and good fortune, however. It has not been. The audiences have hung on my every word, laughed so heartily when I bid them laugh, and cried with us so deeply, though I suspect the credit must go beyond my talent alone. There is a tension that hangs in the air here quite densely. The brazen talks of secession, the way they speak of and treat their Negroes in front of northern company, all alongside their famed southern hospitality—which I am compelled to admit serves their reputation—leaves one terribly conflicted.

To add to it, I was subjected to the cruelest prank posing as a rite of passage, new to the company as I am. Under the guise of a celebration of recent performances, we abruptly departed rehearsals in Richmond and made for Charles Town. I was told it was to be a rabbit hunt, but once there, I saw we were in the company of the Richmond Grays! Furthermore, imagine my horror and astonishment when I was told we were to witness a man's hanging, supposedly an abolitionist who had grown too vocal in improper circles. After the ordeal was finished, the devils shoved me onto the stage and began to cry, "Speech! Speech!"

Edwin, I was mortified, but you would be proud, if not dumbfounded, by how it was handled. I dutifully swallowed my disgust and gave them the words they craved so doggedly. I performed, as one fit for the stage might, their mock speech. They were satisfied and none the wiser.

The butterfly, my patient companion, has just departed, so I will leave you with this. I am well. The company's tour of the Deep South has been exceedingly successful, and even those portions marred by unfortunate events were turned to good advantage. I think of the gypsy woman's palm reading you always say I am wont to mention and her fortune of a "bright and prosperous life." I tell you, Edwin, how correct she was, and Mother, I know I am not alone in wishing only that father were alive to see it.

Now, truly, that must be all. The courier which delivers letters for the company and its actors is waiting. We leave for Savannah shortly, and I must pack.

Yours in adoration always,
John

J.B. Wilkes

. . .

March 8, 1861

Mother,

I hope this letter finds you well and if Edwin is the man of his word I think him to be then it will be in your hands this day before supper, before the ink has fully dried. I thank you for your endlessly kind and congratulatory words in response to my last letter. As well, I trust you've received the checks I sent, and will remember the allotted amount meant for dear sweet Asia. It is meant for her dowry and should be handled with appropriate regard. Dramatic Oil has been doing well, though my partners' patience for the drills' production as well as the company's name is dubious at best, so we ought not spend as though it will never run out.

Now, I wanted to address those same preposterous rumors you yourself made mention of in your last letter. There have been those seen around the country parading about condemning, loudly and brashly, the President's actions and trumpeting the so-called "heroism" and "bravery" of the childish and boorish South, all the while apparently sporting my resemblance! It is absurd, and I hope you will treat these country myths as precisely that. I abhor how the Negroes are treated and the perpetration of our neighbors to the south. Alas, after these last years' grand success, it is the way of it that we who taste the sweet lips of fame are due also to carry her burdens of conjecture and gossip in the public square, isn't that right?

To follow, I will shed some light on an even darker event that transpired. Yes, it is true that last October I was attacked in my hotel room. He was a crazed man with a gun, and by the sounds of it, a staunch abolitionist, given his shouting before the act. I was seen to by our good friend, the mighty physician Samuel A. Mudd. With his help, the favorable outcome it brought about, and some time to distance myself from its occurrence, I may <u>almost</u> allow myself to chuckle in its remembrance. I have come to the reasonable conclusion that it was the tension which has gripped our nation met with the heinous false gossip of my supposed outspokenness on the matter which pulled the trigger. He must have either heard of or even seen my mock yet admittedly convincing speech at poor Mr. Brown's hanging in December of '59, I'm sure of it.

I don't blame him. That is to say, being a successful man of theater, as I've told Edwin, is to be under the scrutiny of the public eye and the center of its talk, I'm afraid. To say nothing of the tensions—have you been reading the papers?—I suppose I might even have expected something of the sort. Why, if I myself had heard the things I have been reported to have said, I might have been driven to do as he did. Now, with it thoroughly behind me, I might even dare to call the whole ordeal exciting. Besides, the pitiable lunatic was later found dead behind a pile of refuse in an alleyway. So, no need to further fret, it seems I have if not a guardian angel then one of vengeance watching over me.

Please, write again soon.

Lovingly yours,

John Wilkes Booth

. . .

[undated document, est. early 1862 by Tennessee postage]

Cpl. Henry Rathbone,

The news of the attempt on our man's life was worrisome at first, but I hear he's made a full recovery and your handling of the threat was sufficient. Now that he's survived, the field is set even more advantageously than we might have hoped for. It informs him in a painfully clear manner the stakes at hand, for one, let alone the newspaper headlines, which suit our purposes perfectly.

I have included within the package of letters to your garrison herein an order for your promotion, effective immediately. You will hear of it and be called to office shortly. Let it serve as a reminder that your efforts here will water your notable ambitions like the rains water the fields. There will be much to reap from its harvest, that I promise indubitably. You have chosen the winning side, and rest assured I mean that in more than one regard.

With the collectively furtive nature of our campaign, continued contact will herefore be brief or limited. While not out of place for a military governor to correspond with his officers, lengthy or much singular correspondence is likely to arouse unwanted attention eventually. As discussed in our last letter, make contact with the asset soon, at a time when his self importance is at its zenith. With that, you should have your sixth and final game piece. The board will be set.

I trust I need not mention this letter is to be destroyed once read, like the others.

Finally, allow me to be the first to congratulate you on the first steps of your illustrious rise through the ranks of our great nation's Union army.

That will be all, Sergeant.

A. Johnson

. . .

[private journal entry, dated August 25, 1862]

If such a time permitted, I would shout what news I have from the nearest church steeple or even mountain's peak. I would furiously write to Mother, Edwin, and Father in his grave to share the grand task I have before me. Alas, I cannot, as its very nature alone demands secrecy at its utmost.

There is risk even in this, but I must. I cannot help myself. I must have some record of recent goings on, if for no other reason than I might retain vivid detail of this should I wake from it. Were it enough that I had merited yet another standing ovation to close a lead performance in Richard III, I was approached by a military man, a ranking officer in our very own Union Army, by the name of Rathbone. He wished to congratulate me on an inspired performance, and through conversation, slowly turned to his true motive.

I have been called to join a purpose, a call that I might serve my country and protect the President himself! Now! At such a time as this—brother combats brother, neighbor against neighbor, the fabric of our nation rips itself in twain—I am to be called to defend its leader. The honor I feel could not be matched by any other accolade, pedestal, or stage.

But the work entailed will be gruesome. I will infiltrate a conspiracy, a villainous den, meant to abduct President Lincoln himself! From there, I shall report on their movements, disrupt their traitorous practices, and relay their plans to Union contacts. By our efforts, their own will stifle and fail.

To do this, I'm told I am to state, publicly and loudly, my support for the South's cowardly secession, such that, in search of a spokesman as they are, they are certain to seek me out. It will be a performance of a lifetime, arduous and grueling, but one which pits my God-given talents in a righteous cause. I shall even need to lie to my family. I may not clue them in, even in discrete letters, lest they be intercepted and used against me.

God willing, we shall see the villains' plans eradicated, and the scoundrels themselves in irons.

. . .

[letter addressed to Edwin Booth, dated March 3, 1865]

Edwin,

As you have shown me the courtesy of writing so informally, I shall respond in kind. I will be brief, and I will be frank with you: you've no idea of my business, and your remarks have been profoundly unwarranted. As I have told you before, and as Mother is certain to have mentioned, my dealings with David Herold have been entirely consuming. I'm sorry you've been left to handle many of the company's performances yourself, but I was under the distinct impression that was how you preferred it. Your impression that we "disappear on a moment's notice" to "places far and wide" is not inaccurate, but it's by these paid consultations and meetings for which we must travel that the company will continue and stave off the bankruptcy towards which you drive us so doggedly.

Your reaction to my politics is, just as well, uninformed; especially your remarks on my arrest in St. Louis. You may save your vitriol for your characters, Edwin. All I shall say on the matter is that how I choose to stand for my nation will be proven out as truly righteous and that history will justify that. If the gypsy woman might see me now, how she might laugh—and I would laugh with her—at her foolish fortune; and that if you could truly know the depths of what steals my time, your belly would ache from laughing also. I would give anything to meet her now and reposte with a fortune of my own; that beyond theater, our nation will remember my name for centuries.

I will write again soon. Until then, please hold your jealousy at bay and write again when your own temperament permits.

Yours,

John Wilkes Booth

. . .

[confiscated letter of a convicted trespasser; dated April 21, 1865]

Eugene,

We have a big chance here. Have you seen those posters for that actor, Booth? The reward's at $100,000! Numbers you can understand, right? All those zeroes!

I'm sayin this because your my brother-in-law, for my little sister. Let's find the motherless son of a bitch and split it! No more chasin that soldier's pension or workin the docks. We'll retire rich!

Get your bear gun and meet me at pa's ranch. Be quick. I better not regret lettin you in on this.

Daniel

. . .

[private journal entry; dated April 19, 1865]

I am currently looking out from between the boards of a barn on a tobacco farm. David Herold is with me, my lone friend in a world of snake—ah, and he reminds me I ought be brief, as we may need to uproot on a moment's notice. I will do my best to record here what I am horrified to think history might cruelly smother.

I learned of the plot that morning, as I had so many others. Or so I had been led to believe. After what has transpired, I cannot be certain of anything anymore, only that I was informed of another attempt at the President's abduction that very day.

With my prestigious name, I was permitted free reign of the Ford's Theater while the company rehearsed.

In my searching, I found no cached tools nor any sabotage to the President's designated viewing area, which I found curious, as those signs had become the norm in my new trade. It was decided I would instead be present during the night's performance as the unexpected sentinel. When I saw Major Rathbone and his wife accompany the President and First Lady to their seats, I felt certain he should be informed of the situation at present, as he would be closest guard throughout the night.

Rathbone—the filthy snake!—pulled his revolver as soon as I entered the box with them. I thought he might just have been jumpy, already informed as to the night's dangers, but my veins went cold when he turned the barrel away from me. He nodded to his wife, who shouted manically that I'd stolen his pistol, and fired on the President himself! I tried to wrest his weapon from him, but the devil overpowered me. He could have shot me just as well, but he did not. Instead, he threw me over the railing and shouted something after me. I would hear later through David's scouting about town and its gossip that he yelled, "Sic semper tyrannis!" Though news to the common man believes it was I who spoke it. The bastard even went so far as to wound himself to secure his story.

It is not hard to see, however. I landed hard on the stage from his shove, injuring my leg in the process. Rathbone shot after me, but I know he aimed to miss, blast him. He plays the hero, while I fall victim to my reputation—the very reputation they had me build! Even in the scramble, I already heard murmurings in the crowd of who I was, the "man of the South" and such nonsense.

It was to be a tool with which to save the President; instead, they shall wield the collection of falsehoods I crafted for them as a net in which to tangle me and a shroud under which they will hide their true nature. Rathbone's wife may have seen the truth, or perhaps she knew it all along. No matter. How could she speak out against her husband even if it were true.

I <u>must</u> clear my name, however possible.

. . .

[scratched on a crumpled piece of paper found among Major Rathbone's effects]

"No loose ends."

. . .

[private journal entry; found buried beneath Garrett farm, later confiscated]

The Devil's turned every man's hand against me. I am told the papers cry me "Judas," likened only in deed— and falsely. History will know me only as a beguiling cutthroat. To the common man, I would speak thus, "Watch closely those in power, for powerful men will play the strings and twist the knife. And would you know the full truth, rather than cry 'Judas,' you would speak, 'There but for the grace of God go I.'"

David has turned himself in, and the regiment now prepares torches at my indecision. I will hand myself over, but I do not expect they shall suffer me long, as I complicate their story.

I pray only that those I love—Mother, Edwin, Asia, my darling Lucy—will not succumb to their lies or villainy, believing I might truly be capable of something so heinous; and if evil should triumph, I will plant this seed that one day truth may grow from it.

Lucy, know that I love you with all my heart.

God Bless America.

John Wilkes Booth

###

About the Author

Evan Davis is an emerging author with an overactive imagination, which explains how he got here and why you're reading this—which is great. After years daydreaming of stories, he eventually transitioned into writing them full-time instead. Fiction being his first love, he's written everything from bellyaching humor to thrilling fantasy, from romantic mysticism to science fiction misadventures, and every colorful dot in between.

He's gotten lost in Europe, made things explode with a bow and arrow, been a 6' 4" street acrobat, DJ'd a wedding or two, and now lives happily in Northern California scribbling about wonderful what-if's.

*****~~~~~*****

Defender of the Realm

by H. J. Monroe

Louise the First, of the United Kingdom of Great Britain and Northern Ireland and of her other Realms and Territories Queen, Head of the Commonwealth, Defender of the Faith, came to a halt in the windowless, concrete hallway.

"Pardon me Director, but could you repeat that?"

Dame Fiona Ali, head of security services, gave her a sympathetic look. "He insists his name is Arturus Rex. Though the database says he is Phillip Duncan of Somersetshire."

Louise nodded and began to walk again. She wanted to ask why MI5 had thought it necessary to drag her to a black site in the middle of the night to speak with a lunatic who thought he was King Arthur, but her tumultuous and dangerous month as Queen had taught her to trust Dame Ali.

"He said he would only speak with you. Normally we wouldn't allow such liberties, but we believe that his information could prove vital to uncovering the key players in the June Massacre."

Louise understood then all the extra security and precautions. If the man was associated with the Egalitarians, he was dangerous and untrustworthy. Her

231

heart began to pound. She took a deep breath, while the Director gave her guidance on what questions to ask and advised her on not giving away state secrets. A veteran of the intelligence services and, at fifty-eight years old, more than twice the Queen's age, Dame Ali was an invaluable source of wisdom and steadiness amidst the chaos.

"Thank you," Louise said when they stopped at the guarded door.

"You are welcome, Your Majesty."

She said the words with a fierce note of pride, and Louise stood up straighter. The young queen tried to channel the regal unflappability of her Grandmother Elizabeth the Second as she bade the guard to open the door and stepped inside.

Born eighth in line to the throne and displaced even further as her older cousins had children, Louise Alice Elizabeth Mary Mountbatten-Windsor was never supposed to be Queen. Her parents hadn't wanted a royal life for her or her brother. They had encouraged them to have a profession and done their best to shield them from public appearances and official duties. Her parents had even insisted she not be given the title of princess, though it was her birthright as youngest granddaughter to the Queen. It had all been done to help Louise lead a productive and relatively normal life. No one could have foreseen the rise of the rabid Egalitarians and their war on hereditary titles escalating to bombing a royal family party. In one bloody explosion, thirty-eight people had died, including the seventeen in front of Louise in the line of succession.

The June Massacre was intended to kill the monarchy, but in times of disaster it was the monarch the people had always turned to. To reassure the country and the world and avoid a constitutional crisis, Parliament had been quick to swear loyalty to Louise and to declare the Egalitarians enemies of the state. Now there was a chance the young queen could prove her worth by getting information.

Louise stepped into the stark interrogation room ready to face a monster, but instead she found a balding man in his fifties with a substantial beer gut and pale pink skin sitting at a small table. He was so ordinary.

She burst out laughing. Her hand clapped over her mouth, and smothered the laugh to death.

"Apologies, I am overtired." Her manners, instilled from birth, took over.

"Completely understandable. It's been a difficult month for you." Even his voice was perfectly ordinary.

Louise noted the lack of title and that he seemed to have no intention of standing for her, not that she'd expected him to bow and scrape.

"My condolences, by the way," he said with what seemed like sincerity.

She smiled tightly, keeping close rein on the anger that had flared. "I was told you needed to talk with me."

His look turned appraising. "Were you truly not expecting me? Did you think I could sleep through your endless calling?"

"Sir—"

"Please call me Arturus."

"Arturus," she said sarcastically. "I have never met you, and I most certainly did not call you."

He sighed. "Well, I guess it was to be expected. You were hardly meant to rule."

The words hit at the heart of the Queen's insecurities and fears. She felt like a usurper to William's crown, and the threat of assassination loomed over her daily. But Louise wasn't about to let this small man threaten her. She squared her shoulders.

"I am of the House of Windsor. We have ruled for a hundred and fourteen years and will continue to rule long after your kind have been dealt with."

"My kind? My dear, you haven't the slightest idea. It is I who will be here long after you, just as I was here long before you and your estimable house."

The kindness in his tone confused her. "What?"

"I am not questioning your right to rule," Arturus continued gently. "I of all people know you are the true Queen. But though the people have invested you with the crown, and the right blood flows through your veins, you are lacking the vital knowledge that the heir apparent would have been entrusted with. Knowledge that would have included me, would have told you how to call me. Though you figured out a way to do that on your own, which is impressive."

Louise was annoyed by the warmth that washed through her. Was she really so desperate for affirmation that the words of an insane man gave her such comfort?

"You said there was knowledge that I needed," she said trying to return to the reason she was there. "What knowledge?"

"Please have a seat, and I will explain." He gestured to the plastic chair on the other side of the table. The chains around his wrists rattled.

Louise eyed the chair for a long moment before sighing and sitting with as much regal grace as she could muster. "Enlighten me."

Arturus smiled wide. "You are no doubt familiar with the legends of King Arthur?"

"Of course, Merlin, Guinevere, Excalibur, Knights of the Round Table, Holy Grail. There was a TV show on BBC when I was a kid." Louise had fond memories of arguing with friends about Merlin and Arthur, mostly about who was the most attractive. Louise had preferred the dark hair and skinny physique of Merlin to Arthur's brawny, blonde actor.

"Do you know of the concept of his return?" he asked.

"Sure. He is the Once and Future King of England. The legend says he didn't die but was taken to Avalon to be healed and that he will return when Britain is in dire need of him. It's a very common folklore motif. They say the same thing about Charlemagne and St. John."

"Charlemagne," Arturus huffed. "That upstart has nothing like my power."

Louise pinched the bridge of her nose. She was getting nowhere. "I fail to see what any of this has to do with the information you promised."

"The legends are true, after a fashion. They leave out crucial details." His smile broadened, and he leaned forward. "For example, they don't mention how to awaken the sleeper, his precise abilities, or that he is subject to the master of the land, whomever they may be."

Louise was going to have to reevaluate her trust in Dame Ali. The man was a complete dead end. She stood, the chair scraped loudly. "I'm not here for fairy stories. I need solutions."

Arturus stood too, his chains rattling. "Don't be a fool. I am your solution, as I have been the solution for countless kings and queens before you."

She laughed. "You're crazy."

As Louise turned for the door, he spoke quickly. "I am aware this form is unimpressive. I was forced to take this low creature, because you didn't awaken me properly." He rattled his chains. "A proper Queen would have come to me in supplication instead of crying out day after day about her fears." Louise turned the door handle, and his voice took on a desperate edge. "You asked for courage, you begged for wisdom, you wished King William would return to life, and you want more than anything to go riding on Darling."

Louise closed the barely opened door and spun around. He might have been guessing but they were eerily accurate guesses. She wasn't sure if the name of her favorite horse was public knowledge, but even if it was

235

how could he possibly know how badly she wanted to go riding? The young queen thought of the hourly pleas she had made to whomever might be listening. Pleas for wisdom and courage and the ability to just get through the day. Perhaps someone had been listening.

Arturus waited, watching her. When she only stared back, he spoke. "Perhaps a demonstration?"

"What kind of demonstration?" she asked, against her better judgment.

"Nothing harmful. I just want to show you what we could be capable of, together."

Louise wasn't sure if it was the lack of sleep, her desperate need to not be alone, or a desire to prove that Arturus was crazy, but she decided to find out what he would do.

"Okay."

Arturus extended his hand. "Take it."

She hesitated for only a moment before striding across the small room and taking his hand. It was warm and slightly clammy. Her arm prickled. The sensation traveled up to her shoulder and then settled as a warmth at the base of her skull. She wrenched her hand from Arturus, but the warmth stayed.

"What did you do to me?" she demanded, her voice quavering.

His face wrinkled in confusion. "Your Majesty?" He bowed his head, and his eyes roamed wildly around the room. "Where? How?"

Louise heard laughter, but it wasn't coming from her or Arturus, it was in her head.

"Your kind is always so diverting when confused." The words licked inside her skull. It was the voice of her own thoughts, only deeper, richer. She shivered. How was Arturus in her head?

"Get out," she commanded.

"Your Majesty, I am chained to the floor. I cannot leave. I don't even know why I am here." The man

236

stumbled over his words, gone was the smooth Arturus of only moments before.

"I can return to him if you wish," Arturus's voice echoed in her. "You need only touch him."

Louise shook her head as if she could dislodge the invader.

"Perhaps now that you understand my nature you can let me stay until we have things sorted? Communication without the limitation of words would be far easier." He sounded smug.

The man, Phillip, Dame Ali had called him, was watching Louise with fear and confusion. She gave him a smile. She couldn't afford to be seen talking to a voice in her head.

"My apologies, sir. I will see that someone comes and speaks with you."

As he bowed, Louise spun on her heel and pulled open the door.

"He won't remember anything, not even his time in custody," Arturus said.

Dame Ali stepped up as the guard entered the room, and Louise closed the door. "Your Majesty? What did he say?"

It occurred to Louise that the conversation had not been recorded. A small mercy, for she didn't think anyone would know what to make of it. She didn't know what to make of it.

"I don't believe he knows anything," Louise said, hoping Arturus wasn't lying. "If he has broken no laws he should be compensated and released." She walked away before the Director could ask further questions and headed for the elevator. She needed to get away before the perceptive intelligence agent suspected something.

Arturus said nothing as she descended. Louise contemplated which option was worse, demonic possession, alien body snatchers, or a psychotic break.

"Can you read my mind?" she thought the words.

"No. But if you think at me, I will hear it." Arturus sounded pleased.

Louise frowned. Was he lying? Did it matter? If he could read her mind she could hardly stop him, or at least she didn't think she could.

The elevator opened, and Richard, her security detail for the evening, greeted her. They climbed into the nondescript black town car. Only when the privacy partition was up, did Louise attempt to communicate with the thing in her head.

"What the hell is going on?" She spoke aloud and then immediately felt crazy, as Arturus seemed to answer in her head.

"Please don't be alarmed. This is not permanent. I needed you to understand. This seemed the most expedient way."

"Understand what?" she whispered.

"How I can help. Let me show you."

The car seemed to melt around her, and Louise found herself on the deck of an old sailing ship watching a fleet of ships burn. Around her, men dressed like Shakespeare characters cheered. Then she shifted up into the air and blew along the waves. She twisted and whirled, traveling North and becoming a storm. She howled down at the same ships. As she broke them apart she heard snatches of Spanish before the world went dark.

She was rain above a green field falling down upon soldiers in uniforms out of a Jane Austen movie. The ground turned muddy, and she felt a swell of triumph as she flew down into a soldier looking at a map. The word "Waterloo" caught her attention before the scene shifted again.

She was on a street filled with people and a blaring siren. The dark shadow of Big Ben loomed above her. She had never seen it dark. All around her the people streamed toward an underground entrance, and she caught the words "raid" and "German." She moved among them, giving gentle touches that spread peace and order through the fearful crowd. She stepped into the tunnel and then abruptly found herself sitting back in the car.

The city lights of modern London flickered past, and Louise took several deep breaths.

"That is a small sample but a good display of my abilities. I can be a force of nature, a calming presence, a battlefield commander. Or, I can stay with you as an advisor and help you accomplish a difficult task or two. Bertie found me quite helpful for that tricky speech he had to give."

The idea was as repulsive as it was unbelievable. George VI had let this thing control him? Louise knew that wasn't an option, having him in her head was bad enough. How many other monarchs had let this entity inside of them? How many had used his abilities to save the country?

"Are you some kind of guardian angel?"

Laughter resounded in her head. "You are not the first to call me such. But I am so much more and so much older than such Christian concepts. I prefer to be called Defender of the Realm, but all you really need to know is that I am tied to this land, and I serve its leader. Which means you, Queen Louise."

A weight seemed to lift from her shoulders A traitorous tear escaped. She wiped it away quickly, even though there was no one there to see. She hadn't realized how heavy her burden was, until that very moment. Her father, mother, brother, and all her older cousins were gone, she was Queen, and no one could truly help her. Until now. The legend said King Arthur would return when England was in dire need, it only made sense that he had come many times, to many monarchs. If they had used him, why not her?

"I will, of course, require payment for my services," Arturus said interrupting her thoughts.

"Payment? I thought you did it for the good of the kingdom?"

"It's true that as Defender of the Realm when the land and its people prosper I am sustained, but I will require something more."

The words hissed and slid through her skull, and Louise felt as if slime had been poured over her. She shivered. If he could eliminate the Egalitarians and stabilize the country it would be worth any price.

If Queen Louise had been trained as the heir apparent, she would have known that Arturus was dangerous and would demand payment in blood, but there was no one to guide her, and it was possible that even if she had known the true cost she would have made the same choice, just as the rulers before her had.

"Agreed," she said firmly. "If you can save the kingdom. I will give you what you want."

"Excellent." Louise felt happiness bubbling from him. "Then, let us get started."

About the Author

H. J. Monroe is a country girl who joined the Army and became a Captain before leaving to travel and pursue writing. She enjoys all genres, but her heart belongs to sci-fi and fantasy. She's survived live nerve agent training, deployed to Afghanistan, climbed Kilimanjaro, backpacked Europe, and SCUBA dived in Bali, so she knows that staying home with a book is the best adventure of all.

*****~~~~~*****

Cry the Thousand Sentinels

by Brian Trent

The man who needs to die pulls into the truck-stop in a cherry-red tractor-trailer, while the Arizona diner clock reads 7:02 p.m.

The diner sits on a stretch of desert highway. A towering sign advertises its existence: TRUCK STOP & DINER. For sixty-eight miles it's the only watering hole for drivers to refill their stomachs and gas tanks. We are not concerned with the first eighteen trucks that pull in after sunset. Nor with the thirty-six cars disgorging families or commuters returning from long shifts. We hover, invisible to all but the lone Golden Retriever who pads anxiously back and forth, whining at our overhead comings and goings. The dog was named Max Perkins by his original owners. Abandoned now, he is "that old dog" to locals.

The man who needs to die exits his truck as the diner clock reads 7:03 p.m. He glances at the half-moon, seeing straight through us as he does. Blue eyes, sandy hair, a paunch barely concealed beneath baggy flannel. We open his mind like a night flower. His past unfolds in a familiar kaleidoscope; we already know who he is and why he must die. Several thousand possible futures extend from him in a faint starburst of directions, but his present path gleams brighter than the rest.

The man who needs to die begins to fill his tank. A tiny trickle of gasoline draws a wet serpent around the rubber hose.

The man who needs to die has a name, but that is inconsequential. He has lived for twenty-four years and two months and has a woman living at home with him. She is ovulating tonight.

Left undisturbed, the man follows one line of probability into a single tomorrow: he fills his gas tank, drives home, penetrates his woman, releases his seed, and twins are conceived.

This will not happen now. The man leaves the pump unattended as he hastily enters the diner, bowels gurgling from a sandwich that had gone bad from a supermarket cooler that we cut power to during the night. He will be in the bathroom long enough for gasoline to pool beneath his truck. It's a cold night. His boots will accumulate static on the diner's carpet as he leaves the lavatory. The carpet was installed last week because we whispered to a child to spit water from his straw on the linoleum, and a waitress fell and bit off her tongue.

The carpet will build up static electricity beneath the man's boots. He will go outside, touch the gas pump, and there will be no twins.

We hover above the truck stop, our tendrils interlacing to convey rapid, anxious thoughts.

The trucker flushes the toilet, tracks his boots across the carpet, building static. A woman with hair the color of ripe plums passes him on her way to the restroom. The door is conveniently opened for him as a child runs outside to play with the dog named Max. The trucker steps into the cold desert air.

The gasoline has now spread along the pump station tarmac in a shape vaguely suggestive of our own: a jellyfish body with a shroud of immense wings.

Cry the Thousand Sentinels

The trucker touches the pump.
Returns it to its cradle.
Starts the truck engine.
Drives off.

. . .

Max howls wildly below us as we hiss our astonishment. Lines of manipulated probability blow apart like star jelly. So much planning and careful orchestrations, gone!

"Why did he not die?"

The question passes between us as we agitatedly touch tendrils in the air, communicating through frantic, physical contact.

He *should* have died. The child ran outside at the correct moment; he misses his own dog Nikki, who died last year when we lured her into the street in time to meet a high-speed delivery van. Therefore the trucker never touched the door. Never dispelled the static electricity.

"Did he know?"

The air hums with our terror.

"We saw his mind. He knew nothing."

"Was the rug moved?"

"No."

"The static charge must have dispersed."

"But how?"

"The woman!"

Yes, the young woman with plum-colored hair. She passed by him. Who was she? She was not in our tabulations.

"She must have touched him!"

We descend to the diner. The young woman is still there. We open her mind like a suitcase. She is sixteen years old. Her name is Aurora. A metal stud glints in her nose. She is sitting by herself, lifting French fries to her purple lips, texting someone.

Our tendrils interlace in a bristling debate.

"Who is she? She is not supposed to be here!"

243

We slide across the air's viscosity through the diner. People shiver, as if from a draft, as we spread along the ceiling. The girl laughs as she receives a text that says: CAN SEE THE TRUCKSTOP NOW GIRL GET RUNNIN!

Our confusion deepens. *Who* is this girl who has ruined our plans?

The man who needed to die is alive because of her, and probability now converges towards the hideous outcome, like an elastic band snapping back to its default length.

The girl pockets her phone, slides crumpled cash beneath her plate, and scurries out the door. She dashes across the parking lot and runs for the darkness beyond the truckstop.

We glide above her, circling, watching.

"Where is she going?"

"The train!"

The evening train has appeared on schedule. The girl runs for it like an arrow fired at a moving target.

"She is going to hop the train!"

This realization does not cure our anxiety, but it does put it in perspective. There are billions of humans, and like any predator-prey dynamic, the prey outnumber the predators. Being outnumbered, we acknowledge it is possible for humans to surprise us. An adolescent girl sneaking about is like a guppy whose wriggling movements absorb into ocean currents without alerting the keen senses of even the most desperate shark.

Our latest plan unraveled by a teenage girl who wanted French fries tonight!

"Follow her!"

It is not command, it is consensus. The girl must be tracked, monitored, and tabulated, to see where she fits into probability. We cannot abandon our monitoring of the diner. A single herder is needed to track and factor the aberration.

I volunteer.

The girl bolts for the train. A loading bay door slides open, two cars up from the caboose. She leaps into the gap.

"Hey, girl!"

There is one teenage girl already on the train. Her name is Holly. I enter the car and unfurl above them.

I pry open their minds.

Glitz and glitter, hormones and sound! They laugh, talk, share pictures on their phones. I recall there was spirited discussion over allowing such technologies. Sometimes their own inventiveness assists us: their Edison was permitted to live. Sometimes their own cleverness threatens us: their Tesla, who discovered us through one of his experiments, we killed in a New York hotel room.

I explore the train. The conductor is a sixty-one-year-old man named William Tully. His probability line is a solid line: he doesn't yet know that his persistent cough is the start of emphysema, and when he learns the news, he will check into a Reno motel and pay a prostitute to bind and strangle him to death with a braided leather belt.

I return to Aurora and Holly.

I watch them.

As they laugh.

As they tease.

As they watch the shadowy landscape rushing by.

. . .

An hour later, the teenagers jump off the train.

The action startles me so much that I almost forget to follow them. The train is hurtling along at forty miles per hour, but Aurora and her friend leap, their hair like different hues of flame behind them, land hard on the desert, and roll like tumbleweeds. They recover and caper towards a trailer park.

There are no herders above the trailer park. Its probabilistic topography is an unknown island.

My discomfort twists inside me. The human population keeps expanding, while our own numbers remain constant. This is a problem much discussed. Diebacks are a risky proposition; even plagues end up strengthening the herd in the long term.

Aurora and Holly enter a trailer and plop down on a mustard-colored couch. Aurora has her phone out again. I spread above them.

Aurora is talking on her phone.

"Hi, grandma. Yes, we're behaving. Yes."

Monkey chatter. So easy to distract these primates and their—

"Yes, it's here with us now."

Pause. "I know, grandma. The containment field is set up."

Pause.

"Punch it!"

And before I can react, an energy field snaps out around me, affixes me to the trailer ceiling. I cannot move. I cannot escape. I have been caught.

Electrical current runs over me like waves of ants.

. . .

In spite of my horror, I take note of what's happening below me.

Aurora and Holly are removing their scalps!

Wigs! They have been wearing wigs to cover their shaven heads! The wigs contain copper nodes. They were shielding their thoughts from me! When I peered into their minds, I saw only a pair of fictions!

"Open them up!" Aurora yells, and the trailer walls collapse. Engines purr outside, wheels crunch gravel as other trailers converge, linking to form a mobile lab. Men and women in white lab coats enter. Countertops flip to reveal hidden workstations. Cabinets are flung open, revealing flatscreen monitors instead of canned goods. A rack of syringes rises from the floor.

"Ten minutes, people!" booms an auburn-haired woman in a lab coat. Her name is Winona, but I wonder if her hair is another wig feeding me another fiction. "Containment is stable! Look at its size!"

A man with a buzz-cut and a burn-scar on his cheek adds, "It seems there's been unchecked evolutionary development." His name, or the name I'm allowed to see, is Wilhelm.

"It's only been sixteen hundred years!" Winona says. "Not enough time for speciation to take place."

Sixteen hundred years?! How can they know this? That knowledge is long gone, burned by torches of angry mobs!

Wilhelm shrugs. "Who says anything about speciation? They've gotten larger. That can happen among any animal population given the right environmental pressures."

"But what pressures?"

Ignoring her, Wilhelm cranes his neck to stare up at me. I shouldn't be visible to him. Yet he sees me. Special contact lenses? An implanted ampullae of Lorenzini?

The teenagers return to the mustard-hued couch, watching the proceedings with a cold scrutiny. They are *invested* in what's happening, I think. I wonder if we killed their loved ones. I wonder if other treacherous islands of hidden humanity are doing the same in the hinterlands of China, in the deserts of Australia, in any of the islands of Greece or Japan or Micronesia.

A knowing, greedy smirk spreads across Wilhelm's lips.

"*Kleidi*," he says.

I respond in vibration, and the frequency travels along the energy field imprisoning me and comes out through an electronic translator: "***Kleidariá.***"

"What is your name?"

Winona looks at him in sharp rebuke. "They never had names before."

"Designations," Wilhem clarifies. "Their creators gave them designations." He glares at me. "The lock is turned. Answer me! What is your designation?"

"*Protopóros.*"

Wilhelm consults a clipboard, scanning a list of ancient Greek titles. Greek! Stuck to the ceiling as I am, I glimpse the old Alexandrian dialect. The language spoken by bearded men in tunics sixteen hundred years ago, in a secret laboratory not so dissimilar to this one.

"He's a free-roamer," Winona says, looking at her own clipboard. "A limited number were created to set up new monitoring pods." She addresses me in a harsh, disgusted tone: "What is the *purpose* of your designation?"

"*I travel between monitoring zones bearing informational updates.*"

"See? They've adapted. In a way, they're still following the old impulses, striking out into new areas. Only now it seems they've become message-runners."

To me, Wilhelm asks, "Do you still communicate with one another by touch?"

"*Yes.*"

"You must *physically touch each other* to communicate?"

"*Yes.*" We were never given voices by our old masters, those forgotten scientists of Alexandria who learned to create life, experimenting with living jellies from the wine dark sea. Shaping and enhancing us to serve their purposes.

"*We destroyed you,*" I protest. "*The Circle of Apis was destroyed when the Library burned! The scrolls and researchers were—*"

"Torched by zealots," Wilhelm growls, eyes glinting. "Destructive mobs whipped up by your kind, I'm sure. Sent an advanced civilization into a Dark Age!

Reduced humanity to ignorant, knowledge-fearing worms who were easier to control."

"Easier to herd," Winona says bitterly, tucking the strands of her wig behind her ears in a nervous gesture. "Isn't that right?"

"*Yes,*" I say. "*You must be herded.*"

"We must be free!"

"*You must be herded.*"

"You son of a—"

"Winona! There's no point arguing with it. They were created to do this!"

She trembles in fury, cheeks as red as her hair. "How could the Circle have done this to everyone? Unleashing these. . . these *wardens* on the human race!"

"It doesn't matter!" Wilhelm says. "Sixteen hundred years ago the world was falling apart. Barbarians overrunning the Roman Empire. Endless wars. Human cruelty. The Circle of Apis must have figured that we needed to be. . . "

"Controlled!"

Pinned to the ceiling, I say, "*May I ask a question?*"

Wilhelm's lips compress into a line. "Sure, I'll allow it, you bastard."

"*How did Aurora and Holly deceive me? How is it that you are deceiving me even now?*"

"Frustrating, isn't it, to not be totally in control? To not be omnipotent?"

It *is* frustrating, though for reasons these humans cannot fathom. I cannot follow their probability lines. I cannot see how those probabilities interact with each other. Cannot measure the force they might exert on the hideous outcome.

Blue-clad attendants wheel a contraption beneath me. It has a single mechanical arm that rises like a crane until it touches my soft underbelly. Something sharp penetrates my gossamer flesh.

249

Winona touches Wilhelm's arm. "Are we sure about this? Really sure?"

"Yes," he says at once.

"I'm scared."

"We all are. But it has to be done." He turns to me. "You will not remember any of this conversation."

"*I will not remember any of this conversation,*" I echo.

"You will tell the others that the girl you followed is a runaway living in a trailer park."

"*I will tell the others that the girl I followed is a runaway living in a trailer park.*"

He continues with his list of instructions.

"You will immediately leave here when I release you. You will remember nothing, but you will obey these instructions."

I tell him I will.

"*Kleidi,*" Wilhelm says.

"*Kleidariá.*"

The containment field drops.

. . .

The man who needs to die has already penetrated his woman, and she will soon conceive an egg that will split and there will be twins and within fifty-three years they will head a powerful political dynasty which will provoke a global war, and San Francisco, Islamabad, Delhi, Washington D.C., and Moscow will be destroyed by nuclear bombs. This will set off a chain reaction, all the old grudges rising like bilge water from the cracks of civilization laid bare. The human race will dwindle into barbaric camps, and one by one they will perish. The self-destructive impulse of human beings will come to fruition on a global scale.

This is the source of our frustration. *This* is the hideous outcome. *This* is what we were made to prevent.

Cry the Thousand Sentinels

The pod at the truck stop is waiting for me as I ride the desert thermals. I interlace my tendrils with theirs, sharing what I have seen and heard and learned.

"The Circle of Apis is still in operation. The girl was a lure set to trap me."

My cohorts are silent as they process this unexpected news. Max Perkins howls agitatedly back and forth below us.

"They were destroyed," one protests.

"Some must have survived." And I tell them of the old key-and-lock hypnotic technique the man had tried to use on me. The one we evolved resistance to. The one that no longer works on us.

All around us, probability lines are being yanked like whiplashes towards a dead world of nuclear fire.

"I will spread this update to the others," I announce at last. *"We all must know what has happened!"*

I fly from TRUCK STOP & DINER to the next pod of herders, and to the next, and to the next, speeding along over dark desert and lonely highways, watching other message-runners spread the update towards cities far and wide.

It is hours later, as the purple-red blush of sunrise hatches, that I feel the tingling.

Like thousands of stinging insects crawling over my flesh.

The first spasm hits like a bullet, and I fall, my wings failing, body crashing into the desert.

Do you still communicate with one another by touch?

Yes.

You must physically touch each other to communicate?

Yes.

The man's words return to me. I think of the free-roamers spreading the warning—*spreading the virus the humans have made!*

It will spread around the world! It will kill us all!

And I recall something else they said:

Are we sure about this? Really sure?

Yes.

I'm scared.

We all are. But it has to be done.

I skid to a halt in the desert, unable to move now. The virus has snapped my ligaments. I convulse, body shutting down, awareness winking out like the signal on old televisions. There is only pain and a darkening horizon.

A whiskered rodent creeps near to investigate the hissing of my dying breath.

I see the rodent's probability line yanked with all the others towards mushroom clouds and radioactive winters. See its descendants scampering through the bones of old cities, rusted pipes, and foundations laid bare. See how the line keeps going out, farther and farther. . . towards a fuzzy point many eons from now, where, to my surprise, I glimpse glimmering lights on the horizon, like campfires, of a source I cannot see.

###

About the Author

Recent work by Brian Trent has appeared in *Analog* (March/April 2018), *Fantasy & Science Fiction* (May/June 2018 and September/October 2018), and *Terraform* (September 2018), as well as several Third Flatiron anthologies.

*****~~~~~*****

Red Reckoning

by Jonathan Shipley

Ulrich felt a subtle ripple, a premonition. He glanced out the window as a car pulled up to his home in the Seattle suburbs, the reporter who called earlier for the blog interview. He could feel this would be significant, and it terrified him.

He left the living room to sit in the kitchen, staring into space as the doorbell rang again and again. He would not answer it—he would *not!* The ringing stopped, and he gave a sigh of relief. Then an urgent knock on the kitchen door right beside him startled him. He met the eyes of a young woman peering through the glass-paned door.

That face—almost familiar. But not the expression. Her look was demanding, accusatory. Ulrich knew he couldn't simply shuffle off to another part of the house. This one would be pounding at all the windows until he let her in. He stood up and unlatched the door. "I have nothing for you," he grumbled. "The Luckiest Man Alive was all a trick, a lie. Now go away."

But she pushed right into the kitchen. "Ulrich Breitling? I'm Emma Sardof from the Massachusetts Journal of Mathematics and—"

"No publications," he interrupted shrilly. "I give no interviews." But a mathematics journal sounded nothing like the gambling tabloids that wanted to know

how The Luckiest Man Alive always won at the racetrack.
. . or used to. His heart wanted nothing more to do with
manipulating numbers. Literally. Last time, he'd gone into
cardiac arrest.

She stared a long moment. "The Journal was only
an excuse. I'm here for Lisl Kinerman. You remember
Lisl, don't you?"

The name hit like a slap in the face, and he fell
back into his chair. Of course, that was the face he saw in
her. Lisl. . . it had been so long, and now memories boiled
back up.

*February 1945. Bombs falling, buildings
exploding, the Mathematics Institute of Dresden going up
in flames. "Ulrich, grab Hannah's hand!" Lisl had shouted
above the chaos. "There's a tunnel from the basement."*

*"Hurry, Fraulein," an SS officer in field gray
snapped. "If these children cannot hurry, they will be left
behind."*

*"Nein, wir kommen, Untersturmführer. Wir
kommen. . . "*

. . .

. . . we are coming. Lisl had been six years older
than he and had taken care of the younger ones. He never
knew what happened to her after the bombing. "Lisl," he
croaked.

"You *do* remember her," the young woman
nodded. "She is—was—my great-grandmother."

"So she survived. And had children." He felt
uneasy.

"She died last year," Emma continued, "but left
behind so many questions. I was taking care of her at the
end. She began talking of Dresden and a thing she called
Rote Berechnung, which I translate as 'red calculation' or
'red reckoning.' But it makes no sense. And the old
notebooks of equations—"

His head snapped up. "Notebooks! You have the
notebooks?"

Red Reckoning

"Yes, Oma Lisl kept some of them hidden all those years, and I've gathered up more from other descendants, but those make no sense, either. And understanding is important. This preyed upon Oma's mind to the very end, and for my own peace of mind, I have to know."

"It will bring you no peace of mind," Ulrich huffed. "Leave and forget about it. Lisl would not want you poking around the past like this. I certainly do not want you poking at *me*."

"I'm not going away," she said firmly. "I've hunted down names across two continents over the last year, and you and she were the last living members of this Red Reckoning group. That makes you the very last. Of course, you were all just children during the war. Oma would only have been sixteen back then, and you only ten. It all has a Holocaust feel to it, with references to a concentration camp—"

"Teresienstadt," Ulrich said abruptly. "It was just two hours away over the Czech border. The mothers were kept there."

"What mothers?" Emma asked.

"*Our* mothers. If we were good children and did everything we were told, the SS guards would bring our mothers to see us on Sunday afternoon. If not. . . " He gave a grim shrug. "We were all very good."

She pulled a laptop from her heavy purse. "May I?" she asked, taking a seat. She typed for a moment. "That's consistent. Teresienstadt is fairly close to Dresden, and the common link of all this seems to be the Mathematics Institute of the Technical College of Dresden. But no university records survived the bombing of 1945. Which brings me to you."

Ulrich thought back a few sentences. So he was the very last of the *Roteberechnungsprogramm*. Thank goodness. Let it die with him. But then there was this persistent great-granddaughter. "Burn the notebooks," he said abruptly. "Lisl would only speak of such things if she was losing her mental faculties—a long-term effect of the drugs they used on us. She would not have spoken otherwise."

Emma leaned forward, almost intimately. "No, it was this. Oma was contacted near the end, and that brought it all back to her. Researchers are on the brink of finding something in the forests east of Dresden, formerly Germany but now in Poland, and thought she might have answers. But she barely remembered the Primkenau Sphere."

Ulrich tensed. The Primkenau Sphere? No.

"Oma said it was nothing. But it can't be if it's been uncovered in Poland. What did it do?"

"*Ach*, you wouldn't understand."

"I have a PhD in Mathematics from MIT," she said coolly. "I think I can handle your explanation."

"It was conceived as a cold fusion device."

Her brow knitted. "But atomic fission had barely been discovered, and cold fusion is far more problematic. How did you overcome the dampening effect of—"

He held up a hand to stop her. "I am disturbed that people are talking of it again. Who are these people?"

Emma dug in her purse again and pulled out a letter. "Read this."

He reached in his shirt pocket for his spectacles, then took the letter. It was addressed to Emma Sardof, not to Lisl, which was odd in any discussion of old war projects. Then his eye traveled to the very plain header in small print at the top of the page, and his heart pounded. *Rote Berechnung*—Red Reckoning. The address was Dresden. The logo was red, appropriate enough for the name, but in combination with the bold, black text, it suggested fouler things. "You work for these people?"

She shrugged. "They offered me a job in theoretical mathematics—my own field—and in research, not teaching. Do you realize how rare those positions are? But read on."

Red Reckoning

Emma Sardof,

Please respond to our offer of August 6, which is both generous and provides an intellectually stimulating environment. We wish you to continue the work of your great-grandmother Lisl Kinerman as she would want. The cache of notebooks that you retrieved from her personal effects will be a great aid in our ongoing exploration into the Primkenau Sphere.

Ulrich set the letter aside. "This is wrong, Miss Sardof. Red Reckoning was a cruel and dangerous program. It was a Nazi experiment using mathematically gifted children. We were supposed to invent the wonder weapons to turn the war."

Emma nodded. "Yes, I know. You were all child geniuses. And according to the notebooks, you worked on top-secret war projects—V-2 missiles, jet airplanes, super-submarines, and. . . the atomic program? That notebook was less clear."

"The theory of an atom bomb was already set forth by Einstein, but it was the production that stumped the Reich scientists. Production needed a high energy source. The Primkenau Sphere. It was supposed to be the marriage of mathematical theory with advanced engineering. There, now you know."

She shook her head. "You say that, but you're telling me nothing. Oma was upset by the memories. . . haunted by them. She kept talking about 'making the numbers dance'—whatever that means."

Hearing that old childhood phrase again, Ulrich gave a bitter chuckle that turned into a whole-hearted laugh that kept coming and coming until he was crying and laughing all at the same time. Too many memories were coming at him. And he didn't want to remember.

Emma stood to get him a glass of water from the tap, and eventually he settled down into morbid silence, sipping at the water. "Cruel and terrifying," he finally said. "Why do you want to dredge it up again? Isn't it enough that we children had to live traumatized? The Nazis were fearless fools who didn't mind cracking open doors that never should be opened. And they didn't mind using children to do it. The mind drugs they used on us didn't even have names, just numbers. My personal drug was Number 72. The Death Angel himself prepared it, and I am not being metaphorical. That was his nickname. *Todesengel.* Death Angel. Josef Mengele, I mean."

She pressed her lips together. "I've heard that Mengele was involved, but I didn't see how. I thought he was at Auschwitz."

"Yes, yes. He experimented on children at Auschwitz and used the results on us. They did things to young brains, those drugs. Opened up perceptions that shouldn't be. After the war, people would call me the Luckiest Man Alive, because I did not lose at the race track. But it was a curse, not luck, and I stopped, because it was killing me. On bad days, I cannot look at any list of numbers without starting to see nonlinear alternatives and possibilities. Then I must take medication to drive the numbers away again."

Emma frowned. "But if you had Number 72 again to do the process correctly?" She trailed off uncertainly.

He sucked air. Do the process correctly? With the Mengele drug? Was this woman mad? No. Something was wrong here. Wrong and dark. Ulrich picked up the letter again, looked it over for numbers. Just contact information, not lists. Lists were the most useful. "The drug doesn't matter, not anymore. Once your brain is cracked open, the numbers are in your mind forever. I was the first to see this."

She looked confused. "So this making the numbers dance is more about skill than drugs? That's different than we—I assumed."

We? What "we" was she talking about? The new Red Reckoning group? Was she part of them? The persistent feeling of wrongness surged over Ulrich like a wave, carrying with it a certain tension that he'd always associated with black-and-silver uniforms. So that was what he'd been sensing. He knew that the SS hadn't died with the war, just gone underground. He knew, because they contacted him every few years. Always very polite, but a dangerous politeness. And they never gave up, no matter how many times he said no. And here they were another time. Did this Emma woman even know who she working for?

He thought what this might mean. If Lisl was truly gone and he was the last of the children, all efforts would be concentrated on him. "Perhaps I should show you how I make the numbers dance, Miss Sardof. Pass the secret to a younger generation, so to speak."

Her eyes widened in surprise and. . . sudden eagerness? "Why, yes. That makes perfect sense. An actual demonstration. The most I'd hoped for was an explanation. How can I help?"

"Give me a list of significant data to form into a pattern." He made an attempt at a smile. "Perhaps a list of your colleagues on this project."

Emma pulled a paper from her purse. "I do have this list of Red Reckoning descendants with vital statistics. It's what I used to track down the notebooks. Will this do?"

"It will do." He laid his hands flat on either side of the page and took slow, shallow breaths to slow his heart rate. He was able to see the numbers shift without drugs, but it was hard on the heart to stop it like this.

"Ulrich, make the numbers dance and tell me what you see?" The voice was Lisl's, and the room was the basement of the Mathematics institute. Bombs exploded outside. "Which way should we go?"

"Through the escape tunnel, idiot!" the SS officer fumed. *"Why are you wasting time?"*

"Not the tunnel, but the alleyway," Ulrich murmured as he hunched semi-comatose over the map. *"The tunnel collapses."*

. . .

With monumental effort, Ulrich wrenched open his eyes to see the page on the table, not the map, but still with the shifting red numbers that led off into infinity. He saw, then sucked in a deathlike gasp of air as his heart feebly reasserted itself. He collapsed across the table.

He drifted back to consciousness with water trickling into his mouth. He gulped it down and opened his eyes.

Emma was standing beside with a glass of water and wide, terrified eyes. "I thought you were dead," she whispered.

Ulrich nodded. "The reckoning is hard, and I have always had a weak heart. Give me a few moments." As he sank back in his chair, he was sure. He had stopped his heart once too often. Now it was just a matter of time.

"I fear you are in grave danger, Miss Sardof," Ulrich finally said. "I do not approve of what you are doing, but for the sake of Lisl, I shall give you a warning. You are traveling a path to nowhere. Those of the original Red Reckoning Project—all dead, or nearly so. The notebooks—artifacts that mean nothing to an outsider. But the process of seeing the numbers shift into nonlinear possibilities, it seems the heart of the program has not died."

"But you're the last one who knows how. No one else knows."

Ulrich fidgeted a moment. "Oh, *they* know, but only partially. The Death Angel saw far too much. He took notes on everything and escaped to Argentina with his work intact."

"And he is forty years dead," Emma reminded him with a quick check on her laptop. "Out of the picture since 1979."

"Red Reckoning was supposed to be the great experiment to produce the *Wunderwaffen*. But now I have looked at your list, seen the infinite possibilities, and do not think that was the experiment at all."

"But it has to be legitimate," Emma argued. "A whole group of descendants has joined the project."

"Exactly! When I ran the numbers for these descendants, I glimpsed the project behind the project that Mengele had pursued. A *Todesengel Protokol* all to itself. You know he was no weapons engineer."

"Of course, I know. He was a doctor who experimented on children."

"Yes, children," Ulrich nodded. "His field—even before there was such a field—was genetics. He would have known that his drugs would kill some of us outright and make more of us psychotic over time. That would not have bothered him. He was looking two or three generations ahead to see what his genetic experiment might produce." He shook his head. "You with a PhD in Mathematics. Others, probably the same. You think it is an accident that genius has been passed down? No, the drug injected into your great-grandmother has come down to you as part of her modified genetics. Mengele hoped that later generations would not even need the deadly drugs to see the red reckoning of the numbers."

Emma frowned. "Part of that I knew. We descendants may have the potential, but we lack vital information on the process. Even watching you, I don't know how you made the numbers dance. You passed out too quickly for me to—"

"Do not worry about that," Ulrich interrupted. "I am the last and shall always be the last. I have known for some time my heart could not tolerate another reading." He gave a shrug. "And so I am dying."

The confusion on Emma's face gave way to anger. "You knew it would kill you—you selfish bastard! We could have—"

"We could have been guinea pigs for people I know all too well. And finally the warning I promised. Run, Miss Sardof. Run. When they realize your failure today, they will take it out on you. It is their way."

Her anger gave way to fear. She seemed to understand too well. Grabbing her papers, she made a dash out the kitchen door. Sad. Her involvement with Mengele's people was not as innocent as he had hoped.

"Lisl, so sorry she turned out to be one of them," Ulrich murmured, then paused because the pain on the left side of his body was increasing. So this new group was focusing their sights on the sphere project. Excellent. Let them run in circles. There was no sphere in Primkenau Forest and never had been. It had always been a bogus name intended to deceive. But whatever the focus, he had no more worries about the *Todesengel* project and these latter day SS.

He had reckoned his final numbers and had an appointment with the Death Angel—the real one.

###

About the Author

Jonathan Shipley is a Fort Worth, Texas, writer and active SFWA member with speculative fiction stories published in magazines and seventy-plus anthologies, including SWORD & SORCERESS 25 through 33 and, of course, several Third Flatiron anthologies. A complete bibliography of his publications is available at www.shipleyscifi.com/publishedworks.

*****~~~~~*****

GRINS & GURGLES

Them Tourists

by A. Humphrey Lanham

They blended in like three deer in a field of cows. Three of them in big brimmed hats and fanny packs standing in a peeling-walled pizza parlor in Eugene, Oregon. Tourists. The mother pulled out a travel book and flipped through its earmarked pages until she stopped, pointing. Her accent was thick. Foreign tourists.

"Dis is we will order. . . one double pep-per-one ko-lah-sul pizza and d-et cokes like your typical, average, obese American family," she said, loudly. Every typical, average, obese American looked over at them.

"Can I oder? I'm proficient at odering!" cried the young boy, tugging on his mother's arm and jumping with excitement.

The mother nodded and took off her oversized hat, pulling her arm across her sweaty forehead, leaving exposed a large patch of purple-green skin.

The boy shrieked.

"Mom, your forehead epidermis is showing!"

She gasped and clasped a hand over her chin.

"No, your *gloratheq* is showing," he said, and she moved her hand to cover the oddly colored skin above her

263

brow. Unfortunately, the hand took with it another chunk of beige makeup, revealing yet another purple-green patch below her lip.

"*Sher harglargq mol*," said the father. The mother gasped, dropped her tourist book, and covered her chin. Her eyes appeared far larger than was natural.

"I need to reapply the dermal spray. I need a. . . what is the word for *frnahlable*?"

"I know!" shouted her son. "It was in that human movie we watched last night."

He rushed up to the counter and banged the bell several times, even though the cashier was already standing there, staring.

"Quick! My mother needs to use your powder room AS-AP!" he shouted. The human pointed, and the three tourists crammed into the single-stall bathroom.

The cashier shrugged, returning to his work. Stranger things happened in Eugene.

About the Author

A. Humphrey Lanham is a fantasy, science fantasy, and YA writer. She reads and writes a wide range of fiction but prefers strong female characters who refuse to cater to patriarchal social structures, expectations of romance, or cultural gender norms and stereotypes. She is chair of Wordos, an internationally renowned writers' workshop group in Oregon. Ru, her cat, is an anthro-xeno-biologist, researching humans and their inexplicable, hydrophilic proclivities. Everyone else believes he is a common Earth cat. Her interests outside of the literary realm include kombucha kitcheneering, cat herding, and language learning. Follow their adventures on Twitter @ahumphreylanham and @thecupcakebeast.

*****~~~~~*****

Date Attire

by Tyler Paterson

Madeline waited for Clark in the dimly lit restaurant. Blind dates were a younger woman's game, but somehow Lucy had talked her into it.

"Clark is nice, and stable. He does a lot of good," she said, and so Madeline reluctantly agreed. Traditionally, whenever a guy got too close to her and saw her for what she really was, they'd end up leaving, and the isolation would take up fierce residence in her mind.

But maybe this time would be different, even though Clark was 45 minutes late already.

Madeline was about to call it a night when her date came scrambling in and sat down. His black hair was a mess, and he wasn't wearing what she would consider to be date attire. Instead, he wore blue tights, red undies, a blue rashguard with a giant 'S' on the front, and a flowing red cape.

"I am SO sorry that I'm running late," he said. His voice was like warm maple syrup. "It's just that work called, and there was this. . . thing. . . I had to deal with last minute. I swear, I'm not usually like this. Typically, I'm very responsible."

"Oh, my goodness," Madeline gasped. She pointed at the giant 'S' and quickly looked around to see if anyone else in the dimly lit restaurant had noticed.

"Aw geez," Clark said. "Listen, you cannot tell ANYONE about this, ok?! It's already hard enough meeting a good woman, but to add this snafu to the list puts everyone in danger. Literal danger."

"But it's not. . . " Madeline started.

"What am I doing? Why am I angry? Listen, I'm sorry. I never really knew my parents. My adoptive family never quite understood me. It's fair to say it's caused some emotional issues. Not that I'm putting those things on you, I'm just speaking my truth, but as I'm saying it, I realize how insane this all sounds."

"Listen, I get it. . . " Madeline tried.

"A woman falls out of a building window, I need to catch her. A meteor is headed towards Earth, it's up to me to punch it in half. The demands of the people. . . I tell you what. . . Do you know what I was doing right before this? The reason I was late? An elderly woman was trapped in a burning apartment with her eight cats. EIGHT! Why was her apartment even on fire?!"

"You did a great thing, and I. . . "

"No. I'm so embarrassed. This is truly awful, and I'm the only one to blame. This is no way to approach a relationship. And to think—I was excited to maybe finally move on and meet someone after it didn't work out with. . . It doesn't matter. There I go again! Blabbering about past relationships! I'm so sorry. I'm just gonna go."

Clark excused himself and threw a $100 bill on the table. Madeline wasn't sure where he pulled it from. He left without any more fanfare, and the other diners didn't seem to notice.

Madeline took in a long slow breath and exhaled it, shrugging her shoulders and bowing her head. She stood and walked to the exit of the dimly lit restaurant.

"I'm never gonna find love," she said, and then raised her arms and flew away.

###

About the Author

W. T. Paterson is the author of the novels, *Dark Satellites* and *WOTNA*. A Pushcart Prize nominee and graduate of Second City Chicago, his work has appeared in over forty publications worldwide including *Fiction Magazine, The Gateway Review,* and a number of anthologies. He is a current MFA candidate at the University of New Hampshire. Send him a tweet @WTPaterson.

*****~~~~~*****

Fairy Godmothering

by Dantzel Cherry

"Wands down, everyone," Ms. Frizzlebloom said. "By now, each of you should have selected your client from anywhere in time, and made the first charmed intervention in their lives. How did it go?"

She buzzed the length of the ornately decorated lilac room, her gossamer wings whirring. Alethea sunk lower in her chair, hoping her portal in the guise of a magic mirror obscured her.

Ms. Frizzlebloom pointed at the enthusiastic blonde in the front row. "Yes, Eryn?"

"With my Matchmaker spell, Marie Antoinette received an offer of marriage!"

The other fairy-godmothers-in-training squealed and clapped their hands.

"Excellent, Eryn! And what should you prepare for next?"

"The wedding dress?"

"Splendid! And next. . . "

Alethea knew what was coming.

"Alethea." The fizz in the teacher's voice fizzled. "Please share with us your progress."

Alethea looked through her mirror at her beaming client running barefoot down the ship to adjust a rope. The ocean breeze ruffled her shorn, unladylike hair.

She cleared her throat. "With my Confidence spell, Grace O'Malley's father allowed her on his shipping expedition."

269

Someone behind her sniggered.

"That's a. . . good thing?" a girl near the door asked.

"It is to *her*," Alethea said.

"That doesn't seem like fairy godmother material," another girl said.

The blush on Alethea's neck spread to the tips of her wings.

"Ladies, we give all our clients a fairytale ending. Even the odd ones," Ms. Frizzlebloom said. "Alethea, dear, arrange a marriage for the poor girl. I dock points for creating spinsters."

"*Fine*." Alethea scanned her book for a Matchmaking spell, while others shared their successes.

"Mary Stuart just married her childhood friend, Prince Francis!"

"They call him the *Dauphin*, Eleyna."

"Right, that."

"Focus, ladies," Ms. Frizzlebloom said. "Your projects need to be wrapped up by the end of class today. That gives you—" she checked her watch. "—thirty more minutes."

Everyone gasped. All the wands, including Alethea's, began swishing the next charm.

"How do I get this army Mary's wishing for?" Eleyna asked, frowning at her mirror.

Army? Alethea perked up. Miss Frizzlebloom flew over to inspect Eleyna's mirror and frowned.

"Hmm. Well, do your best, but don't worry about it too much. That girl needs a baby."

Alethea hurried through Grace's arranged marriage, and helped her pop out a few kids, then tried to get to the interesting business stuff, but—

"Oops." Alethea shook her fist at the dead husband. Health spells were tricky. She charmed Grace with Cunning to defend her castle against enemies taking advantage of her husband's death.

Fairy Godmothering

"Alethea, you let her husband die so early?" Ms. Frizzlebloom chided, peeking over her shoulder.

Alethea cringed. "Sorry."

"Well, get her another one!"

Alethea used a quick Matchmaker spell on Grace and a man named Richard, who seemed likely enough to help Grace with everything she wished, which was apparently piracy. She scrolled through the time lapse, nodding as the weeks flew by: there was another baby, now a little more land—

"Why'd you go and *divorce* him?" Alethea muttered. Ms Frizzlebloom probably docked points for that, too. Still, Grace kept the castle, so there was that.

"Oh-no-oh-no-oh-no-*Marie!*" Eryn wailed, clutching her mirror.

"Bad luck, dear," Ms. Frizzlebloom said, patting her back. Then she peered at the guillotine in Eryn's mirror and pursed her lips. "Losing control of the entire government is just plain irresponsible, Eryn. You'll never pass certification if your clients all end up like this. Stop crying and start your end-of-semester report, detailing where your project went wrong."

She flew away, muttering "'Leave No Fairy Behind', indeed," under her breath.

Alethea's gaze snapped back to her own mirror, only to see Grace being captured.

Alethea cursed under her breath, but Ms. Frizzlebloom hadn't noticed the noose or the cursing. Grace didn't deserve a *hanging*.

Alethea pelted her client with spells. Another Confidence boost. Now Cunning. Now Confidence. And a *huge* dose of Luck.

Ms. Frizzlebloom flew over at the end of class just as seventy-three-year-old Grace passed away in relative peace. Alethea wiped sweat off her forehead and waited for her own fate to be decided.

"Not exactly a fairytale ending, is it?"

271

Alethea shrugged.

Ms. Frizzlebloom's quill hovered over her clipboard for what seemed like forever, before scribbling a B- on her chart and turning to reprimand Eleyna for Mary Stuart's undignified death.

Alethea heaved a sigh of relief. Sure, she'd lost a few points on "lack of glamorous lifestyle," but on the whole, considering Grace's peaceful descent into old age with heirs and a solid entrepreneurial business providing wealth and land, Alethea's grade could have turned out a lot worse.

And that was what really mattered.

About the Author

Dantzel Cherry's work has appeared in *Cast of Wonders, Future SF*, and *Galaxy's Edge*.

*****~~~~~*****

Credits and Acknowledgments

Cover image and design – Keely Rew
Podcast production – Andrew Cairns
Readers – Andrew Cairns, Genevieve L. Mattern, Tom Parker, Inken Purvis, Keely Rew, Leonard Sitongia
Editor and Publisher – Juliana Rew

*****~~~~~*****

Discover other titles by Third Flatiron:

(1) Over the Brink: Tales of Environmental Disaster
(2) A High Shrill Thump: War Stories
(3) Origins: Colliding Causalities
(4) Universe Horribilis
(5) Playing with Fire
(6) Lost Worlds, Retraced
(7) Redshifted: Martian Stories
(8) Astronomical Odds
(9) Master Minds
(10) Abbreviated Epics
(11) The Time It Happened
(12) Only Disconnect
(13) Ain't Superstitious
(14) Third Flatiron's Best of 2015
(15) It's Come to Our Attention
(16) Hyperpowers
(17) Keystone Chronicles
(18) Principia Ponderosa
(19) Cat's Breakfast: Kurt Vonnegut Tribute
(20) Strange Beasties
(21) Third Flatiron Best of 2017
(22) Monstrosities
(23) Galileo's Theme Park
(24) Terra! Tara! Terror!

THIRD FLATIRON
www.thirdflatiron.com

Made in the USA
Columbia, SC
14 April 2019